Born in Twickenham, **Rob Lofthouse** left school at sixteen to join his local infantry regiment, and subsequently served for twenty years in locations around the world. He retired as a sergeant, and writes the military fiction he always wanted to read, but could rarely find.

Praise for The Sheer Nerve:

'A cracking tale that leaves one barely able to draw breath. The story rattles along at break-neck pace and one wills for Hook's commandos to succeed in their audacious plot. The descriptions of the fire-fights are so life-like, one almost has to take cover to read them. A thrilling read.'
– Shaun Lewis, bestselling author of *The Custom of the Trade*

THE SHEER NERVE

Rob Lofthouse

LUME BOOKS

LUME BOOKS

First published in 2018 by Lume Books

This edition published in 2022 by Lume Books
London, Great Britain

ISBN 978-1-83901-181-8

www.lumebooks.co.uk

Dedicated to all those who dared (1939–1945).

Teach us good Lord to serve Thee as Thou deservest.

To give and not to count the cost.

To fight and not to heed the wounds.

To toil and not to seek for rest.

To labour and not to ask for any reward.

Save that of knowing that we do Thy holy will.

And bearing our part in Thine eternal purpose.

Through Jesus Christ Our Lord.

Amen.

The Commando Prayer of St. Ignatius

Contents

Prologue

The bow of U-911 came level with the end of the jetty. Another docker, wrapped in rain gear, waved them in towards the left side. Hook took a deep breath, wiping his sweaty palms on his battledress trousers. Any second now, he knew that 2 Troop would let all hell break loose.

The docker and a man who appeared to be a German officer, were shouting in unison at the crew. The lads standing on the deck looked at each other and shrugged their shoulders back at their antagonists. Rayner focussed on what the officer was shouting. He nodded and gave the officer a thumbs up.

'The German gentleman...' Rayner paused, stifling a little nervous chuckle, 'wants us to make ourselves useful and help get the ship unloaded before she goes down.'

'Oh, *does* he now?' Hook was amused. Traske fought his own nervous laughter by whispering orders down the hatch, for the submarine to stop. U-911 continued to drift as the commandos holding the mooring ropes threw them to the dockers, who stood with their hands outstretched. Meanwhile, the German officer was growing all the more agitated, his body language and his tone suggesting to Hook and his men that they were not working fast enough to assist with the stricken ship. Hook was poised to clamber down the external conning tower ladder.

It was now just a matter of time.

Dockers heaved two gangways onto the deck of U-911, one forward and one aft of the conning tower, just as they had predicted. The German officer, along with two sailors who did not appear to be armed, came stomping down the forward gangway, and his animated arms and dialogue were clearly not expressing welcome.

Yet as the officer verbally assaulted Lieutenant James Rands of The British Commandos, his rant was suddenly cut off with the appearance of a Colt .45 automatic pistol, not two inches from his face. The German officer stopped abruptly, which caused the two inattentive sailors behind to stumble into him. Rands fired one shot, the bullet smashed through the nose of the German officer, blowing out the back of his skull, all over the faces of the two bunched up behind him. The jaw of the sailor directly behind shattered, as the ballistics of a .45 calibre round did what they had been designed to do.

1

Spring, 1943. The Azores, North Atlantic.

'That's the port coming into view now, Captain.'

Lieutenant Anthony Fearl's tone was matter-of-fact as he consulted his chart. The headland had hidden them from the port for as long as it would allow. The Germans within the port area would now be able to see them, and if required, engage them at range.

As the captain pulled his binoculars up to his eyes, he acknowledged the concerned expressions on the faces of the Italian crew manning the bridge of *The Rosa*. The container ship made an easy target for any keen German opposition within the port of Velas, their destination.

The southern edge of the Azores island of Sao Jorge dwarfed the ship and intimidated its crew. The crew had every reason to be scared, for their cargo contained not just torpedoes, fuel and provisions for the U-boat crew languishing in the unremarkable fishing town, but it also held a company of British commandos keen to seize the same U-boat from its current owners.

U-911 was reportedly in the Azores, awaiting a resupply of torpedoes from Italy. *The Rosa*, marked up to look like a Portuguese-registered vessel, had the rather bad luck of being boarded at Gibraltar during a snap inspection, only to have the torpedoes betray her true intentions. The crew, clearly not prepared for tactical questioning by British intelligence officers, gave away their destination with relative ease, since the officers' threat of having them revealed to their German masters as turncoats was too much to bear. The Italian sailors, including their captain, would not want to have to explain how the British managed to take over their ship for their own ends. If what the British had in mind against the German authorities proved to be a success, even without the crew's cooperation, there would be little tolerance for their excuses as to how they came to be involved in the first place. The Italian captain also could not rule out the British killing them out of hand either; after all, Italy was an ally of Germany. The captain of *The Rosa* fearing reprisals against his crew members' families, told the officers everything they knew of the port town of Velas. That included German positions in the town, estimated strength of the garrison, its headquarters and barrack locations. The ship's captain even went as far as describing the structures in detail, as he and his crew had delivered parts and other essentials to other U-boats moored there in the past, bad weather having forced them to stay in the very buildings he was now so keen to reveal to his interrogators.

Captain Paul Hook lowered his binoculars. He watched with interest as the crew began their preparations for the final approach into Velas' harbour. He moved over to the starboard windows, scanning the bluffs above the ship for any German patrol activities. None were to be seen.

'There she is Captain, under the sand-coloured sheeting.' Lieutenant Commander Ronald Traske, a submariner by trade, announced his discovery. In commando fashion, Hook was the overall commander of the mission, Traske, as submarine commander, being his senior outside of that role.

Hook pulled up the binoculars once more. He slowly panned from left to right, looking out for the sheeting Traske had described. He duly picked up the sheets flickering in the breeze; the Germans, in their usual diligent manner, were keen to deny anything flying over the island a good look at their submarine, and to provide their deck-bound crew some shade from the merciless sun. The sheeting did little to hide the vessel from surface ships on their way in. Hook took in the profile of the U-boat, for she was the prize in the first phase of the operation. His men knew they had to take a submarine from the Germans — a submarine and nothing more, for the time being. Hook would reveal the true nature of their mission once they had that submarine, and the opposition was taken care of.

His men knew what was required of them. Rehearsal and planning time had been short, almost non-existent. Recovered back to Gibraltar after a successful yet costly raid on the Tunisian coastline, Hook and his commandos had just enough time to grab a shower and their first decent meal in days, when he was summoned into the operations room. The significance of the container ship he currently sat on was explained to him, and he was told why he needed to get his men onto it that very night, as no time could be wasted. To delay even by a day could potentially give away British intentions to the Germans, who no doubt had their own spies in and around the Gibraltar Strait. British High Command wanted the U-911, and badly. Hook was most displeased at being deployed on another mission before he could write letters home concerning the eight of his men whose bodies were now in the hands of the Afrika Korps.

With the aid of the ship's captain, and such air photography and mapping as could be mustered before they set sail, Hook had devised a simple plan of attack. He was an advocate of the simple plan. Not because his men lacked the intelligence to execute a detailed plan, far from it. No, he kept it simple so that all of his men, regardless of rank or role, knew what was required — but they would have to use a little 'commando savvy' to get it done.

Hook's company was led by its company headquarters, comprising himself and his second-in-command, Lieutenant Mason Kemp, who had been wounded in Tunisia and therefore left in Gibraltar. The original company commander, Major Phillip Bird, had been one of the eight that fell in the recent mission, so it was through a stroke of fate, rather than luck, that Hook stepped up for the U-boat operation. At his side, kicking arse and taking names, was Warrant Officer Neil Gibbs, the company sergeant major. Hook's troop commanders, leading thirty men each, were Lieutenant Bamber Cross leading 1 Troop, Lieutenant James Rands who led 2 Troop and Lieutenant Christopher Joyce with 3 Troop.

Once the ship had docked in the harbour, Hook's men were set to unleash hell. 1 Troop would line the bow of the ship and rain fire down upon any German personnel within the harbour area, as the two remaining troops poured down the gangways. 3 Troop would over-run the barracks and headquarters building before anybody within them could alert German High Command. 2 Troop, along with Hook and his radio operator, were to seize the prize — U-911. Commander Traske and his submariners would remain on board the ship with Sergeant Major Gibbs, until U-911 was cleared of enemy personnel. When called for, Traske was to get himself and his men onto U-911 and familiarise themselves with it, and locate the two Enigma machines and their code books.

'Standby to dock!' called out one of the nervous bridge crew, sweat pouring down his temples. The temperature on the bridge was stifling; despite the fluttering of the sheets covering U-911 indicating a strong tailwind. As they cleared the breakwater, Hook spotted his men crawling on their hands and knees on the deck, beneath the bridge windows. With Bren guns and Thompson submachine guns held ready, they fanned out in preparation to take the fight to the enemy. They were all kitted out in regulation kit, less helmets. Hook was aware of the 'Commando Order' that had been issued by Hitler after the successful raid on the Normandie dry dock at Saint Nazaire, the year before. He insisted that, should any of his men fall into German hands, there was to be no mistaking them for spies, and they were not to be treated as such. If they were to face the firing squad, they would do so as uniformed British personnel.

The Italian bridge crew went about their routine, slowing the ship down. Their deck hands, equally terrified as the British commandos laying about their feet, got ready to throw the mooring ropes to what appeared to be German navy personnel, who had their rifles slung behind their backs. Hook pondered on the fate of those men as they held out their hands to receive the heavy ropes from above. They would stand no chance against his men.

As the ship's engines rose in pitch, pulling up alongside the jetty, Hook got his bearings one last time before making for the door to join 2 Troop as they made their dash for the U-boat, then sat at their 2 o'clock position on the other side of the sea wall. Hook flicked his eyes up to note the two sharpshooters he had up on the overhead crane. He could just about make out their positions, they remained statue-like, for any movement could draw attention from the dozen or so armed enemy personnel now walking about the harbour area between the ship and what appeared to be the headquarters building pointed out earlier by the ship's captain.

The ship was tied to the dock, the crew putting its engines into neutral. As they turned to face the commandos, Hook eyed the two gangways being pushed into place. Using his Thompson, he gestured to the crew what he wanted them to do.

'Down, now!'

They did as they were told.

As they slumped to the deck, those of his men ahead of the elevated bridge sprung up as one, pulling Bren guns onto the rail. Hook wasn't even at the door when the chugging bursts of numerous machine guns announced the arrival of the British.

2

Before the Germans on the quayside could react to what was happening, a number of them were already dead or dying where they fell. The remainder were caught like rabbits in headlights as they tried to shoot back at the commandos pouring down the gangways, all the while looking for suitable cover from which to fight. Cover for the defender was sparse, but that also proved a problem for the assaulting British. With the lead commandos firing from the hip as they went, they could do nothing more than press home their attack, and overwhelm the German sailors before they could catch their breath and react to the threat pressing down upon them.

Hook and his radio operator, Private Alfie Parch, were hot on the heels of James Rands and his men, the bullets of 1 Troop snapping over their heads, whizzing and screaming off the concrete, flicking through nearby buildings. Tracer bullets ricocheted away into the distance. They sprinted as fast as they could, under their combat loads, around the quayside towards the U-boat that now had many figures leaping on and off it.

Hook knew that casting off a submarine was not a quick job, but was mindful the crew could be trying to remove — or even destroy — the Enigma machines and their code books. As the front runners of Rands' troop got near the bow of U-911, its crewmen on the deck fought frantically to load the 88mm deck gun. The sheeting flapping wildly above their heads prevented the sharpshooters high up on the ship's crane from picking them off. Some of Rands' men skidded to a halt, opening fire on crewmen running away from the U-boat. Two of them fell, and whatever they were carrying clattered to the ground with them. Several commandos sprinted on to overwhelm them as they crawled away. Others engaged the deck gun crew, hitting one in the chest in a burst of pink mist, the remaining two threw up their hands as more bullets smashed and flicked off the boat. They knew that to continue to operate the weapon system would swiftly result in a violent death.

With commandos covering the deck gun crew, Rands and the remainder clambered onto the submarine. The deck hatch forward of the deck gun was open, so Rands had some of his men go for that one, whilst more clambered up onto the conning tower. As the forward group swarmed the deck gun and its operators, whose hands were still up, another crew member attempted to pull the hatch closed, but was quickly dispatched by a burst of Thompson machine gun fire to the face. The surrendering deck crew gasped at the violence, but thought better than to protest. As the commandos surrounded the hatch, Thompson barrels all pointing inwards, they could hear shouting and crying within the submarine. The commandos were taking the submarine, one way or another.

Captain Paul Hook and his radioman, Parch, jogged to a standstill on the quayside. Hook surveyed the submarine before him. Rands had his men, with Thompsons, gathered at both the bow and stern deck hatches, and men up on the conning tower. Even from the quayside, and despite the small battles 1 and 3

Troop were having, he could hear pandemonium within U-911. Now it was time to push home the advantage. While they did so, 2 Troop's Bren gunners provided security against German counter-attack onto the submarine.

'Grenades, now!' He shouted to Rands' men.

Rands' men knew they were to drop in only one grenade per hatch, and leave the hatches open. Commander Traske's submarine expertise meant he knew that to leave the hatches open would allow the concussion of the grenades to cause cosmetic damage only, and eliminate risk of both long-term damage to the boat and overpressure issues for the crew hiding within.

Rands' commandos sent their grenades clattering down the hatch ladders, the shouting within the U-boat becoming even more hysterical as the grenades detonated. Two of Rands' men stormed the hatches, clambering down the ladders as fast as they could, to exploit the shock action of the grenade attack. Hook moved from the quayside onto the U-boat, taking up a position at the base of the conning tower. He could hear his men hollering at the concussed crew to get up the ladders. The German they used was textbook basic; they didn't have to worry about regional dialect. They shouted what was required of the crew, and that was all they needed to know. After thirty seconds of mayhem reining within U-911, the first defeated submariners emerged into the brilliant morning sunshine, shielding their eyes as the commandos up on the deck continued to harass and bully them out of the hatches.

Content his men had things in hand with the U-boat crew, Hook called up to Rands in the conning tower. The din of battle still raged amongst the port buildings.

'Mr Rands? What can you see? Any of 1 and 3 Troops?'

A short time passed before he got a response. Rands peered down the starboard side ladder at his boss.

'Can't see a bloody thing, this sheeting is in the way.' He prodded it with the barrel of his Thompson.

Hook turned to Parch, who was never far from his side.

'Give me the handset.'

As well as the headset Parch was wearing, he also had a handset attached via a lead to his set. He knew the boss often spoke for himself on the radio, and so whenever he prepared for a mission, he ensured the captain had a handset available to do just that. He handed it to the officer, who nodded his thanks.

Before he made the call to his rather busy troop commanders he returned to the quayside to make room for Rands' men to hustle their prisoners off the U-boat and search them properly with plenty of room.

Hook opened his call to the commander of 3 Troop, Chris Joyce.

'Hello Charlie Three Zero, this is Charlie Zero Bravo, send sitrep, over.'

'Sitrep' was an abbreviation of 'situation report'. It saved time on the radio, especially in the middle of a gunfight.

A few seconds passed before the radio burst into life.

'Charlie Three Zero. The headquarters is secured, prisoners and casualties taken. We are in the process of clearing out the barracks. Will give you a call when complete, over.'

Hook nodded approvingly at Parch. He knew the mission wouldn't be without loss, but that was the nature of their job. He then called Bamber Cross, 1 Troop, asking the same from him. The response was swift and measured.

'Charlie One Zero, roger. No casualties, we are watching out for any enemy counter attack. We can see Charlie Three Zero clearing the barracks area; we are stood by to assist if they run into trouble, over.'

Hook was happy at the result. 'All stations, this is Charlie Zero Bravo. Good effort men, I don't think we will get counter-attacked, but stay on your game, we are yet to ensure we have the whole crew here. They could be lurking in the back streets, out.'

'Captain Hook, sir?'

Ever since his promotion, just before the Tunisia mission, Paul Hook had heard all the *Peter Pan* jokes and one-liners, not only from his fellow officers but from the men, too. Unlike regular units, where such relaxed familiarity was seldom enjoyed, commando units were much more informal about such matters, due largely to the type of characters found within the outfit, but harsh in terms of standards and training.

Hook turned to see Rands' troop sergeant jogging over to him. Clarence Grice was a fearsome looking fellow, his piercing eyes suggesting menace even when he was off-duty. Hook was at a loss as to why his parents had felt that their son deserved the name Clarence. Built like a prize fighter, with the tattoos to match, Grice was, however, one of the unit's originals, extricated from the Channel by a fishing boat off the Brittany coast long after the Dunkirk debacle. All of Hook's 'originals' were Dunkirk survivors, keen to get back at the Germans for what they had done back in '40.

As the sergeant pulled up, Hook was pleased to see the man had a rare grin on his face.

'Sub is clear, sir. Not all the enemy crew are accounted for, only one officer amongst them.'

Hook rubbed a hand over his six-day-old stubble. The lone officer must have been on his duty shift. He pondered. Why *would* everyone sit on the sub whilst waiting for their supplies to arrive? He knew he would have to send out patrols once the barracks was cleared anyway. He couldn't just sit on the quayside enjoying their victory if the town was not secure. Another factor to consider was the loyalty of the locals. He was unsure how pro- or anti- German they would be. A barman for example, he probably didn't give two hoots where you came from or what side you fought on, just as long as you put money over his bar, and left his women alone.

'How about those we killed by the container ship?'

'We haven't checked them yet, sir. Mr Rands felt they could just be a small navy attachment sent there to help with resupplying U-boats when they came into the area. Not a bad little number if you ask me, sir.'

'Until British commandos turn up, and ruin your little number,' Hook was quick to add. The sergeant nodded as he sniggered.

'Yeah, bloody bastards that they are.'

'Okay, Sergeant, have the bodies at the ship checked, they may be part of the crew. We need to sweep the town, once 3 Troop have finished in the barracks.'

'Yes, sir.' With that, Grice jogged back to join his men, as they had the U-boat crewmen on their bellies, spread-eagled as they were searched.

Hook turned to Parch.

'Call the sergeant major please, have Commander Traske and his men join us here. We need to get this boat ready to go, and dig out the Enigma machines.'

3

U-911 was now in British hands — sadly, Hook reflected, at a price. A number of German sailors had died in the thankfully short action to seize it from them. Hook acknowledged that the Germans had been sensible enough to surrender, once they knew they were overmatched by his men. His own casualties were remarkably light; minor wounds, largely due to ricochets and grenade splinters. Despite their swift success, he still had a town to search, for all but one of the enemy's submarine officers were unaccounted for. The one that was captured had proved rather helpful in revealing where he and his fellow officers liked to drink and relax. Hook wasted no time in having men from Chris Joyce's troop go and pick them up. In a backstreet bar there was something resembling a Mexican standoff between the U-boat officers, including their commander, and 3 Troop Sergeant Daryl Pelton and his men.

Foolishly, one of the German officers had sought to impress his commander by cocking his pistol. That officer was promptly shot dead by Pelton, and the remaining Germans in the bar put their weapons down. An unfortunate situation that could have been resolved without bloodshed, but they happened now and again, and Sergeant Pelton was not the man to test. The officers, less their now-dead weapons officer, joined their crew on the quayside later in the afternoon. Hook's men supervised the German submariners' burial of their comrades in the harsh, dry soil of the town's cemetery, which abutted the port's sea wall. No fanfare, just a quick burial in the interests of hygiene, and mutual respect to the fallen. The captured crew were allowed to attend under armed guard, they offered no resistance. They were all devastated at the sudden attack, and the foolishness of one of the officers.

Whilst Sergeant Major Gibbs and a small security party herded the U-boat crew onto the container ship to keep them under lock and key, Hook, Commander Traske and his radioman, Lieutenant Frederick Rayner, went about looking through the diligently-maintained Enigma log books kept by the U-boat commander and his radioman. Hook tried his best to make sense of the hand-written entries, which were, naturally, in German. Rayner got to grips with both the log books and the two Enigma machines that they had recovered from the commander's safe. Rayner had managed to persuade the commander of U-911 to open the safe with the promise that when the British left the island, the German submariners would be allowed to remain. The U-boat commander did not want his boys penned up in a camp somewhere, and the Azores were nicely out of the way. The German officer was pleased that the British might leave them there — minus any means to communicate, of course.

Hook watched as young Rayner went about his work with the Enigma machines, as if it was something he did on a daily basis.

'Rayner, where did you learn about all this stuff?'

Rayner grunted as he gave the captain a sideways glance.

'Don't worry, I'm not German.'

Hook rolled his eyes. 'I can see *that*, man, but where did you learn to get to grips with these machines, and where did you learn German?'

Rayner, remembering his place amongst his present company, sat up to address the questions.

'I was seconded to the Cypher School back home, before being posted to Gib. My job was to monitor German traffic going in and out of Tunisia.'

Hook was a little puzzled. 'So you are not a submariner?'

As Rayner shook his head, Traske spoke for him.

'No-one in my recent command had the know-how, so we pressed young Rayner here to join us on this little adventure.'

'Was subs your last command?' Hook asked him. Traske nodded.

'Yes, she needs a lot of work done right now. She's sat in Valletta at the moment, providing the Luftwaffe hasn't sunk her yet.'

'What do you mean?'

'Valletta has no bloody pens. We are tied up for the whole world to see. Easy prey for the bloody Luftwaffe. It's been the air defence gunners up on the city walls that have kept her afloat. My crew and I just sat in the shelters all day. We need dry dock maintenance, but when that will happen is anyone's guess.'

'Sorry to hear that,' Hook murmured. Traske nodded.

'That's why I got this job, commanding a submarine. Never thought it would be a *German* one.'

Parch came into the wardroom where the officers sat, with a tray of hot drinks.

'Here you go, sirs, sorry it's not tea. The Germans drink that god-awful crap they call coffee. I brought the sugar too, I think you're going to need it.'

'Thanks Parch. Could you have the troop commanders meet here at twenty one hundred please?'

Parch nodded as he left. Hook knew he was a good man. Dependable. A little older than most of the boys in his company. Married too, which made Hook uncomfortable, since the missions his men were used to getting were, in their very nature, not without their hazards. The officers sat back and enjoyed the burnt, yet sweet, scent of German coffee.

The man was right, the coffee was crap. All three of them saved face by adding more sugar.

Rayner abandoned the coffee and got on with reading the log books. As he did so, he had the top cover of one of the Enigma machines open, and was pulling out what looked to Hook like metal rings, eight in total, slotted in side-by-side with letters of the alphabet randomly embossed on the rim of each.

'What are those?' Hook enquired.

'Key settings,' replied the lieutenant. 'The army and Luftwaffe only use three key settings; their U-boats use eight.'

'Why?' Hook pushed.

'The Kreigsmarine are paranoid that their U-boats may be detected and sunk. Understandable, really.'

Hook was receiving an education, there was no denying that. He leaned across the table, pulling the second machine towards him. He had seen how Rayner had pulled up the top cover on the first, and followed suit. Rayner raised a hand abruptly.

'Please... don't remove the key settings in that one.'

Startled, Hook slowly lowered the top cover, pushing the machine away.

'Okay, fair enough.'

Rayner apologised for the unnecessary outburst.

'Apologies sir, the U-boats have two on board. At twenty-three, fifty-nine hours Berlin time, all U-boats running either on the surface or at radio transmission depth received the key settings for the next twenty-four hours.'

'Okay.' Hook gave the lieutenant his undivided attention, interested in what he had to teach him. Rayner continued.

'They leave one machine on the key setting of the previous day, and set the other to the next.'

'Why?'

'Some U-boats will not have received the key change, they may be either too deep or engaged in an attack, perhaps. They would send their next message or request the key change on the unchanged key setting.'

'Does their command not ask them to authenticate themselves, fearing the likes of us having their machines?'

The commando officer was really getting his teeth into the subject. Rayner shook his head.

'I doubt it. From all the traffic I have been listening to in the Med, they appear to answer in good faith, and the boat in question then adjusts key settings accordingly.'

Both Hook and Traske were now nodding to each other. The submariner shrugged.

'Makes sense, I suppose.'

'Also, there is one other factor.' Rayner offered. 'Messages for a trained German operator take a while to encode or decode. I am proficient enough in both the use of the thing, and the use of German, but I am not as quick as some users. U-boat command could deliver a long message for 'captain's eyes only'. The operator, normally the boat radioman, has to decode the very message that tells him the text is for the captain only. He would then have to take the machine to the captain, who would then take it to his own bunk to decode the remainder of the code for his solitary reading.'

'What information would he alone be privy to?' Hook asked. 'Surely his radioman is discreet?'

Rayner grinned. 'Usually the radio man is one of the boat's company. One of the boys. The rest of the crew know that he is the ultimate source of information. Cigarettes can loosen the tongue of almost any enlisted man. Information such as enemy convoy locations and predicted routes, other U-boat casualties, party updates, supply rendezvous, sensitive stuff.'

'Why would the radioman not decode enemy convoy information, surely the captain would want that information sooner rather than later?' Hook knew in his own mind that he would rather Parch told him the message sometimes, rather than just shove the handset at him.

Traske added his thoughts.

'Imagine you are the radioman on a U-boat that is on day 60 of a 90-day patrol. You've been attacking convoys for the last week, and in return, the Royal Navy has been depth-charging the shit out of you... would you rush to tell the captain there is another convoy to hunt?'

Hook now understood. Some information is just not welcomed by the boys. He found irony in Traske's explanation, for he himself had some potentially rather unsavoury information to pass to the men when the time was right.

Before long, Rayner closed up the Enigmas and placed both machines, along with their log books, back into the safe where they belonged when not in use. Rayner also added that when at sea, one of the machines sat with the radioman, ready to receive messages.

Hook took his leave and climbed up out of the conning tower. Out in the open, the sheeting still in place offered welcome shade, as he sat against the rail at the rear of the conning tower. The anti-aircraft gun fitted to the boat was locked in its stowage position, unloaded. From his map pocket, he pulled out his notebook. The notebook had pages missing, for the details of the initial attack were committed to memory. The real purpose of the capture of U-911 was sealed in a large envelope in his canvas bergen rucksack. Hook had much to remember, for shortly he would be giving his commandos the second part of their mission. It was up to the troop commanders and their sergeants to decide how they were going to accomplish their part of it.

Before the troop commanders joined him on the conning tower, he had Perch call the aergeant major, Commander Traske and Mr Rayner. He felt it only proper that all of his command staff were privy to the mission, before he delivered it to the men. Traske had officers commanding departments aboard the U-boat, but they would not be part of the planning and command hierarchy, despite their status.

With the sun leaving them over the western horizon, Captain Paul Hook took in the faces of all those invited to the briefing.

Their beards, like his own, were starting to take shape. He was pleased, for they would have need of them soon enough.

'Gentlemen, we are to raid the U-boat pens at La Rochelle.'

There were no open mouths, no gasps of shock or surprise. They just blinked their tired eyes, awaiting more information.

Hook did not disappoint them.

'We will be taking this submarine into La Rochelle. Our mission is to deny the pens to their U-boat fleet, and cause as much damage as possible.'

'When?' asked the Sergeant Major.

'As soon as we feel we are ready. They know U-911 is expecting a delivery.'

'How do you want us to do it?' Mr Rands enquired.

Hook grinned.

'I'm glad you asked me that.'

4

At first light, whilst the sun was low and the temperature cool, Captain Paul Hook had all of the company, less those guarding the prisoners aboard *The Rosa* assembled in the captured headquarters building. The interior of the structure bore the scars of close quarter fighting. Blown out windows, empty bullet casings all over the floor; and bullet holes in the walls. Hook also recognised the tell tale scorch marks and fragmentation damage due to grenades. The captain stood before his men, all rough and ready, with mugs of tea and cigarettes hanging from their lips. He nursed the large sealed manila envelope which held information regarding their up and coming mission.

Content all the men were present, even those in fresh bandages from the earlier fighting, Sergeant Major Gibbs called for them to be silent.

Hook nodded his thanks.

'Gentlemen, you will shortly receive orders for a deliberate raid on the U-boat pens at La Rochelle, on the coast of Nazi-occupied France.'

The men only stared back; the only motion was cigarette smoke drifting upwards. Happy that he now had their attention, he continued.

'We will be taking U-911 into the pens and launching the attack from within. Our mission is to cause as much damage to the facility as possible, thereby denying its use to the German U-boat fleet.'

Hook noted a few nods amongst the audience, and a solitary cough. He continued.

'Once the raid is complete, we will withdraw into the French interior, linking up with SAS units for follow-on operations and recovery back to England.'

Again his men kept their own counsel. They had been on some tough missions before, Hook told himself, so why should this one be any different?

'When do we go, sir?' One of his NCOs asked.

'As soon as we are ready. German Command knows U-911 is due a delivery, so we have time to formulate our plan.'

'So we are using the boat as a Trojan horse?'

'Yes.'

Murmurs began among the audience, Hook was relieved to see most of them were nodding, as if the plan was to their liking. One of Hook's sergeants raised a hand.

'Who is to do what, sir?'

Hook held aloft the bulky envelope. 'I will break this target pack open with the troop commanders, along with Commander Traske. We will build our plan, and troop commanders will then deliver details to you.'

The murmurs grew louder, as if the boys were already planning the raid themselves. This pleased Hook, for he knew the men under his command approved of such a mission. After all, that's why they had volunteered to become commandos. Before the chatter grew out of control, the sergeant major called for order.

Hook was content that he had given the men enough information for them to begin getting their minds and equipment ready.

'Thank you gentlemen, please ensure those on guard duty get the information.'

The men took that as their cue to get up and file out of the building. As with most briefings, officers and sergeants stayed behind. The NCOs were more than able to run things in their absence. As the last private soldier left the building, Hook broke the seal on the envelope and tipped the contents onto the table.

Many hands swooped in, grabbing the documents as they came to rest. Hook and Sergeant Major Gibbs stood back whilst the troop commanders and their sergeants got together and talked about what was before them. The majority of the target pack was made up of aerial photographs of the pens, some pictures clearer than others. Most had been taken at high altitude by bombers, but a few of them were low level and of better quality. The images had chinagraph arrows and text scribbled on them, highlighting key features within the facility.

Hook also noted the hand-drawn sketches detailing the interior and layout of the pens. The level of detail told him that the artist was either currently working there, or was part of the construction team, one of several risking their lives to provide the British with such information. It was not lost on the captain that a large volume of slave labour had probably been drafted in to build the facility for their Nazi masters. He prayed that those extraordinary people would not be present during the raid, for he couldn't guarantee their safety.

One particularly large envelope remained untouched on the table, marked as being for 'Hook's eyes only'. The captain frowned at the terseness of the address as he picked it up. It was thin, as if it contained nothing but a few sheets of paper. He stepped back away from the men, breaking the two wax seals holding it closed. Hook pulled out a number of leaves of paper, the top one lacking any header, the text getting to the point without pomp.

As he read the document, he quickly realised that it contained details of the SAS squadron they would be linking up with, post-raid. The information was comprehensive enough to give him the name of their squadron commander, Major Dan Simmons. It also went into detail about the squadron's work in Nazi-occupied France, and their current modus operandi in the region. Hook scanned the document at first, mentally highlighting key terms and phrases, before returning to the front cover. He then read the entire document again at a deliberate pace. With the document absorbed, he ignored the address protocol demanded on the envelope, passing the material to Gibbs.

The sergeant major took it as his cue to find a corner and read it for himself. Hook mulled over the details of the SAS mission statement as it applied whilst on deployment, knowing that the work his own men were about to undertake would really upset what they had achieved thus far. It would make the commandos' secondment to the SAS squadron tense, to say the least. Gibbs returned the document to the captain, his cheeks puffed out, eyebrows raised in response to what it had revealed.

After some time watching the men absorb the information before them, Hook called for order and began to address the planning issues in turn. Traske was the first to throw his hand in.

'The boat is German; I need young Rayner here to label all the vital equipment and controls in order for us to have a clue on how to use the thing.'

Both Hook and Rayner nodded. The submariner had a valid point. Traske was not finished.

'My department heads need crew, so I suggest the sharper men amongst the company are given to them, so we can sail both on the surface and submerged.'

Hook had to agree. He eyed Bamber Cross. '1 Troop are about to become submariners.'

Cross grinned. 'I'm sure they will be delighted.'

Traske got Cross' attention. 'We need those torpedoes off that ship, and into the sub, as soon as possible. My weapons officer, Mr Pryce here, needs to teach them how to get the boat ready to shoot.'

Lieutenant Pryce gave a casual wave as an introduction.

Hook nodded at the young officer. 'I want the boys like slick gun crews. I need them drilling around the clock, for they need to be bloody quick feeding them fish into the tubes.'

Pryce agreed. 'No problem, sir. They will be torpedo men before you know it, whether they like it or not.'

Traske then turned his attention to Lieutenant Anthony Fearl.

'You will navigate throughout, same as you would back on the *Marlin*.'

Fearl agreed. 'Of course, sir.'

A tattooed, barrel-chested petty officer, Roger Toil, leaned in. 'I need two of your boys to drive the thing. All they have to do is what I tell them, when I tell them.'

Hook looked at Cross. 'Who are your best drivers?'

Cross scoffed. 'Have you seen them drive *anything*? Usually ends bad for everyone.'

The whole group chuckled. Hook took the opportunity to instruct them to go and grab some tea and come back as quickly as possible. They needed to get the finer details of the mission down before any of them could rest.

*

With the planning group refreshed, Hook then addressed the next dilemma they had to overcome: getting to La Rochelle with such a large force crammed into the U-boat. He looked to his submariners for guidance. Traske was quick to assist.

'It will be cramped, make no mistake. Our key issue is the boat's performance. Because of the additional load, her diving, manoeuvring and surfacing speeds will all be slower, resulting in additional fuel consumption and leaving us vulnerable to attack en route..'

'That ship is full of fuel for the sub,' Gibbs reminded the group. Traske nodded.

'Yes, but La Rochelle is a fair trek away. Over a thousand miles, easily.'

'Surely U-boats can hold more than enough fuel for such a distance?' queried Hook.

'Sure,' Traske responded, 'assuming we are looking at ten knots surface running and four submerged, it will take us about seven days to get there. If we run submerged for long periods, it will really put strain on the batteries.'

'Batteries?' Hook asked, already sensing that the selected route and method of reaching the target would not be without challenges.

'The submarine runs on battery power when submerged. Underwater, we will manage four knots at best, but will only have battery power for about ninety miles, after which we will have to run on the surface for a while and use the diesel engines to recharge the batteries before we can go back down.'

Hook grinned. 'Well, that sort of knowledge explains why you are a submarine captain and I am not. That part of the mission will be your headache.'

'Indeed.' Traske's reply was deadpan.

The group fell to silence, until Hook had another question.

'Will we get there, providing we go direct?'

'Yes, providing we *do* go direct. If we encounter convoys we will have to stop and wait for them to move on. Boxing around them will not... '

'What if we are attacked by a destroyer?' Rayner interrupted. The room fell silent once more.

'*What?*' grimaced the sergeant major.

Rayner composed himself after his outburst. 'What do we do if we are attacked by one of our own bloody destroyers?'

Hook looked to Traske, who had placed his open palms on the table.

'We blow the tanks and surface, making ourselves known.'

'Won't they be shooting the hell out of us as we come up?' asked James Rands, his cheery attitude waning.

Traske nodded.

'Yes, most likely, but to try and out-run them submerged would be our death sentence.'

Hook could see by the demeanours of a number of his group, that things were about to get out of hand. Fearing his commanders would lose confidence in the mission, he stepped in.

'That settles it then. We run on the surface for as long as we can risk it, saving fuel and time. We run submerged during the day. We stop if we detect any convoy activity, and surface if we feel we have been detected. Agreed?'

The captain looked at all the faces around him. The men were all looking to each other for reassurance, yet nodding their approval. That was good enough for Hook.

'That's that taken care of. Despite what we do for a living, I'm not in the business of getting my men killed before they get on target, never mind getting sunk by the flaming Royal Navy.'

A few of the group chuckled. Hook gave Traske a gentle nudge. 'Present company excepted, of course.'

'Of course.'

Rayner brought the group back to earth with another concern. 'How will I know what is a convoy, and what is a destroyer? I'm not a submariner by trade. Sonar is not my area of expertise, sir.'

Traske waved a hand dismissively. 'If it sounds man-made, it probably is. As soon as you hear it, tell me, and we will go quiet. I will then join you and together we will fathom what it is.'

'Thank you, sir.' Rayner felt reassured.

Hook leaned across the table, rearranging the target pack so the aerial photographs were spread out for all to see. He focussed on one photo in particular. A low-level pass, just as a U-boat moved through what was labelled as a 'lock', into the main basin outside the hardened pens. About the facility he could make out strategically-placed barrage balloons and their tenders, which were, ironically, designed to prevent low-level attacks. He squinted at the grainy image of the submarine itself.

'The crew is up on deck. I can make out figures in the conning tower.'

Traske pulled the image towards him, scrutinising the picture to verify the commando officer's claim, then nodding.

'Usual protocol. We do the same out of Valletta. Dignitaries and locals come and see you off — or welcome you back.'

'Why would the locals come and see them bastards in or out?' grunted the sergeant major.

Traske looked up at the man. 'The Germans have been there since '40. I would not be surprised if some of the local girls have married their German lovers.'

A worrying thought washed over Hook. There was every chance that they would be welcomed 'home' by the wives and girlfriends of those currently held on *The Rosa*. He was not keen to have civilians caught up in the action when shooting started. However, he kept this thought to himself; if expressed, it would only divert attention from what they were there to do. He would have to just trust his men's judgement when the time came.

He focussed on the current conversation.

'My guys will be on the deck ready to go,' announced Rands, and Sergeant Grice nodded in agreement.

'Make sure your men don't shave until further notice,' said Traske. 'They are submariners returning from patrol, so beards will be the norm for all ranks.'

Hook had a question. 'What's this long building to the right of the lock? Looks like a covered access.'

Traske scrutinised the image. 'Could well be a protected lock facility. Bugger knows why they are not using it. Given the context of the image, I would not want to be caught in the exposed lock in daylight.'

Hook examined the photograph again. Traske's point certainly had merit. Why did the enemy not use the facility?

'It could be damaged, but we can't see how, or by what.' Cross suggested.

The sergeant major broke in to disrupt this train of thought. 'What about uniforms?'

Hook had already thought of that. 'We use their rain gear, with our own uniforms and equipment underneath. Weapons slung underneath the rain gear. The soft caps worn by the Germans will have to be used, along with our beards, to buy us a little time before they realise that we are not the crew they were expecting.'

'Does that apply to everyone?' asked Rands. Hook shook his head.

'Just those that can be seen from the quayside. Everyone else will be in British uniform and equipment, ready to go.'

The group nodded. Hook could feel the mood begin to darken. It always did when they planned when the shooting would start. Hook looked at the photograph once more. He studied the crowd on the quayside, some of whom appeared to be running away, fearing attack from the low-flying aircraft. The image inspired another question for Traske to answer.

'Will any of the dignitaries board the boat? Will they insist on a formal handshake, or anything?'

Traske puffed out his cheeks as he slowly shook his head. 'Not sure. *We* would do it now and again, but I'm not sure if the Germans deal in such pomp.'

Hook viewed a mental image in which he had to shake hands with a man he would then have to shoot, in order to clear the gangway for his raiders. The grim nature of the job.

With the formalities of the arrival in the pens discussed, it was agreed that they would just have to go with Traske's expertise when they arrived. Photos were fine, Hook concluded, but they could only tell you so much. It was decided that Rands and his men would be the crew lining the deck, clad in rain gear and soft-ridged, peaked caps and ready to cause mayhem. Standing with them would be men from 1 Troop, who would crew the deck gun as soon as the shooting started. Meanwhile, up in the conning tower, Hook and Rayner, along with Traske and two other 1 Troop men, would be dressed in rain gear and capped accordingly. The two 1 Troop men would get the AA gun onto action and engage any German flak units capable of shooting at the sub.

Both 2 and 3 Troops, Hook's command group and those 1 Troop members that were not on U-boat tasks would disembark as quickly as they could and fight their way into the pens. Traske and his submariners, along with the commando crew, would push off and reverse back towards the lock in order to get beyond the minimum arming range of the torpedoes. 'Hang on,' said Rands as discussions were underway. 'What if the pens are dry docked? You won't be able to hit the U-boats sat in there.'

'Then we shoot at the dry dock gate.' Traske's response was immediate. 'If it is in dry dock then it is likely that the sub is undergoing heavy maintenance. By allowing the water in, we could very well flood and sink the boat in place.'

Rands nodded in capitulation. Hook then challenged the submariner.

'Is the basin long enough for the torpedoes to arm?'

'Yes, but only just. The Germans have recently improved their torpedo reliability. They have upgraded their pistols over the course of the last year or so, hence the tonnage going to the bottom as our convoys cross the Atlantic.'

'Pistols?' queried Hook.

'The easiest way to describe it...' paused Mr Pryce, is as the fuse to the torpedo.'

Hook relaxed a little, his question answered. Traske continued.

'My intention is to shoot off all the torpedoes into the pens as quickly as we can, with the deck gun and anti-aircraft gun covering us as we surface fire. Once we have shot all the torpedoes, I will ram that bloody sub into the nearest pen. We will then disembark and join you again, as you shoot your way through the place.'

The commandos in the room eyed each other and exchanged childish grins. They liked Traske's bold, yet simple, plan. His fellow submariners didn't smile so much and this reticence prompted the sergeant major to step in.

'You gentlemen need to familiarise yourselves with all our weapons. Once you are off that tub, you will become infantry.'

Traske nodded his understanding; his department heads accepted their lot.

5

Hook allowed a leg stretch and more refreshments before they got onto the finer details of what they were to do once they had got into the pens.

Once back from refilling mugs and relieving themselves, they looked carefully at the photos that gave them a good view of the jetty, the quayside and the hardened shelters that protected the U-boats inside. Previous bombing raids had caused considerable damage to the less robustly-protected buildings in the pen area, but the main bunker had withstood all punishment. The craters on its broad, flat roof were shallow and fragmented, unlike the deeper, more devastating ones that straddled the smaller structures.

Hook turned to Traske.

'These sketches aside, do you have any idea what the inside looks like?'

The commander shook his head. 'I've only worked out of Valletta. I can only imagine the pens are wide enough to accommodate one, maybe two, U-boats at any one time. Overhead cranes for torpedo loading, heavy maintenance and so forth.'

Hook nodded his understanding, aware that information regarding the layout of the pens' interior was vague at best. He posed another question, whilst scrutinising the sketches.

'Would they have a magazine bay for their torpedoes, deck gun ammo, et cetera? We can't point out where they are, on these.'

'Most likely, hence the lengths they have gone to to make them as good as bomb-proof.'

The sergeant major waved a hand dismissively. 'We haven't got the explosives to blow up the magazine, even if they do have one. So let's not dwell on it too much.'

Hook nodded his agreement. 'The sergeant major is right. Let's not worry about what else they have in there. Our main effort is to be directed at damaging the U-boats enough to render the pens unusable — for the short term, at least. Besides the torpedo option, what can we do with the deck gun?'

'Depending on the height of the dry dock gates, we could have that thing shooting holes in the conning towers. They can't go out on patrol if they can't dive.'

'Are the subs armoured?' Rands chipped in. Traske shook his head.

'Not particularly, they can't afford to have them too heavy in the water, hence the very issue we are facing. The outer skin of the sub could be pierced by the deck gun, making diving without repair extremely risky, due to water pressure, flooding and so forth.'

'What calibre is the deck gun?' Hook asked aloud, throwing the question open to anyone that knew.

'Eighty-eight millimetres.' Rayner jumped in. 'Some of their flak guns have that size round. Reports in from North Africa say that the Germans have been knocking out a lot of our tanks with their flak guns firing in the ground role. Bastards.'

'Right then,' Hook concluded, 'we can use torpedoes and the deck gun to shoot up what boats they have in the pens. Both can also be used on dry dock gates, should they be up. We flood the pen; they still lose the boat within it.'

Everyone nodded. Hook then put the next issue to them.

'We need to destroy their means of communication with the outside world. By the time we get into the pens, every German in the garrison will probably know that an attack is in progress. Any information they get will be vague initially, so we need to knock out their main offices as part of the plan. In doing this, we stand a better chance of getting out of La Rochelle whilst they are all still trying to get the facts sorted out, so they can deploy their forces effectively.'

'There will be a lot of Germans in La Rochelle, not to mention outside the town.' Rands spoke in a low voice and the others exchanged glances, nodding their agreement. Hook banged a fist on the table, making them all flinch.

'Doesn't mean a thing! Sure, they are many in number, but that means many people will be trying to find out what is going on. With their communications flooded with requests for information, they will be inert until they know where to go, and with what resources. Large numbers of troops are slow to react, and they miss opportunities.'

His statement seemed to lift the men from their doubts. Commandos took comfort in chaos, usually of their own making, hence the type of missions they were customarily employed on. They worked on minimal information, maximum initiative, guts, aggression and the will to win. Hook leaned in, his expression menacing.

'We are going into where the enemy rests, and we are going to tear that place apart. By the time the enemy have pulled their collective finger out and are reacting to the situation, I want that U-boat pen to be a flooded, broken, smouldering shell.'

Hook was greeted with smiles all around. Even the submarine officers were beaming with the excitement of it all. Hook turned around to his sergeant major.

'Have we got any thermite grenades?

Gibbs shrugged. 'Some of the boys might still have some from the Tunisia job; we didn't get the chance to sort out what we had left over before leaving Gib.'

Hook nodded. 'I'm thinking that if we have enough, we can drop a couple in any open hatches we encounter on the boats. Won't sink the things, but it will give them more repairs to take care of before they are seaworthy once again.'

Everyone agreed, except Traske.

'That won't be enough. Sure, I will fire the torpedoes, but that means we will be trying to hit the boats on the nose, when they could just glance down the length of the hull. If they don't detonate at all, at least they then pose a problem for their bomb disposal teams.'

'What has that got to do with thermite grenades?' asked Hook.

'I can't assume the torpedoes alone will do enough damage, same goes for just dropping thermite down the hatch. If your boys can board the subs and open the outer torpedo tube doors, they could perhaps attach the thermite grenades to the torpedo hatches?'

Hook looked at the sergeant major, who shrugged his shoulders, nodding at the same time. Traske continued.

'If they could wedge one in the hatch locking wheel so it would burn a hole in the hatch, it would give the men time to get out again, before water began to pour into the torpedo room.'

Hook sat back, running his fingertips through his beard. He imagined the locking hatch, the grenade wedged in between its spokes.

'If the lads could ensure the base of the grenade was in contact with the hatch, I see no reason why it wouldn't work.'

'I will have the NCOs redistribute their ammo and grenades before we depart,' Gibbs said, making a note.

Traske raised a hand, which calmed the excited chatter.

'Apart from enemy soldiers, we must be mindful of civilians that work on the facility, particularly those in the pens.'

'Why?' Gibbs asked in a surly tone.

Traske shot a disapproving look at the commando warrant officer, before turning back to Hook — but any support he was expecting to receive from the captain was not forthcoming.

Hook blinked slowly, then spoke.

'We are to kill all key personnel within the pens. Civilians who work on U-boats fall into that category.'

'Captain Hook...' Traske was cut short by the mission commander, despite his junior status.

'Commander Traske, my men and I will ensure that the La Rochelle fleet will not be fit to sail into the North Atlantic for the foreseeable future. If that means killing civilians who are key to preparing them for sea... then so be it.'

Hook's bold yet pragmatic statement rendered everyone in the room mute. The submarine commander, a combatant in his own right, was most uncomfortable with what the commando captain had put to him. Holding his hands out in front of him as if it could appease the commandos, Traske made his plea.

'I am not comfortable with the concept, that's all I am saying. I'm not in the business of killing civilians if I can avoid it.'

'What is your tonnage score so far, Commander?' Hook challenged a man of superior rank.

'I beg your pardon?' Traske was most put out by the question. Hook leaned in aggressively.

'When you have patrolled the Med, Commander, how many ships have you sent to the bottom?'

Traske composed himself before answering. He knew he could not fight his way out of it threatening the captain with charges for insubordination — that kind of threat didn't really worry commandos much.

'More than my fair share.'

'How many Italian and German merchant seamen went to the bottom with those Afrika Korps supplies?'

'You make a fair point, Captain.' Traske conceded. 'War is dreadful.'

Hook nodded, content not to drive home the advantage. Instead he sought to defuse the situation quickly, by having the men about him begin to plan their troops' tasks within the pens. Hook reminded them that the main objective was to damage the boats, and knock out communications. Concurrent to that, they would be fighting German military personnel, and perhaps a fair number of pro-German French citizens.

'Remember gentlemen, if they are there to welcome us home, choose your targets wisely. If they are in the pens, they are part of the German war effort.'

Traske, along with his submarine officers, nodded in satisfaction. Hook would just have to trust the professionalism of his men. Hook knew that innocents could die in the raid, but he was not going to drag his men over the coals about it.

As they pored over the sketches, the commando officers and their sergeants agreed to have 2 Troop make sure that the moored U-boats were out of action; 3 Troop would clear the offices, and provide fire support as 2 Troop boarded, sabotaging the torpedo tube hatches with thermite.

Traske then pointed out a glaring problem.

'Gents, you are forgetting that I intend to send torpedoes into the very pens you are fighting in, I can only apologise in advance if the bang in there is a little too big. May I suggest you only move into each pen in turn, after I have fired the torpedoes into it?'

'How will we know?' asked Bamber Cross.

Traske grinned and gave him a wink.

'Believe me, you will know when a torpedo goes off in there.'

The commandos agreed. Traske went on to describe his solution in more detail, fingering the grainy photo of the low-level pass.

'When you get off the boat and it all gets very noisy, I will push off and shoot up the pens from right to left. That way the torpedo strikes remain ahead of you.'

They all nodded. Gibbs leaned in, putting a finger on what appeared to be pens to the right of the jetty.

'What about these?'

Hook leaned in to study the part of the image that the sergeant major was pointing at. The roof of that part of the facility appeared open to the elements. Not jagged, as if it had been damaged, but rather it looked to be incomplete.

He shook his head. 'Under construction. Sure it would be great to knock them out, but I don't want to split the company, bearing in mind that some of the lads will still be on the boat shooting torpedoes.'

Everyone agreed. Hook made another point.

'Commander, if you could ram U-911 into the far left pen when you have finished shooting the place up, we can then rally there before we fight our way out. The images suggest there is a railway line that takes you out of the facility and the town to the north east. However, we must ensure we keep our distance from the small airstrip to the north. There are bound to be a fair few Luftwaffe personnel in that area, not to mention German army units.'

'We stand a better chance following the rail line through the town before striking north for our RV,' stated Rands. 'Sure, we are still in the town, but buildings offer cover if the fight follows us out of the pens.'

Everyone agreed. Traske and his submarine officers watched as the commandos began to make their own sketches of the area between La Rochelle and their proposed RV in Marans. Hook looked up, noticing they were not doing the same.

'We are only human, gentlemen, better men than us have fallen. You might want to note key towns and villages. It may only be you that meets up with the SAS.'

The looks the submariners gave each other said it all. There was no guarantee that the commandos would make it to the RV, never mind them.

With the sketches complete, Hook didn't need to remind his troop commanders to have their men copy those sketches, for they knew they could end up separated and still have a job to do. In the grand scheme of things, if the whole company was scattered over the French countryside, it made it harder work for the Germans to chase them all. Each of his men was a confident and competent navigator, or else they would not have earned their green berets in the first place.

'Right then, let's talk about our move to Marans,' Hook said. His own men knew the protocol, the announcement was more for the benefit of Traske and his officers. 'You are armed, and just as dangerous as those chasing you. Fight them where you can, take their weapons if you can, do whatever it takes to slow them down. They won't stop, but they will be more cautious if they know you are willing to fight.'

The submariners were uneasy as they looked at each other. Hook understood; they were about to step out of their comfort zone. He continued.

'If you are near the RV, and you are still being chased, don't go to the bloody RV. The SAS will not thank you for it. They've been there long enough without the German army catching on to them.'

They understood. Hook reassured them.

'More than likely you will be tucked in behind some of my lads, so you will have some muscle with you for the move to the RV. If we break into small groups, it makes chasing us all the more difficult for them. They will split their units, which make the chances of ambushing them all the greater.'

'What happens when we link up with the SAS in Marans?' asked the Chief Petty Officer, Roger Toil.

Hook shrugged. 'We work with them until such time they can assist us with our recovery back to England. However, there is every chance they will get you guys out, whilst we get seconded to them long term, or re-tasked via agents and couriers. Nothing we haven't done before.'

'Well then,' shrugged the petty officer, 'it's a good job we didn't wear our usual rig for this mission, then.'

It wasn't lost on Hook and his officers that the Royal Navy Submariners sported the very same battledress as they did. Gibbs was right to point out that as soon as the submarine part of the mission was over, they would become soldiers for the foreseeable future.

The officers planning the raid into La Rochelle U-boat pens mulled over the images before them, trying their best to tie up any loose ends. Hook reassured them that should any questions or issues spring to mind during their preparations over the next few days, they were to be discussed and examined, leaving no stone unturned.

'Hang on a minute!' bellowed the sergeant major. All heads turned towards him as one.

Gibbs nodded his apologies for his sudden outburst. 'Excuse me gentlemen, but...'

He had their attention and he pressed that advantage home.

'We have a ship parked outside full of torpedoes, fuel and provisions for this very U-boat, correct?'

'Correct.' Hook's expression was impassive.

'Then why on earth would we need to come back to La Rochelle?'

'I don't understand.' Rayner's response was apologetic. The other officers looked no more informed than he. The sergeant major put a finger on one of the photos.

'If U-911 was out of torpedoes and low on provisions, she would have returned to La Rochelle autonomously, would you agree?'

'Yes', Traske nodded.

'I don't think their sub commanders have the freedom of movement as perhaps ours, or I dare say, the Americans, have.'

Hook blinked as he leaned in, placing his hands on the table, eyeing his warrant officer.

'Sergeant Major, what are you driving at?'

'I'm saying we need a *reason* to return to La Rochelle, or else our sudden arrival could be seen as suspicious. They have been told to sit here and await re-supply. I think the German top brass want to keep as many of their boats in the Atlantic as possible, or else why would they go through all the trouble of having an Italian ship marked up as Portuguese, just to get past Gibraltar?'

Silence fell upon the group. Gibbs knew he had a point. Rayner raised a hand slowly.

'I will look through their radio log; see if we can find a way in which we can ask La Rochelle for authority to return.'

The petty officer suddenly stood bolt upright, eyes wide, mouth agape. Hook acknowledged his apparent 'eureka moment'.

'Chief? C'mon, show us officers up some more!' Hook winked. Toil addressed his request to Rayner.

'Sir, if you please, check their log for recent depth charge attacks on U-911. See if they have reported them in.'

'Okay' Rayner replied. "What am I looking for?'

'If they have reported them in, then La Rochelle will be more likely to allow a return to the pens for, let's say, dry dock inspection. We already have a poor performance case to put to them. With all of us on board for the run in, our diving and manoeuvre performance will be affected anyway.'

All the officers stood upright, there were grins all around. It *could* work. Gibbs threw a comment into the mix.

'Just don't mention the part where it's full of British commandos.'

Chuckles erupted from the group. Rayner nodded.

'I will go through the log. Since she is out of torpedoes, I'm sure she has been chased and battered by at least one destroyer recently.'

The discussion continued for some time, with members of the group reassuring each other as to the rationale behind their fictional need to return to home base. Hook allowed it to continue a little until he called for order by slapping the wax-sealed envelope on the table. It wasn't heavy enough to make much noise, but Hook's over-dramatic action had all the men pause and look at him.

'We need to talk now about the SAS.'

The faces staring back at him frowned, before looking at each other. Their expressions told Hook that they had no idea what he was referring to.

Hook rested clenched fists on the table, eyeing them all as he spoke.

'What we are about to do is going to really piss them off, not to mention their French allies.'

The looks back at him remained vacant. He continued.

'The squadron in question has been deployed in the region for about six weeks so far. Their commander, a man called Simmons, has managed to build a network of trust and co-operation with local resistance units, who have recently agreed to a cease-fire of sorts with the local German garrison commanders.'

'Why would they do that?' Rands asked.

'In return for captured aircrews and an end to mass arrests and searches, the local French forces have agreed not to attack German troop trains taking personnel on leave back to Germany, nor those coming into the area from the Russian front, to rest. The French have also agreed not to attack local girls who happen to be dating German soldiers.'

'Our plan is really going to upset the apple cart, isn't it?' Traske's question was rhetorical. Hook nodded.

'So as you can imagine, I will have to really jump into bed with this Simmons chap when we RV with them. I can't imagine they will be pleased to see us. That could well play to our advantage.'

'How so?' asked Rayner .

'They will be keen to get us out of their hair as soon as possible. They will have their contacts sort out our return to England sooner rather than later.'

'Do you really think our mission will break the ceasefire?' Sergeant Daryl Pelton asked. Hook eyed him with a weak smile.

'If you were the German commander in the area, would you be in the mood to play nicely after what we have planned?'

The SAS discussion ended as abruptly as it had begun. Hook and his men had work to be getting on with.

'Right, gents,' Hook began. 'We have a plan in principle. The finer detail is down to you. You now have the remainder of the day, including all of tonight, to formulate your plans. Since the target pack is not to leave this room, I suggest that you plan and deliver your orders to your men in here too. Mr Cross, you will deliver your plan to your troop first thing in the morning.

Bearing in mind, they will be learning how to load and drive a submarine; they can then crack straight on with preparing the boat and training.'

Bamber Cross nodded.

'The remainder of the company will go through their equipment checks, before receiving their specific orders for the mission once 1 Troop have got theirs. Agreed?'

The officers and NCOs nodded. There was much to do, so it was vital to be proactive and concurrent with what time they had. The captain and the sergeant major left their commanders to plan probably one of the most audacious raids of the war so far.

6

Both Hook and Gibbs took a stroll along the quayside, leaving the officers and men to go about their planning and mission preparations. Traske and his officers were aboard U-911, assisting Rayner with the labelling of key equipment and controls in English.

With their Thompson submachine guns slung across their backs, both men stood with hands in their pockets looking at *The Rosa*.

'We need to move that bloody thing, if we intend to get the torpedoes aboard,' Gibbs observed.

'I'm happy for it to be moved in the morning,' Hook replied. 'I just want the troop commanders to get their plans in order first. I will attend all the briefings, just so I know what they are up to.'

Gibbs nodded. The experienced warrant officer was never one for showing a softer side, but he felt it was time to show his cards to the captain.

'It's one ballsy mission sir, I'll give you that.'

'You not confident it will work?' Hook would always listen to Gibbs' reservations, which were few and far between. Gibbs scoffed in reply.

'It'll work, the boys will see to that. The Germans will be fucking pissed off if they grab any of us.'

Hook and his commandos were all too aware of Hitler's new directive, ordering the execution of any commando captured in or out of uniform. The German leader knew they were dangerous men, and had to be disposed of. Gibbs had been a troop sergeant on the Saint Nazaire raid the previous year, returning to England with only a fraction of the men that he went out with — but not before destroying the dry dock gate that prevented the German battleship *Tirpitz* from having a repair facility on the French coast. He knew the risks, so did his men. A few of the NCOs within the company were on that very same raid.

'That's a thought...' Gibbs chirped up. 'Where are we meeting the SAS, once we get to Marans?'

Hook shrugged his shoulders. 'No idea. They are expecting us within the next ten days. So that gives us, say two days to get ready, a week getting there. The raid, then perhaps a day after getting to the RV.'

'What if we are late?' Gibbs pushed. The captain turned to his sergeant major.

'Mr Gibbs, your guess is as good as mine. I felt it wise to leave that part out when we were chatting with the others. Our main effort is the pens, getting to Marans is just something we are going to have to pull out of our hats when the time comes.'

'Excellent,' said Gibbs, with a grin from ear to ear.' I can't remember the last time we made it to an RV on time anyway. I have no intention of dancing to the SAS timetable, either.'

Hook winked. 'My thoughts exactly. If the sods aren't there when we get there, we will just make our own bloody way home.'

The pair of them were then distracted by a small group of German prisoners loitering up on the rail of *The Rosa*. The ship had become their stockade for the time being. The U-boat crew, along with the Italian merchant men, had neither means of gaining access to the torpedoes or provisions, nor the means to set sail. Gibbs had ordered his sentries to shoot any prisoner that touched the mooring ropes. Once Hook and his men were gone, they would have the run of the place again. The captain doubted they would be in any hurry to get back into the war. Some had their soft-ridged caps pushed on the back of their heads, which reminded the sergeant major of the pending ruse.

'If you want us looking like German submariners, we are going to need their caps too.'

Hook nodded as he turned to scan the sheer cliffs towering over them.

'I'm sure you have the flair for that. Offer them medical attention, their personal possessions and any booze that they have lying about the sub and the barracks. I don't want any more of their crew dying. We have what we came for.'

*

Little sleep was to be had that night. Hook wandered in and out of the troop commanders' planning sessions as Gibbs went about ensuring the lads were guarding the ship and their prisoners, whose behaviour was impeccable, despite the loss of a couple of comrades in the initial attack. They were ordered into the bow storage bay and were to remain there until the torpedoes and supplies were unloaded the following morning. Gibbs was originally concerned with the possibility of enemy crew members sabotaging the torpedoes and fuel, but his concerns were groundless — they knew they were on to a good little number and that once the British departed, they could remain on the island and sit out the rest of the war. Gibbs ensured some of the men were keeping an eye out for any locals that may try and stir trouble. He even went so far as to send patrols into the town. The locals kept themselves to themselves. Those commandos not tasked with anything were to rest, for things were shortly about to get very busy.

The following morning, nothing remarkable happened in the Azores town of Velas. Hook was in attendance as Bamber Cross issued orders to his men, whilst the remainder of the company went about their morning ablutions. The risk of the men shaving was not a concern, as the commandos seldom brought luxuries on missions. Just the means to wage war, weapons, ammunition, explosives if they had any, water and maybe some food.

The morning routine involved a change in manpower guarding the ship, whilst everyone else, i.e. those not in 1 Troop, got on with cleaning and checking their weapons. As concurrent activity, Gibbs had the Italian crew move *The Rosa* alongside U-911. 1 Troop would shortly be getting their first lesson in submarine warfare, moving torpedoes from ship to sub. The Italians were happy to comply with Gibbs' demands, for they were not enjoying the company of the Germans who joked at their expense. Gibbs was not overly concerned for their safety; if they couldn't handle a little heckling, then they were certainly in the wrong job.

With the ship now moored alongside the submarine, Gibbs became acutely conscious of the steep learning curve his men were about to follow. The crane controls were in Italian, the instructions on the torpedoes and the sub were German. With a grunt, he acknowledged the perks of being the company's sergeant major.

As 1 Troop finished receiving their orders for the raid, they clambered aboard the ship, their NCOs quickly putting their boys to task with the crane and the torpedoes under the direction of Lieutenant Pryce, the submarine weapons officer. Gibbs watched as the young officer pulled off his battledress jacket, rolling up his sleeves as he approached the crane controls.

'Fear not, Sergeant Major,' he said with a cheeky grin and a wink. 'In Valletta, the controls are in bloody Maltese, so we are all stuffed.'

Hook took the opportunity to refresh himself with tea before going in to oversee James Rands' orders. Thankfully, his orders were much less complex than those given by Cross, who had to include all the submarine factors.

Rands had to get off the boat and generate havoc in the pens. It would be his men that would concentrate on dealing with the U-boats moored in the pens, should Traske have not done them in good and proper with the torpedoes and deck gun. Sergeant Grice had managed to canvass the whole company, collecting what thermite grenades they had left in their bergen rucksacks from the Tunisia mission. Rands now had enough for each U-boat should there be two subs in each pen. They were to board the submarine, killing any opposition as they made their way forward to the torpedo room. They would manually wind open the outer torpedo tube doors, and the thermite grenades would be set to burn a hole through the lower tube access hatches, resulting in catastrophic flooding. It would be enough to sink the U-boat, if Traske hadn't put holes in them beforehand.

Because the U-boats were the focus of main effort, Hook and his radio operator, Alfie Parch, would be with Rands and his men. The company sergeant major would accompany 3 Troop as they swept through, destroying enemy communications and any offices within the facility, not to mention killing anyone that stood in their way. If there were civilians in the pen area, they were contributing to the German war effort. Hook wasn't happy about the prospect of killing them, but if it saved the lives of many coming across the Atlantic... then it was justified.

Before long, all company personnel were briefed on what their tasks would be once the shooting started within the pens. With that confirmed, the men went about ensuring their bodies, minds and equipment were ready to go.

Hook wandered along the dock wall on his own as he thought through various parts of the mission, for much was riding on its success. If they put the pens and whatever U-boats were moored in there out of action for a while, then in theory more shipping could cross the North Atlantic unmolested. He was also mindful that this was not a suicide mission, to be carried out for the sake of prestige. He wanted all his men to make it out of La Rochelle and make the RV — but he knew that was going to be a tall order. The Germans would be stunned initially, but he had fought them enough times to learn that they tended to get themselves re-organised very quickly.

The raid needed to be quick, they had to destroy what they could, and get the hell out of there in true commando fashion.

His solitary walk took him around the top of the port sea wall. The Atlantic was calm, yet the breeze sent a chill through him. He came to be looking down at the town's small cemetery, the hastily-dug graves of the German sailors killed in the initial attack, still evident. On each of the five graves stood a simple cross that had been fashioned out of thin strips of wood. Hook assumed the text written upon each was the dead man's serial number, rank and name. Their identity tags would have provided such information, not to mention the close bond they would have had with their fellow submariners.

Someone had already visited the graves and laid flowers upon them. The islanders appeared to cause no trouble, and had some rapport with the Germans who no doubt had been using the island for some time. He doubted it made the locals pro-German, they were just living with whoever happened to be there at the time. Hook turned, giving the graves one more cursory glance before slowly heading back towards the U-boat and the activity on its forward deck.

Some of his men were rehearsing how to operate the deck gun. Others were up in the conning tower, doing the same with the anti-aircraft gun, ensuring they could lower it enough to fire at ground targets. Other men streamed off the submarine at a fair pace, throwing off their rain gear as they went. He was pleased to see his men leaving nothing to chance, even rehearsing the initial disembarkation, when the shooting would begin. He glanced up at *The Rosa* towering overhead. He could see the crane lifting torpedoes slowly, manoeuvring them into position for their eventual destination, which was U-911. The boys nominated to become ad-hoc submariners were taking it all in their stride. It was what was required, just for the raid. Once back on dry land, they would soon be back in their old commando routine. Hook caught sight of a lone figure, jogging up towards him. Then

Parch's familiar profile revealed itself. Hook continued to walk towards him.

'Captain Hook, sir. Mr Rayner has something to show you.'

7

'She was depth charged three weeks ago.'

Rayner smiled excitedly; sweat dripping from his nose in the stifling confines of the submarine. Hook removed his battledress jacket as he sat next to him. On the table before them were log books and other documentation held by the captain and radio man of U-911.

'Go on.' Hook was impassive as Rayner pointed at the log entry in question. Hook noted that all the entries had been made in pencil, the handwriting a challenge to fathom, let alone translate into English.

'It's states in the log book that she was tracked and engaged several times over a period of about six hours.'

Hook puffed out his cheeks. 'That's a long time to get hit with depth charges.'

'You are not wrong sir, if I was a betting man I'd wager they only gave up trying to sink her when they were running out of the damn things.'

Hook remained emotionless. 'Was it called in?'

'Yes sir.' Rayner nodded, pointing at the log entry column further to the right. 'They even responded to the message, which tells us that they know U-911 was under attack.'

'Any damage control reports logged anywhere?' asked Hook

Rayner shook his head.

'Can't find any, which gives us an opportunity to call performance issues in and get permission to return to La Rochelle for dry dock inspection.'

Hook agreed, but then another question suddenly reared its head.

'What if they direct us to another pen facility?' His question was more or less rhetorical.

Briefly, silence fell. Then, as they sat still, the air around them filled with the sounds of commandos rehearsing their roles in the mission. Shouting, swearing, orders to 'do it again!' filled the hot, cramped interior of U-911.

It was the young Lieutenant that broke the deadlock.

'Well, sir, it means some poor sod is going to get his sub pens smashed up, wherever it is.'

Hook shot the man a surprised glance. He had a point. The mission was to hit La Rochelle, but if they end up going to other pens, then they would feel the sting of the British instead. Hook put a hand on Rayner's shoulder.

'Get on that Enigma thing and call it in. We go, once they have given us clearance.'

Leaving Rayner to get on with encoding and sending the message, Hook did the rounds. Traske was in the control room overseeing his men as they took the commandos through the basics of operating a submarine. Crudely-translated labels were stuck all over the place; with the English version written in bold capital letters. When any of the men got a sequence wrong, the chief petty officer would correct them in a manner that was forceful, but not all barking and shouting. Lieutenant Fearl was busy consulting the note books and charts that his opposite number had been using, prior to his capture.

Hook nodded at the officers in question before moving further forward. He found himself in the vile, squalid space the German sailors would have called their home. The bunks were unmade and the smell ripe from numerous unwashed bodies. Their personal effects were still in place. Photographs of families stuck on the walls, a raunchy colour poster of half-naked dancing girls. Even their reading books were as they had been left, face down on the bedclothes, the page saved for the reader's return. Hook made a mental note to remind the sergeant major about the German sailors' possessions and to hand them over prior to their departure.

As he moved further forward, Hook reached a bulkhead door. Behind it, he could hear all manner of profanity and chaos. As he opened the door, he was consumed by the sight and sound of numerous men cursing and sweating as they lowered a torpedo in through the external loading hatch. Hook could see that to try and move amongst them would only warrant a rebuke from his own men as they fought to get the troublesome weapon on board. He felt that in this case, discretion was the better part of valour and went to close the door when he spotted Mr Pryce in the melee. They locked eyes as the captain waved him over. Pryce called on the boys to take a breather. All were stripped to the waist, glazed in oil and sweat from their efforts. Pryce was similarly dressed, smiling as he dried his hands on a rag.

'That's two in already, just getting the third in now.' His voice was raised over the din of soldiers cursing each other for being lazy, clumsy bastards.

'How many can we hold?' Hook was intrigued.

'Twelve, if we stow them right. Won't leave much room for comfort, but she can take twelve. Two can be stowed in the stern. We have a tube for firing rearwards too'

Hook's eyebrows rose as he looked about the already cramped interior of the torpedo room. Pryce nodded, sensing his thoughts.'

'The life of a submariner. At least you commando chaps can get on dry land and stretch your legs.'

'When do you think you can have the boys drilling with the firing sequence and all that?' Hook didn't know the jargon associated with the whole rigmarole of loading and firing a torpedo.

'Once we've got all twelve on board, I plan to teach them step by step how to feed them into the tubes. With four put in the tubes, that will free up some space. I will then drill them to run the torpedo out and in a few times until they get it right.'

Hook was satisfied with Pryce's reasoning, and left him to it. As he stepped out of the door, Pryce called out after him.

'Your man... Corporal Maker. Turns out he was a docker before he joined you lot. He told me to leave the crane controls alone before I killed someone. He's up there, moving things about.'

Hook grunted. He had known Phil Maker for a while. Good NCO, a little rough around the edges. He leaned back in towards Pryce, to make himself heard.

'I'm sure he was most polite when he told you to do so.'

Hook got himself out of the way as more of 1 Troop began to offload tinned food from the ship, and under the guidance of their troop sergeant, Albert Ross. They had to literally cram it into every nook and cranny of the submarine. He knew they would be at sea for the better part of a week, so it was certainly a logistical effort getting it all in. Ross acknowledged the captain and made his way over.

'Hello, sir. Just getting the tins and stuff on board. The perishables will have to stay in the ship's cooler until nearer the time to sail.'

'It's not going to leave us much room to do much else, apart from sit upright.'

The NCO sniggered. 'Tell me about it sir, but then again, I don't think they designed her for what we have in mind.'

Hook agreed, and took his leave to let the men get on with all that submariners had to do prior to a patrol. As he strode across the gangway, Rayner fought his way out of the aft deck hatch and jogged after him.

'That's the request to return to La Rochelle sent. Won't get an answer back for a while, so I thought I would get out of that overcrowded tin can and enjoy the fresh air while I could.'

'Do you think they will fall for it?' Hook asked.

'No reason why not. Our reason to return is credible. Can't inspect the boat all the way out here.'

'Could you do me a favour and pop your head in the control room and ask for Commander Traske, please? I need to ask him something.'

It wasn't long before the submarine commander was sitting with Hook on the port sea wall. Traske felt it necessary to inform the commando captain of his men's progress. Hook was pleased to hear they were getting on fine. They were not of war patrol quality, but with constant guidance on the route, they would do okay.

Hook asked his question.

'I've been thinking about what you said, regarding civilians getting caught up in the fighting.'

Traske kept his mouth shut, as he could tell that Hook was finding it hard to phrase his question.

'Would it be out of the ordinary for U-boats to arrive back in the pens after dark? After all, it reduces the threat of air attack.'

Traske merely shrugged his shoulders. 'I wouldn't know. I prefer coming into port in the dark. I honestly don't know. I can't see it being that much of a big deal. If anyone gets funny about it, it won't matter when the shooting starts, anyway.'

Hook mulled the idea over in his own mind, but Traske then put to him another factor they hadn't yet considered.

'We don't know what the RAF has planned for La Rochelle. They could well be plastering the place when we arrive, certainly after dark.'

Hook could only agree. If they were already hitting the town, or perhaps the pens themselves, the entire garrison would be alerted, and they would have one hell of a time trying to get out after their raid. Darkness had its advantages, but it was when the air raids tended to happen.

'I will think about that as we get closer. I would prefer a night attack, but as you have rightly pointed out, we have no idea what the flying boys are up to.'

'Is it normal for British commandos, just to hope for the best?' Traske's tone was jocular and Hook could see the funny side of it.

'We normally plan our missions with other services, but this one, as you well know, left us with little or no time to prepare. We hadn't even got our boots off when we got given this mission.' He pointed at the U-boat. Traske stood up.

'I'm going back aboard. Lots still to do.'

'Thanks.' Hook smiled.

'What for?'

'Helping us get ready. Why would they even think my men could drive a bloody submarine?'

Traske smiled as he turned to board U-911. Hook watched him board, before the circus act that was the loading of torpedoes into the sub distracted him. It was all coming together. Slowly, but it was coming together. All he needed was permission for U-911 to return to La Rochelle for dry dock inspection, and they could get going.

8

The day ended with the last of the torpedoes being stowed aboard just before last light. The submarine officers had really worked 1 Troop hard, for they clambered their way out of the boat dripping with sweat. They all rested on the sea wall as the cool evening air whipped around their soaked bodies. A few of them acknowledged both Hook and the sergeant major.

'Who in their right mind would want to serve on submarines?'

Some members of 1 Troop had a few choice words for their instructors, who had worked them to the bone all day. They were quick to temper their views when the sergeant major glared at them. The submariners may have not been commando officers, but they were officers nonetheless. Gibbs threw in a little reminder.

'Just remember lads, when they get off at the other end, they are in *our* world.'

Many of the men grinned at the very thought of the submarine officers having to fight like infantry once U-911 had been rammed into one of the pens. It was that very idea that reminded the sergeant major of an important point.

'Need to have them trained up on our weapons too, sir.'

Hook agreed.

'Indeed, but they just need to know how to handle them. We don't have the time or the ammunition to see how well they shoot, so just the basics I think.'

Gibbs took his leave and went to check up on the rest of the company. Hook eyed his watch, mindful that at 2059 hours local time, Berlin would send out the Enigma key setting for the next twenty-four hours. As 1 Troop got on their feet and made their way back up towards the barracks for food, Bamber Cross perched on the wall next to the company commander. Both Rands and Joyce wandered up to join them. Both were holding tin cups, a lump of bread balanced on each.

'It's not silver service, but it's not bad either.'

Hook and Cross thanked them for the soup, and went about their meals without conversation. The commando officers ate and admired the view. Less perishables and men, U-911 was pretty much ready to go.

'You and your boys are good to go?' asked Hook of his troop commanders.

All three nodded. As they finished off what soup remained in the bottom of their cups they highlighted areas that were of concern to them. The chief concern, which they shared, centred upon getting lots of men out of one hatch quickly once the shooting had started. The conning tower would not be an option as the anti-aircraft gun would be firing at ground targets, and the forward deck hatch would have the deck gun firing over it. Hook listened to their observations and reservations, and could only agree with them.

'I'm leaning more towards a night-time arrival. Minimal opposition on the quayside, hopefully. Get as many off as possible before we open fire or are fired upon.'

The troop leaders liked the idea of this, but the captain pointed out that both he and Traske were unsure if it was German protocol to arrive after dark, and could arouse suspicion.

'There is one certainty,' Rands commented, 'at least all the bloody lights would be out.'

'But would they not put all the lights on when the shooting starts?' Cross asked.

Rands shrugged.

'Sure, but if they can see us, then we can see them, right?'

All of the officers, Hook included, could only agree. It was settled in Hook's mind.

'We attack after dark. Exploit the confusion, and then melt into the dark interior of the town before striking north for the RV. Agreed?'

Christopher Joyce held aloft his empty tin cup.

'Here's to all that have the sheer nerve to try this shit in the hope some good will come of it.'

The commandos chuckled, as their mugs clattered together. Rayner popped his head out of the stern deck hatch.

'We've got the new key setting for the next twenty-four hours.'

Hook smiled in the fading light. 'Thanks, great work.' Rayner wasn't done. His smile was full of mischief.

'We've also got permission for dry dock inspection at La Rochelle.'

*

Sergeant Major Gibbs had the company woken just before first light, less those that were guarding the ship. As Hook drank some sweet coffee, he watched as his men got themselves prepared for what would be one of their most audacious missions yet.

There was no commotion, they all got themselves organised. Breakfast was a quiet affair, as soon as the men had eaten their fill and washed it down with tea, they began to take themselves and their equipment over to U-911, her overhead sheeting-cum-shade now removed. Hook took himself and the mission documents and photographs behind the sea wall, burning them all before he boarded. With the exception of the sketches his commanders had made, he ensured that all official documentation about the forthcoming mission was destroyed, as per their standard operating procedures.

Traske and his department heads were already aboard, going through their checks. It took a while for the majority of the company to get on board. It was not lost on any of them that the journey to La Rochelle would be long, hot and claustrophobic, not to mention downright dangerous. Hook overheard more than a few of the boys commenting about the chances of the RAF sinking them.

As Hook clambered up the external ladder of the conning tower, he found himself looking over to where *The Rosa* now sat. Moved during the night to permit a departure, its crew, along with the German submariners, lined the rail watching the enemy take their submarine away from them. They didn't appear too bothered by the event — now they could languish on the island for as long as they wished. They had a ship, minus its radio, but no weapons. They had enough provisions to get by, as the ship was still loaded with plenty that the British had been unable to cram into the submarine.

Hook acknowledged that if he had been the German sub captain, he may have felt similarly reluctant to rush back to war.

Hook felt it wise to keep out of the way and stay up in the conning tower whilst Traske got the boat set to sail. The commando officers were pretty much redundant until they got to their destination. 1 Troop would be the crew; the remainder of the company would just be passengers, keeping out of the way as much as possible.

Gibbs joined him.

'Too much going on down there, more use up here, out of the way.'

Before long, the diesel engines of U-911 rumbled into life. The mechanical effort vibrated through the conning tower before settling down to a continuous buzz. After a while, Hook noticed two of his men standing on the deck.

'What are you two lemons waiting for?' bellowed Gibbs.

'Waiting to cast off, sir. You know... sailor stuff.'

Both Hook and Gibbs laughed aloud. They were good lads, would take anything in their stride. Hook was immensely proud of them, their ability to turn their hands to pretty much anything, and just get on with what was required. In time, Hook and Gibbs were joined by Traske and Mr Fearl, the navigator. The floor plate of the conning tower was now getting a little crowded.

'We need four people up here at a time when we surface run. We need to be constantly alert for both shipping and aircraft.'

Traske let that sit with the commandos, as he called for the two men on deck to cast off the ropes. They did so clumsily, but managed it. As U-911 slowly pulled away from the quayside, the men clambered back inside, closing the hatches behind them. Hook was merely a spectator as Traske spoke into a handset, giving orders to those below. As the submarine began to make its way past *The Rosa*, Hook was a little shocked to see the German submariners waving.

Hook was then overwhelmed with dread.

Do they know something about the boat that we don't? Is the propeller about to fall off?

Too late to worry about stuff like that now.

'They've got it easy, if they want it.' Gibbs pointed at the men on the ship. 'Their war is over for as long as they wish it.'

'Did you have their personal things handed back to them?'

'Yes sir. It's only proper.'

'I just don't want their girlfriends or wives waiting for them when we arrive. Hopefully, by arriving after dark there will be no fanfare, and very few people to meet us.'

Gibbs nodded. 'I agree, sir. It wouldn't be fair on the boys to have to fight through them just to get on with the job.'

As U-911 cleared the breakwater, Traske spoke to those around him.

'We will follow the coast to the south east, and when we run out of island we will be striking a course north east for La Rochelle.'

'Do you think we will encounter convoys?' Hook asked. Traske nodded.

'Maybe traffic coming to and from Gib, but other than that, most of the convoys will be much further to the north, bound for England.'

'We need to see how she will dive, should we need to in a hurry.'

Traske agreed with the captain. 'We will do that when we get out into open water. Not much water under us until we are clear of the island.'

'How much room is there below, now we have everyone and everything aboard?' Hook asked.

Traske, with a chuckle, grinned. 'It's snug, let's put it that way.'

9

With the sheer cliffs of Sao Jorge to the port side, U-911 steamed east along the length of the Azores island. Hook was resigned to the fact that his own men were now in the hands of Traske and his officers. The men were far from being competent submariners, but they would just have to go with what they had. Much was still to learn on the way to La Rochelle, and to top it off, schooling would have to take place under the threat of attack from their own side. They had no way of letting the RAF or the Royal Navy know who they were, so they would just have to avoid them as much as possible.

Traske instructed those in the conning tower in the art of scanning their sector.

'Not saying you chaps don't know how to use a set of binoculars, but it is equally important that you scan the horizon, not just the clouds.'

Hook nodded as the submariner continued.

'Remember, if you can see shipping, it could well be armed and therefore we are already in range of their guns. I would prefer to dive should we spot any, for they could have already seen us running on the surface, and call in aircraft to attack us.'

Hook acknowledged that the commander had a point. Traske leaned in towards the captain.

'I intend to conduct diving drills on the way, but not too much, so as not to have us cry wolf, if you get my meaning?'

Hook agreed with enthusiasm. 'By all means, put us through our paces, we need to see how she fares in the dive anyway.'

'Absolutely. The chief has already instructed the boys not at a post on what to do. Any spare man-power is to get as far forward as they can as quickly as they can, so we can get the bow under straight way. Anyone on bunks is to stay where they are, they will only get in the way and slow things down.'

Hook grinned. 'It will be farcical, but if it needs to be done, the boys will oblige.'

'I should bloody well hope so', chuckled Traske, 'dive or get sunk, it's quite a motivator.'

Traske kept U-911 on an easterly course until they had cleared the island, before setting a course north east.

'I'm going below to see how the boys are getting on,' Hook stated.

Traske and the others did not answer as they scanned the skies.

As he climbed down into the Control Room, Hook was immediately hit by the familiar aroma of sweating bodies. Fearl followed Hook down the ladder, and excused himself to squeeze past and consult his charts.

'Two lookouts to the bridge.' Traske's voice crackled over the intercom.

Hook suddenly realised he had left Traske short-handed up above. He knew submarines were not his area of expertise. He nominated two NCOs who were trying their best not to get in the way of anyone. They clambered up the ladder, the fresh sea air more inviting than the stifling, dense atmosphere they were trying to get used to.

Content with what he had seen in the torpedo room the day before, Hook went aft to see how the men were faring in the engine room. As he clambered through the control room hatch, he became aware of fresh produce hanging from netting all over the place. Some of the men had crammed loaves of bread into any space that was available. Small wooden crates of bananas and lemons were stacked up on one of the bunks, and as his men were accommodated there, they tried their best to make the area liveable. Hook patted one of the NCOs on the shoulder as he stepped through.

'If you eat it before it goes bad, you'll get more room to yourselves.'

Hook stopped at the door to the engine room. He could hear the two diesels chugging away. As he opened the door, he was greeted by the horrendous din of both the engines and the chief shouting instructions to his new apprentices. His men were stripped to the waist, glazed in oil and sweat, their hair and beards matted. They already had the appearance of veteran submariners. Hook decided not even to bother trying to make conversation amid that racket and simply gave the chief a friendly wave as he went to shut the door. The chief gave him the thumbs up before following the captain out of the room. Glazed in sweat, Roger Toil grinned at Hook.

'Lead on, sir, they will be fine. I can't be in two places at once. I need to be with the boat drivers.'

Hook fought his way though both men and fresh produce swinging in his face as he made his way back to the control room. The chief was once more with the drivers, scrutinising the gauges. Hook was three ladder rungs up when he was greeted by one of the NCOs shuffling down, almost landing on top of him.

'DIVE, DIVE, DIVE!' Traske crackled over the intercom.

Hook fell to the floor of the control room in an undignified heap, scrambling away in time as four men crashed down the ladder, Traske slamming hatches shut behind him.

'TAKE HER DEEP!' he roared as he secured the last hatch.

Hook was now on the verge of being trampled by those men the chief had already briefed, as they stomped towards the torpedo room. Around him, men pulled levers, cranked wheels as if they had done it their entire lives. The captain was impressed.

'GO,GO,GO, or I will kick your arses!' roared the sergeant major as he tucked himself just inside the radio room along with Lieutenant Rayner, allowing the chastised men to crash forward, some earning a fatherly clip around the back of the head from Gibbs. Hook straightened himself up as he fought to grab hold of something steady as U-911 went below the waves. Chief Toil staggered a little, grabbing the shoulders of his new boat drivers.

'Good effort lads, now just listen to what I say, okay?'

The two commandos nodded as they kept their eyes on the dials and gauges before them. The depth gauge moved, indicating the boat's progress. Both the chief and Traske looked at each other before shaking their heads.

'That'll do, chief. Level her off at one hundred metres. We will do some manoeuvring shortly.'

'Aye sir, levelling off at one hundred metres.'

Traske came over, speaking quietly to Hook.

'We are very slow in the dive. We really need to have the lookouts on their game if we have to do that again for real.'

Hook could only agree. As the boat levelled out, he could already see the men making their way back from its front, resuming their duties. Traske got his attention once more, leading him over to the navigation charts taken care of by Mr Fearl, his finger tracking their intended route as he spoke.

'We will do some moving about, just so we know how she handles. Then we will run shallower as we pass the western side of Angro Do Heroismo. We can't chance running on the surface too much; I have a feeling we are going to encounter convoys running in and out of Gibraltar. The RAF will have that covered.'

Hook looked at the chart. Given the route they intended to take, they would face the potential convoy issue shortly.

'If we see them?' Hook asked.

'We stop and observe at periscope depth during the day. We can chance observing on the surface after dark. We cannot afford for an escorting destroyer to pick us up. You have just seen how sluggishly we dive. They will be all over us before we know it.'

Hook bit his bottom lip. He was aware that convoy traffic could badly delay their timetable, but there was not much they could do about it. The sergeant major joined the group, a piece of paper in his hand.

'The German tonnage scores from last night apparently. Mr Rayner has just been decoding it.'

Both Traske and Hook read the paper. Six U-boat numbers were scrawled on it, and next to them were numbers in the thousands. Traske sighed, shaking his head.

'Six wolves, lots of deer.'

'Where was the convoy when it got attacked?' Hook asked Gibbs.

'Just south of Greenland. Convoy out of Canada, judging by their position.'

'That's a lot of men in that freezing water.'

A silence hung over the group; it was Traske that finally broke it.

'What on earth were their escorts doing, for them to rack up that tonnage score?'

No-one answered. Traske knew the Germans were cunning bastards. They must have drawn the protection away from the merchant ships in their attempt to sink the attacker, only to allow other U-boats in to wreak havoc.

Traske addressed both Hook and Gibbs. 'Better you gentlemen get some rest, we will be putting her through her paces for a while.'

Hook and the sergeant major found a spot in the officers' wardroom. The name did not entirely suit it, for it was merely a couple of benches that ran either side of a high, rimmed table. Just enough room for the officers to sit in relative comfort and eat their meals. Even when seated, those sat in the gangway would have to stand to let men pass as they went about their duties.

Living space was at a premium when serving on submarines, nowhere more than aboard the overloaded U-911. With their backs to the bulkhead wall they could lean on the table, should they need to sleep. Rands and Joyce were already trying their hardest to get some sleep, but with all the commotion on board, it proved to be impossible.

'Where is Mr Cross?' Hook enquired.

'In the torpedo room.' Rands replied. 'He's helping Pryce drill the men. Not like he has a week of doing nothing else.'

Hook could only smile. He felt a little for Rands and Joyce, all their men could do was rest and try not to get in the way of 1 Troop as they drove the boat to France. With a company crammed aboard, and next to no room to do much except think about the mission ahead of them, Hook was a little concerned they could lose their edge. Confined in such close quarters for a week, and then expected to come out fighting — it was going to be a real eye-opener. His men were used to exercising when they had time to themselves. They would think nothing of climbing Ben Nevis, or getting their assault gear and swimming in a loch, before tackling the assault course prior to going to the range to practice on all the weapons they could get their hands on. Always looking to improve. Despite the efforts by all three services to stifle their flair, ammunition was never in short supply. Hook insisted that all exercises were done with live ammunition. Accidents did happen occasionally, but that was the nature of their job — in fact, the company had lost more men to mountaineering accidents than through negligence with weapons.

Hook recalled when Prime Minister Churchill had visited them at Spean Bridge in early '41. He was shocked to see that the only accommodation afforded to his new band of military misfits was a row of large, snow-laden canvas tents, with a wooden shack that served as a latrine, surrounded by concertina wire.

'We train without luxuries for operations, sir,' stated the now-captain, then second in command. Major Phillip Bird, his superior until his death in Tunisia, backed up the statement.

'If the conditions we live and train in are too much for the man, then he has no business in a commando unit.'

Never did Captain Paul Hook expect his company to go from the sparse, cold expanses of Scotland to the hot, moist and cramped innards of a submarine. Such challenges just went with the job, whatever and wherever it may be.

'You okay, sir?' Mr Joyce pulled Hook from his reverie.

'Huh?'

'You appear to be out of sorts.'

'Mr Rayner decoded a message that boasted last night's tonnage score from an attack on a convoy coming out of Canada. Six U-boats ate them alive, judging by what went to the bottom.'

'Ah, yes. I understand. Whereabouts was the attack?'

'Just south of Greenland.'

The troop commander winced. 'That is bloody cold water.'

'That's what we said,' nodded Hook.

'Do the U-boats allow a rescue?' asked Joyce. Hook shrugged his shoulders.

'No idea. I'm sure the ships still afloat just get the hell out of there, and the U-boats are unlikely to help.'

Joyce conceded that his company commander had a point. Joyce himself felt there must be honour among sailors, regardless of nationality. He was certain in his heart that the German submariners were only interested in the tonnage, not the taking of lives.

'That dive we did earlier was a little lively, wasn't it?' Rands was keen to change the subject.

'Not lively enough,' shrugged Hook, 'according to the commander.'

'Oh, well, we knew her performance could be an issue.'

Hook agreed. 'Traske is keen for lookouts to really be on their game when we run on the surface. If you see a ship, call for a dive, as they will already be within range of us, and as for aircraft, we can't hang about. We have no friends out here, other than U-boats perhaps.'

'Fair enough. When are we surfacing?'

'Not for a while yet, Traske wants to move her about a bit, see how sluggish she really is. He's keen to only surface at night, and I can fully understand why.'

The officers and Gibbs all nodded. They would rather take their chances against the might of the La Rochelle garrison, than get sunk by their own side in the middle of the North Atlantic. Rands couldn't help but frown.

'So a week to get there could be a tall order, if our esteemed sub captain doesn't want to run on the surface during the day?'

Hook was a little irritated by the lieutenant's comment, but chose to let it pass. It may well have been his mission, but whilst they were at sea, it was Traske's boat.

10

Time passed slowly as U-911 was put through her paces. Overloaded, her speed submerged was only four knots on a straight course. Manoeuvring about as if to evade a destroyer, her speed halved, rendering her almost static as she turned — this infuriated all the submariners on board. Hook and his commandos could only keep out of the way, with the exception of 1 Troop which was her ad hoc crew until they reached their target.

The commandos not operating the boat went about checking their weapons over and over; all ensuring they were all unloaded. If a shot were to be fired accidentally in such a crowded environment, the results could be disastrous. There had been a little cosmetic damage to the boat's internals when they rolled grenades in during her initial capture, so they replaced the shattered dial covers as best they could; fortunately, the German crew kept a plethora of spare components due to their own experiences of naval warfare.

Whilst the men kept themselves occupied with the cleaning of weapons and packing and repacking equipment, the officers and NCOs took time to study the sketches they had made, conferring and memorising as much as they could. Hook found himself recalling what the photographs had shown him, prior to their destruction. He hoped the Germans were not as thorough as the Civil Defence Service back home, with their policy regarding the removal of road signs. The very thought that the German Special Forces community would be fooled by such a stunt infuriated him. They may have been the enemy, but Paul Hook acknowledged professionalism, regardless of nationality. The removal of the road signs had only served to make life for everyone at home more awkward.

He thought of what would become of his company when they linked with the SAS. He knew they could well be taken out of France via a series of agents, but he quite liked the idea of joining them long term, and magnifying his men's impact on the occupying German forces for the foreseeable future. Sabotaging key installations, raiding soft targets such as German headquarter elements, intercepting communications and troop reinforcements. He was in no rush to get home, for he was single and his parents understood his reasons for joining the British Commandos in the first place. As a student, he had been a troublesome young man, always arguing with his teachers and lecturers, demanding to be told the method to the madness when it came to certain policies.

At school, Hook was forever at odds with his housemaster, who happened to be an old army pal of his father's from the Great War. Bob Stacey and his father had served in the Middlesex regiment in Flanders, and both were delighted, albeit for different reasons, when Paul chose to join the army. His father was happy that his son was following in his own infantry footsteps when he accepted a short service commission with the East Surreys in 1939, and Bob was glad that the jumped-up little git would probably be taken down a peg or two.

A regular battalion was not to be for Paul Hook. He became a subaltern with one of the territorial battalions, the 2/6th East

Surrey Battalion. Shipped out to France as part of the British Expeditionary Force in 1940, Paul soon found himself trying to fight Rommel's panzer forces whilst still employing the methods of the Great War. Static trench attrition had given way, at least on the German side, to highly mobile offensive doctrine. Instead of fighting the East Surreys toe-to-toe, Rommel's units would just keep out of range of their old generation anti-tank guns and bypass them, shooting up the logistics units trying to keep the outdated and outclassed British Army in the fight.

Hook was one of a handful of battalion officers who attended a meeting in Rouen, where they tried to establish two things, namely who the hell was in charge of the situation, and where on earth was Rommel heading next? With little progress made on either issue, the colonel of the battalion had Hook and his driver make their way back to where their unit was now fighting a defensive action. The 2/6th East Surrey Battalion, along with the 51st Highland Division now had their backs to the channel at St Valery. The aggressive, mobile German panzers had cut off their avenues of withdrawal. Hook and the colonel could not get through to their men; all they had to fight their way through the vanguard of the blitzkrieg was a Webley pistol each.

A Stuka attack forced their car off the road. With the deadly wasps hovering above the battlefield, to press on with the car in daylight would have been suicidal. Unable to stay on the road, even on foot, instead they picked their way through field, orchard and forest towards the coast. If they couldn't reach their unit, they had to find a ship that could get them back to England.

On their way to the coast, they encountered more and more British and French troops hiding in barns and haylofts. Hook thought to rally the men and attempt breaking through to the besieged division, but he was stunned to find that all the men he encountered had already thrown away their weapons. Amongst the men were officers, talking of ships taking men out of St Nazaire. The colonel pulled out his map; in a straight line, St Nazaire was just shy of three hundred miles away.

That first night on the run from the German army was one of the longest of Paul Hook's life. They would chance walking on the roads, up to a point where they felt they could be captured at any moment, and all their effort thus far would have been for nothing. Their driver was starting to feel the pace. He was only in leather shoes, unlike the colonel and Hook, who had wisely chosen to wear their boots. The driver was starting to fall behind, and the colonel had known the young corporal long enough not to want to leave him to be captured. So they decided to stay on the roads and make as much distance as they could before first light.

In the twilight of early dawn, having walked throughout the short summer night, they came across what appeared to be a storage depot, holding all manner of military equipment. The place was crawling with Royal Engineers, getting the facility ready for demolition. The driver managed to get himself a pair of semi-worn boots, but had picked up a pair that was a size too small. With German advance units, and the daunting prospect of Stukas shortly arriving in the area, no more time could be wasted finding boots that would fit, and they had to move on. The driver would just have to suffer. Fewer than ten minutes after Hook, the colonel and his driver had left, the depot was blown sky-high.

Thirst began to take hold of them. The locals refused to give the British soldiers water. Soldiers who had already collapsed, or had been wounded in earlier fights with the Germans, were left slumped at the roadside. French citizens spat on the soldiers marching west, calling them cowards.

It was in response to the spit of one elderly French man, that their driver broke his hand on the jaw of the assailant. The devastating right hook knocked the man clean out, but the driver now cursed not only the pain ravaging his feet, but now also that of a broken right hand.

They resorted to joining the fragmented, broken groups of British soldiers as they scooped water into their mouths from a nearby stream.

As the day came to a close, and with their strength draining from them, the colonel, Hook and the corporal decided to shelter in nearby woods, resisting the temptation to hide in the barns which were dangerously close to the main road. Each taking a turn to stay awake, their night was long, their sleep fitful at best. At first light they were shocked to see German troops surrounding the barns, shouting at those within to come out. Some troops came out with their hands above their heads, only to be cut down in a hail of bullets. The German troops then went about throwing grenades into the barns. The hysterical cries from within them were cut short as the grenades pummelled the life out of all hiding within.

The three of them had moved, quietly, further into the wood to avoid attracting attention. The Germans were overtaking them, because they kept to the road, but by keeping in the woods for as much of the journey as they could, they got to live longer and get closer to St. Nazaire.

It was ten days later that Lieutenant Paul Hook, the colonel and their almost-crippled driver made it to the outskirts of St Nazaire. Surprised to still see the port in British hands, they made for the jetty that ran alongside the huge ship that sat low in the water, its decks crammed with troops escaping northern France. *The Lancastrian*. Paul's heart sank — she had already cast off and was making her way out of the port. He and the colonel looked to each other for inspiration. They had risked all, marched for days to get on board... and they were too late. They both knew the reasons for their delay; the colonel had been resolute throughout their journey, that they would not leave the corporal behind.

It was whilst watching 'their' boat for home move out, into open water, that they spotted the Stukas diving in. The large lumbering ship was hit numerous times, listing heavily to starboard before lunging to port and slowly turning over. Hook could see people falling into the water, only to be crushed by the massive superstructure. Some had even managed to clamber over the uppermost railings and establish themselves on the ship's belly, which was now pointing skywards.

But the Stukas were not yet finished.

The German pilots saw fit to strafe those in the water, numerous times. Their cannon fire set fire to the oil and fuel that was pooling out of the shattered ship. The colonel wept as they watched helplessly from the side streets of the town. Paul was just as distraught, yet privately thanking the lame NCO. He turned, giving the corporal a nod in acknowledgment. The man was in tears. Hook wasn't going to mock anyone for that.

They had yet to get out of hell, but they were going to, one way or another.

*

It was by sheer chance, a few miles further south, that they came across a small fishing boat and its owner. For what money the three of them could muster, along with others who had made it there after the *Lancastrian* tragedy, the Frenchman (who claimed to have fought at Verdun) agreed to take them to England after dark, providing no German troops were nearby. In *that* case, the deal was off.

The voyage back to Plymouth was not without its moments, with one of the exhausted soldiers giving in to sleep then falling overboard in the night. It saddened Paul that the man had made it all that way, only to fall asleep for the last time, and no one noticed. Once home, struggling to find the strength between them, they carried the crippled corporal off the boat, thanking its owner, only to find themselves under arrest by the Royal Military Police for desertion. In a fit of rage that almost killed him, the colonel let fly at the redcaps, informing them that his battalion had been destroyed weeks ago, and the three men in their custody *were* the 2/6th East Surrey Battalion. Medics tended the corporal, and ultimately resorted to cutting the boots from his feet. This revealed the reason for his ongoing agony — all of his toes were dislocated.

It was whilst recovering in Roehampton Hospital in Surrey that Lieutenant Paul Hook came to hear of a new branch of the army. The British Commandos. Currently without a unit to call home, Hook needed a sponsor in order to apply. He spent a while tracking down the colonel, who was now stationed at Bassingbourn. The colonel, who was now rested, had been branded a pariah by his peers and the top brass, who were embarrassed by the retreat from France. A scapegoat, put out to pasture. The crippled corporal was still his driver, but no longer fit for any frontline duty. Hook was invited to visit the colonel, and was pleased to do so.

Hook received a glowing sponsor recommendation from his former commanding officer, and with that, volunteered for the British Commandos.

11

'Captain Hook, sir?' The voice was hushed and soothing.

'Captain Hook?' The voice a little sterner now, but still hushed, and it was a hand touching his right forearm that had him jolt from his slumber. At first he was dazed and confused; the space around him was dark, with the exception of a dull red glow that reached around the dark figure in front of him. The figure spoke to him once more.

'Commander Traske would like you to join him on the bridge, sir'

As the captain gathered his senses, he recognised the voice as belonging to Parch. Hook looked about him; he was the only one at the mess table.

'What's going on?' he hissed. Parch leaned in closer, his features beginning to come into focus.

'We've surfaced, sir; we have a convoy in front of us.'

'Why are the lights out?'

'It is dark outside.'

'Captain Hook to the bridge,' came the whispered message, passed along by a chain of hushed voices.

Parch stepped back to allow his company commander to edge his way out from behind the snug mess table. Hook was still drunk with sleep as he slowly clambered through into the control room. The confined area was dimly lit with red bulbs. Men stood about, not speaking at all. The officer received a respectful nod from the darkened profile of the chief as he staggered past. Hook took hold of the conning tower ladder, and climbed up. Still not firing on all cylinders, he was tapped on the shoulder and handed a pair of binoculars by Sergeant Major Gibbs. The man leaned in close to his ear.

'The wolves are circling the herd once more.'

Hook was stunned at Gibbs' statement, and a little confused.

'Captain Hook?' a voice above him whispered.

'Yes?' he whispered back.

'You'll want to see this.' Traske was the owner of the voice above him.

Hook made his way up onto the bridge of U-911. There was a full moon, that floodlit the calm ocean from between large cloud banks. He found himself in the company of Traske, Fearl and Rands; all had their eyes to binoculars.

'Convoy,' hissed one, as Hook pulled his own binoculars to his eyes. On the horizon he could make out the unmistakable silhouette of ships. Most had a familiar shape; tankers. Others were low in the water but not as long. Supply and troop ships.

'How long have we been here?' Hook whispered.

'Couple of hours,' replied the sub commander. 'We were given their location and course from other U-Boats moving in to attack.'

'The wolves are forming a pack,' hissed Rands.

Hook continued to observe the distant convoy, now exposed by the large pale moon. He panned slowly left and right; the convoy stretched as far as he could see.

'Are they usually that big?' he asked no-one in particular.

'What?' asked Traske.

'The convoy. A lot of ships, but I can't make out any escorts.'

'Me neither. I can't see any protection, unless they are doing a sweep on the other side.'

'Maybe they have detected U-boats already and are chasing them off?' Fearl suggested.

'Maybe. Ensure two of you are keeping an eye out behind us, their escorts may sweep very wide of the main route.'

Hook turned to look over the stern of U-911. In the calm waters, with the moon out in full force, she appeared huge and sat high in the water. The moonlight glinted off the superstructure. Hook used his binoculars to scan the horizon once more, feeling very exposed. If a destroyer detected them, the U-boat would still be diving when they came under attack.

The weather was beautiful for the RAF, too. Hook respected them enough also to focus on the skies above. All seemed quiet.

Traske, Hook and the other officers remained on the bridge for some time, watching the distant convoy slowly lumber on towards its destination. Hook assumed it was an American convoy, bound for North Africa. They hadn't sailed far enough north to miss them.

Both Traske and Hook were then captivated by a flash on the horizon, followed a few seconds later by a muffled thud.

'Torpedo attack!' hissed Traske. A second detonation rippled over them, but this time there was no flash.

'Make that two,' added the commando captain.

All of the officers were fixated on the attack in progress. With the moon now behind a cloud bank, it was difficult for them to determine which ships had been attacked. Another flash, followed by another thud of detonation, confirmed that a third torpedo had found its mark. As the moon lit up the convoy once more, Hook spotted a tanker listing to starboard, black smoke chugging from the stern of her long profile. None of the other ships appeared to be coming to her aid.

It was then that they heard an explosion. Perhaps it was a fourth torpedo strike, but none of the officers could vouch for it.

'Prepare to dive,' hissed Traske.

'Why?' Rands enquired.

'Whoever is in charge of protecting that convoy is going to paste this whole area with depth charges. Multiple hits could mean multiple U-boats, and I don't want us picked up as one of them. Prepare to dive!'

Hook sided with the submariner. 'You heard the man, let's go.'

Traske was the last to clear the bridge, closing the outer hatch behind him.

He only followed Hook down the ladder so far, stopping at the attack periscope station.

'Chief, take us to periscope depth.'

Without so much as a hesitation the response came. 'Periscope depth, aye sir.'

As the chief mentored the commando drivers down to periscope depth, all Hook and his officers could do was let Traske and his crew get on with things. The control room was cold, moisture hung thickly in the close confines, condensing upon everything it came into contact with. Mr Fearl used a rag to wipe the clear laminate that covered his charts. With the boat sitting silent in the water, Hook could hear the slight whirring of the motor that power traversed the attack periscope station. Hook knew in his heart that he would never make a submariner, he just didn't have the patience for the long, cold watch beneath the waves. He had joined the British Commandos for action, but he accepted that this was combat for the so-called silent service, as the submarine arm of the Royal Navy was known.

A long, sharp, scraping sound began to echo through the submarine. Hook and the men around him exchanged enquiring glances, only the chief kept a poker face as the sound grew louder and harsher. Hook looked to the veteran submariner, who could read his facial expression in the dim red light.

'Bulkheads breaking up. Whoever those bastards hit, they are now sinking.'

The din that was pulsing through the boat rose, in pitch and ferocity. To Hook it sounded like the roar of a dinosaur along with the crushing of metal. Never did he ever imagine the death of a ship could sound so terrifying. He couldn't help but feel for the men on board. Other bulkheads were also singing their death songs as they collapsed under the weight of their own cargo, and the relentless cold sea that would soon devour them. If the Germans had hit one of the troop ships, that meant a catastrophic loss of life before those aboard had even had the chance to fight.

The horrendous soundtrack of dying ships was enough to drive Hook's men to the control room, to find out what on earth the sound was. Even Sergeant Major Gibbs came to ask, and the look of horror on his face was enough to tell Hook that Gibbs was humbled by what was unfolding out in the cold dark water. A series of dull, muffled crumps echoed through the boat.

'Explosions,' hissed Rayner, loudly.

'More torpedoes?' asked the captain. Rayner shook his head, leaning further out of the radio room.

'Smaller, more frequent.'

'Depth charges,' said the chief. 'Their escorts are pounding where they think the other U-boats are.'

'Will they come this side of the convoy?' Gibbs asked.

The chief shrugged. 'Depends if there are other U-boats attacking from this side.'

'Commander Traske,' Rayner called. 'I hear propellers. Far off to starboard.'

Hook relayed the information up the ladder. Traske was clambering down as soon as he heard.

'Chief, take us to one hundred metres.'

'One hundred metres, aye sir.'

Hooks stomach turned. 'Destroyer?'

Without answering, Traske headed for Rayner, taking the headset from him. He listened intently to the sounds coming through. The faint crump of depth charges, the screeching of dying ships that everyone could hear. What got Traske's attention was the rapid chopping of propellers growing louder in his ears. He pulled the headset off, calling to the chief.

'Make our depth one-five-zero'.

'One-five-zero, aye sir.'

Traske re-joined the men in the control room. He remembered to answer the captain.

'They are doing a sweep. They are not looking for us, but we can't tell if there are other boats around us, so things could get a little rough in a minute.'

'Now at one-five-zero, sir'

'Thank you chief, all stop.'

'All stop, aye.'

The chief continued with his on-the-job training, keeping his voice down as he pointed at certain levers and valves, telling the commandos about him what to do.

U-911 was now at the mercy of the sonar man on the destroyer marauding above them. Everyone crammed on that boat couldn't help but look up as the Royal Navy destroyer chopped overhead. Even Traske was glazed in sweat as the propellers began to fade, closing his eyes tight. He knew that if the depth charges were on their way down to them, they would soon know about it.

As the propellers faded off their port side, a series of explosions punched the side of U-911. It was enough to have the men unsteady on their feet, as they grabbed for fittings that would hold them upright. Traske held the conning tower ladder with one hand, calling for calm.

'They are just fishing. We would know if they were after us, as they would drop them either side of us.'

As reassuring as the sub commander was, Hook and his men couldn't help but feel apprehensive. It dawned on Hook that their sinking would go unnoticed, and without record. He knew their missions were hazardous, but this was something else. The sting of the depth charges were still being felt by all those aboard, as more went off further away, rocking U-911 as she drifted ever so slightly in the water like a large, silent, inert hole in the water.

Over the next three hours, the officers and men aboard their stolen U-boat could do nothing more than just sit silently, whispering to each other as the Royal Navy continued to pulverize the water around them with their depth charges. Some went off a little closer than was comfortable, but no damage of note was sustained. A few of the men were caught off guard and suffered cuts and bruises when they fell against the harsh surfaces that made up the innards of the German U-boat. Function, rather than comfort, had been in mind when she was designed and built.

Content the convoys and their escorts had moved on, Traske felt it was safe enough to at least go to periscope depth. Hook and all those gathered in the control room watched in silence as the commander took his time and slowly traversed a complete turn with his eye to the 'scope. Hook watched for any sign of shock or surprise as he turned. Everyone aboard U-911 listened for anything that sounded like propellers chopping towards them. No such sound reached their ears.

Traske made a complete turn, then turned quickly back for half a turn. He breathed deeply, his chest expanding under the off-white roll-neck woollen jumper that he wore for all his patrols. His eye dropped from the eyepiece, his forehead resting on the brow pad.

What has he seen? thought Hook. Traske noticed the captain looking at him. He nodded slightly as he gave his orders.

'Surface.'

'Surface, aye.'

'Captain Hook, Sergeant Major Gibbs and myself only to the bridge.'

The chief petty officer returned the order as trained, even though his facial expression told Hook that it was out of the commander's character to go off-jargon.

'We have surfaced, sir.'

12

Traske unlocked the hatch to the attack periscope station and the outer hatch of the conning tower. The sudden influx of sea air was welcomed by all those in the control room.

Hook and Gibbs followed Traske up the ladder. The commandos were not halfway up when the dark profile of the commander gave way to a moonlit night sky. Gingerly, Hook pulled himself up the last of the ladder rungs, his sergeant major grunting and puffing beneath him. What greeted Hook could be described as nothing other than a panorama of hell.

At least three ships had been hit, Hook couldn't locate a fourth. One was the tanker they had seen hit first, the other two were big enough to be troop ships. All the ships had their backs broken and sat very low in the calm, yet deadly, water. What remained of the dying ships was consumed in flames, flames that licked high into the dark sky, illuminating the killing area for miles, enough for the body work of U-911 to glint brightly. Huge areas of the sea were ablaze, as the precious fuel and oil carried by the tanker poured out of her shattered body.

Traske put his binoculars to his eyes, taking his time in scanning the scene before him.

'Look! Just in front of us!' gasped Gibbs.

Hook had forgotten his binoculars, and had to squint into the bright flames where the sergeant major was pointing. He could see material floating. As his eyes adjusted to what he was supposed to be looking at, he noticed more debris floating outwards, not only from the flame-licked water, but also from either side of their bow.

Hook was intrigued enough to clamber down the external ladder and walk the deck towards the front of the U-boat. As the debris bobbed alongside, it became clear that not all of the men who had gone into the water had been rescued. Some of the lifeless men drifted face up past the captain, their exposed clothing and life jackets smouldering, their faces nothing more than charred skulls. The aroma of charred meat and fuel burned the back of Hook's throat as he gagged, trying to take a gulp of clean air.

The bodies kept coming.

Hook sensed someone behind him. He turned to see Gibbs slowly moving towards him. They locked eyes, they didn't need to speak. The picture before them spoke more than a thousand words. Most of the bodies were face down, many glazed in a black, shining tar. Some were naked or in various states of undress. They had not stood a chance. Both commandos gave up counting the bodies after a few minutes, there were so many. The wolves had done their work, and done it well. Fuel and enemy soldiers had been sent to the bottom, at the cost of probably four torpedoes. No-one, not even Commander Traske, could know whether any of the U-boats involved in the attack were sunk, despite the great number of depth charges launched.

Up on the bridge, Traske could only watch the two men on the forward deck. He knew they would probably have questions, but as Hook had pointed out earlier, how many men had he sent to the bottom? On previous patrols, Traske hunted alone; there were not enough submarines in Valletta, or the Med for that matter, to form a 'pack'. He would sit on the western side of Gozo, waiting for the right time to surface run eastwards at flank speed, only diving to periscope depth when he could see the convoy, void of protection with the naked eye. He would then revel in the havoc he would wreak amongst the Italian cargo ships. He was a hunter, feeding his insatiable appetite for a high tonnage score.

Back in Valletta, the shore-based officers' wardroom on Manuel Island would run a tonnage scoreboard. Traske was in the top three, his score inspiring awe among the new, young and impressionable submarine officers who had yet to deploy on their first war patrol. Many officers would spend most of the daylight hours sitting in air raid shelters as the Luftwaffe tried their hardest to sink their boats, which were undergoing maintenance and thus moored up on an exposed quayside. Traske would have done a great deal for some pens like those built by the Germans.

Both Hook and Gibbs clambered back onto the bridge. Traske attempted to offer some comfort.

'It's no less than what we do.'

'What if there are survivors?' asked Gibbs.

'We can't take them with us,' the commander replied without emotion. 'We are stuffed to the gills as it is.'

'So we leave them?'

'Yes, Sergeant Major Gibbs... we leave them.'

Then, all three of the men flinched as one, as a huge explosion punched out of the tanker in a massive fireball, the concussion rippling waves over the bow of the submarine, the blast winding all three of them. Through a slight ringing in his ears, Hook registered what Gibbs was shouting.

'What the fuck happened there?'

'I think there is more than just fuel on that thing.' Traske coughed as he spoke. 'We need to get moving.'

As the three of them went below, the tanker finally gave up its fight for life and allowed Poseidon to claim her as his prize.

*

Between the three of them, Gibbs, Hook and Traske agreed not to mention the bodies in the water to any of the crew. It served no purpose and wouldn't do morale much good. Traske ordered the sub to run submerged for an hour before surfacing once more. Whilst the sea was calm and the sky now dark, with the moon blocked out by gathering storm clouds, they allowed each troop to get out on deck for some air and a leg stretch. As the men of 2 Troop took advantage of the calm seas, Hook and Rayner, along with two members of 1 Troop, manned their lookout positions on the bridge overlooking them. Mr Rayner informed him of the latest message decoded.

'According to the weather reports from a German weather station in the Channel Islands, there is a storm coming out of the Gulf of Mexico.'

'When will it be with us?' Hook looked up, sensing that it was not too far away.

'At the latest, day after tomorrow. It could well be with us all the way in to La Rochelle.'

'Well that's no bloody good to *us*,' commented Hook, irritated. 'They won't open the fucking lock gates in a storm, and we won't be able to get off without most of us falling in the bloody sea in the process.'

'Yes sir, it is unfortunate.' Rayner sounded apologetic as he spoke. 'We will have to sit it out in deep water until it passes, and who knows how long that will take?'

With the men having finished their light exercise and back inside U-911, Traske had her run on the surface until there was enough daylight to warrant a dive. The sun was nowhere to be seen as the storm coming out of the Caribbean began to pitch and roll the submarine, enough for some of Hook's most hardened men to vomit. With a smoother ride beneath the waves, Traske joked about the irony of the situation.

'In bad weather, no threat from the air, and seldom any threat from surface ships either, but the ride is awful, and you end up begging for the boat to dive.'

The submarine officers chuckled as their green-gilled commando colleagues fought to keep their breakfasts down. Hook, who was also not feeling too great himself, pointed out another issue.

'We run submerged, we run slower, and that knocks everything back with regards to linking up with the SAS guys.'

The officers around him could only agree. Hook wasn't done.

'We will have to surface run at some point, rain or shine, to recharge the electric batteries.'

Traske knew the man was right. 'It's going to be a long ride,' he said.

13

The ride was much smoother beneath the surface, but the trade-off was slower progress. Other than those tending to their new-found duties, Hook's commandos could do little more than chat amongst themselves. Some spoke of the forthcoming assault, reminding themselves of what was required, others chatted about anything but. Some slept, others played cards. The smokers in the company had to endure yet another form of torture, the no smoking rule. Traske felt that a constant haze of cigarette smoke hanging at head height would make the living conditions on board much worse, so it was no surprise that the smokers always volunteered for lookout duty as soon as the senior officers had been up on the bridge.

The officers sat around the tiny wardroom table, eating. All except Rands tucked into a pile of bananas, lemons and bread rolls piled up before them. Jokes about scurvy being rife amongst the Royal Navy's men had prompted Traske to insist that fruit be the primary source of nutrition on the way to La Rochelle. The officers had agreed that bread and potatoes be consumed the day before arrival, to ensure the men had the right fuel in them for a big fight and a long walk afterwards. That is, those among them who could manage to eat before a mission.

Rands eyed Rayner suspiciously. He had a question on his lips, but was picking his moment. Hook, looking up from his second banana, sensed that all was not well. He spotted Rands' menacing glare before tracking it to Rayner, and flicking his head back with a frown.

The troop commander became aware that his company commander had spotted the pending assault. Rands smiled at Hook to ease the tension, and went about pulling a bread roll in half. Rands knew that Hook was not one to be shaken off easily, braving a look up from his roll. The captain continued to stare him down, an eyebrow raised. Rands knew he had to say his piece.

'So, Freddy... ' Rands thought the least he could do was open with as friendly a line as he could, given what was on his mind.

Rayner looked up, surprised, lemon peel resembling a boxer's gum shield in his mouth. Hook's frown was back.

'If you can decode German Enigma traffic...' Rands' question tailed off, the speaker uncertain if he should pursue it. Hook held his glare and Rayner pulled the peel away from his lips. Rands took a deep breath.

'If you can decode what they send, why did we watch them sink ships earlier?'

That was it, he had said it. Rands relaxed his posture. Hook blinked hard a few times, before breaking away from his troop commander, focussing with a softer gaze on the appointed radio officer. Rayner cuffed the lemon juice from his lips with his undershirt sleeve, now aware that all the officers sat around him had stopped eating and were looking at him.

'I'm sorry?' said Rayner, apparently perplexed..

'You heard me. If we now know how to read their stuff, why are we still letting U-boats run amok?'

If it had been any other unit, Hook would have scolded Rands for his aggressive tone towards a fellow officer, but given that this unit was somewhat different to most, he let the question stand. Hook hand-picked his officers not just for their toughness, but also for their intelligence. Rands, love or hate him, was no fool.

The captain focussed on the young lieutenant, awaiting his response. Rayner, to his credit, kept his composure and his reply was measured.

'If we interdict every U-boat, if we tell the Soviets every German division's plans, every raid on Valletta...'

Rayner could feel the submariners around him bristle. He knew he had painted too colourful a description, but there was no going back for him now. He swallowed hard before continuing.

'...all that the Cypher School has achieved up to this point would be for nothing.'

Traske's hands, which, had been relaxed on the table, were now fists, his knuckles white.

'Are you telling us that they know *everything* the Germans are going to do, and say *nothing*?' Traske was failing in his attempt to keep the anger from his voice.

Hook interjected.

'Why? *Why* do they not tell anyone?' The tone of this question was inquisitive, intrigued. Rayner continued.

'I can't speak for the Cypher School in general, but every message I decode in Gibraltar is vetted. I am allowed to reveal some messages, but not all.'

'Why the hell *not*?' Rands was now speaking through clenched teeth, his own fists on the table. Rayner looked him straight in the eyes.

'The Germans will know that we know. They will go silent, and have a new code by the end of the week.'

The explanation did little to ease the atmosphere at the table. Hook was angry at the revelation, but understood why it had to remain a secret. Rands had not finished.

'Why you, Rayner?'

'Why me?'

'Yes, why would you volunteer to come out from behind your cosy little desk in Gibraltar to come on a mission as mad as this one?'

'I... don't underst...'

Then Rands was over the desk like a prop forward, and the sudden burst of movement had all around the table lurch back in surprise. Rands grabbed Rayner with one hand by his undershirt, each man's face level with the other's as he shoved Rayner's head back against the wood panelling. Hook had to force Rands off his victim.

'What the *fuck* are you doing?' Hook bellowed. Rands released his grip, sitting back down, his glare locked on his target. Rayner straightened up his shirt, whilst rubbing the back of his head.

Rands glanced left and right, keeping his voice to a venomous hiss. 'You sit there, bold as fucking brass, acting like you have the power and the intelligence to play God.'

'Don't be so fucking naive, Rands,' Rayner snarled. 'Why do you think *The Rosa* was allowed to get as far as bloody Gibraltar before we picked her up?'

'You knew what she was carrying?' Hook asked.

Rayner nodded. 'We already knew she was going to resupply U-911. We just had to give her crew a little squeeze, so they had something to report to the Germans later.'

'Fucking bastards,' said Pryce, no longer feeling the desire to eat.

'That's why my men and I had no time to sort ourselves out after Tunisia,' said Hook. 'You knew that ship could not be late, the Germans would suspect we had got hold of her.'

Rayner nodded. Rands leaned in slowly; simultaneously, Rayner leaned back, prepared for another assault.

'You knew that if the Germans suspected British interference with that fucking ship, we would not have permission to return to La Rochelle?'

'Yes. It was vital we got permission to return. They have so few U-boats in the north Atlantic at the moment; they would rather risk shipping to re-supply them whilst on patrol.'

'So our mission, is that a calculated lie as well?' Hook asked.

'No.' Rayner shook his head. 'La Rochelle is to be destroyed. They have several U-boats in dry dock right now; we must render them useless to the enemy.'

'Strange how you never mentioned that shit when we were planning this job,' sneered Rands. 'Anything else you want to share with us?'

All of the officers, Hook included, looked at Rayner. So far his only ally had been the commando captain. Hook leaned on his right elbow, looking Rayner in the eyes.

'No bullshit, what do they have waiting for us in there?'

'I didn't want certain factors to influence your plan, Captain. If you had known too much, you may have chosen not to attack.'

'Go on.' Hook was impassive.

'La Rochelle is crawling with troops. By that I mean thousands.'

'Mr Rayner,' Hook's tone became stern. 'My men may look like a bunch of misfits on a good day, but they are not fools. I deliberately never tell them how many enemy troops are defending a target, and the boys never ask.'

'Why not?' Rayner was puzzled.

'Because we train them to believe they are invincible, and to do whatever it takes to get the job done.'

Rayner didn't know what to say. Hook continued.

'We know there will be plenty of enemy troops, which is why we play to our strengths. As I said in Velas, if there are lots of them, they will have lots of officers and NCOs with a radio trying to direct men and material all over the place. That fact alone jams up their radio network, which buys us time to get on with what we went there for, and time to get out. By the time they have pulled their fingers out and organised a concentrated response, we are gone.'

Rayner remained silent, he quietly acknowledged the fact that the commandos were up for the job, and that there was no need for smoke and mirrors.

'It was me that approved the linking up with the SAS within the French interior', confessed the captain. 'Our past missions have seen us chased to the coast, where we wait for pick up. That's what killed Major Bird and the others in Tunisia. I vowed not to let that happen again. Whilst the enemy scours the coast for us, we will continue to wreak havoc upon their rear echelons. It's what we do, Mr Rayner. *It's what we do.*'

Rayner nodded slightly and the mood around the table was beginning to relax. Even Rands' demeanour grew a little tamer, and he forced an over-enthusiastic grin.

'Right then, whilst we are on the subject, let's talk about the enemy. Who, where, what and why?'

'High numbers of Luftwaffe manning air defence batteries all over the facility and the town,' Rayner volunteered.

'What about Kriegsmarine?' Joyce threw his hand in.

'Mainly U-boat crews. They have some shore-based personnel there, but they tend to employ local labourers and dockers to assist in the running of the place.'

'Why?'

'Keeps the locals onside. Puts money in their pockets. Any fighting-aged males not of any use to the facility have already been shipped out to labour camps further inside France.'

'Makes sense.'

Rayner nodded.

'What about SS? Gestapo?'

Rayner shook his head. 'All Waffen SS units are either in the Soviet Union, or are resting in the north at Pas de Calais. They would take too long to come and assist. The Gestapo do have offices there, but not much chatter comes out of them.'

'Any other garrison forces?

'Yes.' Rayner nodded. 'They are stationed on the coast. They run exercises often and are well drilled in responding to an incident.'

'Are they front line quality?'

'No, they are just well practised in what they do. The army does not respond to exercises involving the town or the pens.'

'Why not?'

'The Kriegsmarine have command and control of the area. A joint operation only complicates things.'

'How the fuck do you know all this, when you said you just listen to shit bouncing around the Med?' Rands was on the verge of launching himself at the man again. Hook waved him down without so much as looking at him.

'So...' Hook paused. 'We are looking at just sailors and airmen. No high calibre troops?'

Rayner raised an eyebrow at the men around him, before addressing Hook's question. 'You say "only", Captain; there are *thousands* of the bastards all over the place.'

It was now Hook's turn to give him a menacing leer.

'It's not the dog in the fight, Mr Rayner. It's the fight in the dog.'

14

The commando officers tittered, as Rayner smiled sheepishly. Rands then returned to his more measured style of questioning.

'So, the question still stands.'

'What?' Rayner muttered.

'Why *you*?'

Hook held up a hand as if to bring the aggressive troop commander to heel, his voice now jovial to the point of sarcasm.

'James, do you not see why young Freddy here is with us?'

Even Rands was now at a loss as he looked at the captain, who turned slowly to the tormented Rayner.

'Like us... he is expendable.'

Rayner could do nothing more than agree with the captain.

'I decipher hundreds, if not thousands, of codes every bloody week. I know what the Germans are up to before they do.'

'*Just* you? Surely not?' scoffed Rands.

'No, there are many decoders all over the world. Anyone east of Suez listens to Japanese traffic. The Enigma machines, as we call them, are patent pending instruments, so getting them is the easy part. Getting the key setting rings not so much, that's why we are careful when selecting which information we act on.'

'How do you choose what to tell our forces?' Traske was intrigued.

Rayner shrugged. 'I don't, that's Cabinet Office-level stuff. It gets to whomever needs to know through their mysterious methods.'

'So, they would sacrifice a ship full of civilians or troops in order to keep the Germans from getting wind of our eavesdropping?'

Rayner nodded.

'Yes, we were all warned that if we were to reveal what material we were privy to, we would end up in Antarctica counting penguins for the rest of our lives... or words to that effect.'

Comedy is all about timing, and Rayner wasn't a comedian. The officers around him remained silent. Hook asked more questions.

'Why are you on this job? Why were you recruited to the Cypher School?'

'I had no intention of joining up if I'm honest. I was in my final year at university, finishing off my French and German courses, when I was approached by my housemaster and two serious looking gentlemen, who were keen to talk to me.'

'Why?' Rands pushed. 'Who were they?'

'The chap in uniform was a colonel from the Royal Corps of Signals. He informed me that he was a talent scout for the suited gentleman, who just glared at me, not so much as a handshake.'

'Who was he?' Hook asked.

'He spoke little, but the Signals colonel said he was from the Cabinet Office.'

Hook frowned at the young man before looking about the other officers. They too were a little perplexed as to why the Cabinet Office would want the skills of someone not even out of education. Rayner continued, the silence among them was growing uncomfortable.

'I was invited to attend a practical interview in Blandford. They wanted me to demonstrate my French and German skills. Upon arrival, the very same Cabinet Office chap only spoke to me in German, whilst a woman who was sat with him spoke in French. Nothing significant, just general chit chat.'

'Why would they do that?' Rands' question was certainly on everyone's lips, he just happened to beat them to the punch. Rayner shrugged.

'I wasn't sure at first, but it wasn't long before I began to dread the prospect of being sent to France or perhaps Germany on some special mission.'

Rands felt a little foolish, embarrassed at his turn of phrase. He was barely out of university, sat among men who had done more than their fair share of special missions. Hook leaned forward, getting Rayner's attention.

'So you passed the interview?'

'Kind of.' Rayner was a little hesitant. Hook frowned, his expression persuading the young man to elaborate.

'The Cabinet Office chap and the woman left without giving me any feedback. I sat in the interview room for the better part of an hour before the Signals colonel came in. He told me that my French and German was too textbook for intelligence gathering within France and Germany, as the German authorities would pick me up by the end of the first day.'

'Bet you was happy to be told that,' Rands sniggered, his menacing mask slipping a little. Rayner smirked as he nodded.

'Yeah, I don't think I would be able to hold my nerve doing that kind of stuff. The colonel was given carte blanche to employ me as he saw fit, and that was how I got assigned to the Cypher School.

'And you got the eavesdropping job? Just like that?' Traske sounded sceptical. Rayner shrugged.

'More or less. I did my full term at Sandhurst, but they were only interested in having me listen to German radio traffic. I've not long been seconded to the Cypher School. Gibraltar was my first posting.'

The commandos, not to mention the submariners, around him looked at each other, as if to decide whether the young officer was telling the truth. Rayner was uncomfortable, and tried his hardest not to catch the eye of Rands.

Hook broke the silence with some rather sobering information.

'Freddy, I think despite the natural talent you possess, you are seriously out of your depth here. When we get to La Rochelle, you will witness the darker side of what is demanded of our skills. There will be no heroic cheering from the British public, no pats on the back if we pull this off. It will be just another mission in the interest of the war effort.'

'Captain, I understand...'

Hook raised a hand, he wasn't finished.

'If this whole thing goes bad, and you are captured...' Hook tailed off. He looked at the faces before him. He no longer felt the need to spell out what would happen in that scenario. He decided to switch to more productive issues.

'You know how to fire infantry weapons?'

Rayner nodded. That was good enough for Hook.

'If you run out of ammunition, just pick up whatever is available, whether it be ours or theirs. Just pick it up and bloody well use it.'

*

After the very revealing conversation with Rayner, there was little else to do but continue to plan the mission in the pens. The officers now saw that Rayner was, in fact, an asset to the mission, and no longer just a suspicious addition to the grand plan. Now they were in possession of more information, but it didn't really alter the plan. Hook knew they would be hugely outnumbered, but he was still confident that his company could do what was required.

Business concluded for the time being, Hook dismissed them so they could go and check on their men and their submarine duties. They remained submerged whenever the electric batteries allowed them. It made for smooth, but slow, sailing.

Some time later, Traske brought U-911 up to periscope depth. He conducted his careful traverse to ensure they were not about to surface among an armada of Allied shipping. He knew Rayner would have warned him of any propeller noise, but it was better to be sure. Once complete, he pulled his eyes away from the periscope optics and grinned at the men cluttering the control room.

'It's rough up there, chaps; hope you have the stomach for it. We won't stay up for too long, just enough to recharge and then we will dive again. Lookouts, prepare for first watch.'

Unsurprisingly, some of the smokers were already fighting their way into the rain gear. Traske chuckled.

'Good luck lighting your cigarettes up there.'

The storm from the Caribbean was in full force. Never had Hook seen such rough seas. The pitch of the U-boat was so extreme, he thought the whole thing would tip over. Anything not secured now crashed about the interior, causing those buried in the avalanche of equipment and food to curse aloud. Mr Fearl, despite not having to take a bridge watch, was in full rain gear because his chart table was at the base of the conning tower ladder. Every time the boat ploughed nose first into another huge wave, he was soaked. The charts were protected, but it still made navigation a challenge for the young officer. Hook found Traske wedged behind the mess table, reading a book he had pulled from somewhere. He didn't stop to talk with the man; instead he clambered through to the control room to check on the chief and those manning their posts.

Hook came across the chief petty officer laughing his head off as one of the commando drivers vomited once more. Hook caught his eye and grinned back at him. He knew the boys were feeling rough, but they would just have to endure it until the storm passed. Another downpour over the navigation officer directed him towards the chart table, where Fearl was grabbing hold of anything firmly fixed, as U-911 climbed out of another trough.

'Nothing like the Med, eh Lieutenant?' he hollered, as tins of food clattered about them, most rolling down to the rear control room hatch.

'You're telling me. The bloody Med is a fucking lake compared to this. Bloody hell!'

'Are we keeping on course?'

'Difficult to tell. Need a sun shot with the sexant to be sure. We are maintaining direction, but the storm is pushing us towards Portugal. I can't confirm our location until this bloody storm passes.'

Hook was stunned by a torrent of freezing Atlantic sea water as it engulfed him. The cold took his breath away, but in a few seconds he managed a numbed chuckle.

'Fuck, that was cold. I wasn't ready for that!'

Fearl tried his hardest not to laugh, and pointed. 'Rain gear is in that locker, sir.' The soaked commando nodded, his skin so numb it could have belonged to someone else.

'Help us to get him down!' came the roar up in the conning tower. As both the officers at the bottom of the ladder looked up, they were met by another flurry of sea water in the face. Hook was not so upbeat the second time. As the water cleared, he could see someone's feet being lowered towards him, and it dawned on him that the men were carrying one of the lookouts down.

As Fearl and Hook took hold of the inert frame of Corporal Steer, a 1 Troop NCO, they noticed watery blood pouring from the side of his head. One of the lads carrying him down called out for medical kits and dressings.

With Hook and Fearl clumsily holding the NCO between them, a task made all the more difficult by the pitching and rolling of the submarine, the commando helping them spoke loudly.

'Flak gun securing strap broke; the whole thing clobbered him in the head. We can't keep watch with that bloody gun swinging around unsecured.'

That was good enough for Hook. He called to the chief.

'Prepare to dive!'

As the chief turned towards the unfamiliar voice, the commando on the ladder bellowed the order up to the two commandos still up on the bridge. The chief looked a little put out.

'I beg your pardon, sir?' This was clearly against the protocol he had been accustomed to throughout his career as a submariner.

'You heard me, Mr Toil. Prepare to dive.'

The chief petty officer turned hesitantly back to the drivers.

'Prepare to dive. Aye, sir.'

As he relayed the order, Traske appeared in the hatch, a frown etched on his face. He visibly relaxed when he noticed the unconscious and bleeding man held in the officers' arms.

As the men from the bridge came down the ladder, Traske called to them with thumbs up.

'Hatches secured, men?'

'Yes, sir.'

Traske turned to his chief. 'Make our depth one-zero-zero metres.'

'Make our depth one-zero-zero-metres, aye sir.'

Traske looked back at Hook and the men around him.

'Let's get him looked at and patched up.'

15

'He'll be okay in a few days. Just as well we don't have much else to do in the meantime.'

The sergeant major applied a last strip of tape to hold the dressing in place. Steer was awake, but sounded almost drunk in his speech and was in no mood or condition to sit up, let alone do any work.

Gibbs looked up at both Hook and Cross.

'He's got concussion. Judging by what the boys told us, he took one hell of a whack to the bonce with the flak gun. If he is sick, that will confirm concussion. All he can do for now is rest.'

The officers backed away to let the NCO recuperate. 'Thank you, Sergeant Major.'

They left the captain's bunk to return to the control room. It was Gibbs' idea to put Steer in the bunk as the torpedo room was crowded enough, and with loading drills going on all of the time, if Steer were left to rest there, the man would soon wish the swinging flak gun had finished him off.

Traske stood with Fearl at the chart table; there was no longer any need to cling on for dear life. Hook chose not to bother them whilst they plotted with the compass and made notes. He felt it only proper to tip his hat to the chief.

'Mr Toil?'

The chief turned, eyebrows raised slightly at the call.

'Hello sir, how is the corporal?'

'He is fine, thank you. Concussed, cuts and bruises.'

'That's good. He'll be fine I'm sure. How can I help you, sir?'

'I would like to apologise for taking on matters that were outside my remit, earlier. I should have put it to Commander Traske to take the required action.'

The chief petty officer put up his hands, palm outermost, at chest height.

'Not a problem, sir. It took me by surprise I must admit, old habits die hard and all that.'

Hook grinned. 'Yes, well I'm sure you understood the rationale behind the order, given the state of poor Corporal Steer.'

'Aye, sir. I understood alright. We fellows in the silent service are a strange bunch... and that's coming from a submariner.'

Hook grinned as he put a friendly hand on the chiefs' shoulder.

'Thank you, chief.'

'Besides, sir, in a few days, I will be one of your troops. Imagine that!'

Hook was struck by the statement and his smile faded a little.

'Yes. Imagine that. The things we have to do for our country.'

'Indeed, sir.'

Hook left the chief to his duties and turned to Traske, who had now finished consulting with his navigator. Hook could sense that all was not well.

'The storm is pushing us east, closer to Portugal. Not ideal, for we run the risk of not only running into our own navy, but their aircraft coverage too.'

'I see.' Hook nodded. Traske continued.

'We will surface run once the storm passes, so Mr Fearl can get a sun shot, and we can make our adjustments from there.'

'Whatever we need to do, Commander Traske, you are the man to do it.'

The submariner smiled slightly as he passed, heading towards the stern. 'I found some gramophone records left behind by the German crew, shall we listen to them?'

'Sure,' Hook answered, a little surprised.

The first track crackled into life, with Rayner allowing it to broadcast over the boat's tannoy system. Hook was expecting some brash, loud Nazi marches, but was pleased to hear just a gentle melody, and a soothing voice of a lady who sounded to be barely out of her teens. He had no idea what the woman was singing about, all he knew was that it sounded rather lovely. As her velvet tones drifted through the submarine, the singer rendered even the most boisterous commandos mute as she commanded their undivided attention. Despite the relentless soundtrack of electric engines, her voice seduced everyone.

With every soothing song she sang from the gramophone, the men who were crammed aboard U-911 on their way to conduct their most daring raid yet, fell more and more in love with her.

When the record finally finished, Rayner went to change it. The men roared their demand for it to be played again. Rayner looked to the officers slumped around the mess table, themselves seduced. Hook leaned into the gangway.

'Mr Rayner, unless you want a mutiny on your hands, you will keep the boys happy.'

As the lovely German girl began to singagain, she was overwhelmed by a cheer from her new fans. Hook and the officers smiled as they shook their heads. War was hell, but sometimes, a little piece of it was lovely.

*

Eventually, two days later, the storm passed. Traske went about his usual routine of coming up to periscope depth, checking there was nothing on the surface to surprise them. Before giving the order to surface, Rayner confirmed he could not hear anything untoward. Hook and Gibbs, dressed in rain gear, were at the foot of the conning tower ladder.

'We want to have a look at this troublesome flak gun,' announced Gibbs.

Fearl was fighting his way into his rain gear. 'Sure, when you are ready, give me a shout so I can take a reading and find out how far that storm pushed us.'

When they were given the order Gibbs led the way up the ladder, unlocking the hatches as he went. The outer hatch let in crisp, cold sea air which felt good on his exposed hands and face. He looked up and could see the blue sky, devoid of any clouds. As he climbed the last rungs of the ladder, he saw the swaying gun behind the periscope mount. Gibbs was not in the least surprised that the heavy weapon had knocked Steers' lights out. He checked the ammunition bins to ensure they were secure, too.

As the captain stood upright, Gibbs grinned. 'No wonder poor Steer was knocked for six, feel the weight of this bloody...'

'Listen!' Hook hissed, holding up a finger for silence. Gibbs looked about the boat, trying to see what the captain was alerting him to. Both of them hushed the other two lookouts as they clambered up onto the bridge. The two lads from 1 Troop stood stock still as Hook began to look upwards and around.

'Tell me you can hear that?'

The others began to scan the bright blue sky, the sun forcing them to shield their eyes. The sea was much calmer now the storm had blown through, but it too had its own unique relentless din.

Before any of them could react, cannon fire straddled the U-boat, sending thin geysers of water high and wide. No sooner had the men flinched in time to take cover, a loud roar of engines overcame all the ambient noise. A shadow, almost like a giant bird, eclipsed the sun for a moment as the attacking aircraft pulled out of its dive.

'Dive, dive!' roared Gibbs, on his way into the hatch.

'Wait!' shouted Hook. He managed to find the aircraft as it climbed into the sun once again. Its distinct shape revealed it to be a Catalina flying boat. Probably on anti-submarine duties, the crew had found some long-awaited prey.

The swaying of the flak gun caught his attention. Hook grabbed the barrel, swinging the gun around in order to use it.

'Get the ammo for this thing.'

'What?' Gibbs bellowed.

'Ammo, get the bloody ammo for this gun!'

Gibbs immediately got the two commandos to fetch a box of belt ammunition for the captain. They fought their way into the stowage bins. The captain kept track of the Catalina as he shouted over his shoulder.

'Hurry up with that bloody ammo you two.'

The men got the ammunition tins and staggered over to the flak gun.

'You've been shown how to use the bloody thing, get on with it. Shoot at that plane, before they sink us.'

Hook leaned against the rail, to allow the men to get into position so they could use it. Gibbs helped by breaking open one of the ammunition tins.

'It's coming back!'Hook roared.

The conning tower rumbled under their feet as cannon fire splashed about them, most of it hitting the water. The two commandos carried on loading the gun, and then began to track the Catalina as it pulled up to circle around again.

'Why don't we just dive?' Gibbs called to the captain.

Hook shook his head. 'We are too slow to escape, if she drops depth charges, we are done for.'

Gibbs looked up at the aircraft as it circled into the sun once more, then back at the officer.

'I would rather chance that.'

Hook shook his head. 'We are too shallow for depth charges; all we have to do is scare it off.'

The flak gun opened fire, chugging out a few shells, which clattered, spent, about the men's feet. The firing took Hook by surprise, his ears ringing. The men fired off another short burst. The Catalina knew how to attack. Out of the sun. The men continued to fire short bursts *into* the sun, in the vain hope that it was enough to put the attackers off.

More cannon fire straddled the U-boat, but it was not as concentrated as the first two assaults had been. As the Catalina pulled out of its dive, a burst of flak gun registered a hit on its left waist gun bubble, shattering it, along with a portion of wing. Hook thought he detected a left engine hit.

'Good hits men, good shooting. Hopefully, they will fuck off now.'

The crew concentrated on the Catalina, awaiting its climb into the sun for another dive. As it grew smaller, all four of them could see the tell-tale oily streak coming from its left engine.

Hook puffed out his cheeks.

'Hopefully, the buggers won't be in a rush to come back.'

'They had RAF markings, sir', one of the gunners pointed out.

Hook nodded.

'Yes, Temple, it was certainly the RAF. We just happen to be on a German submarine, why would they *not* attack us?'

'They have probably already reported our location to the whole RAF and the bloody Royal Navy,' Gibbs snorted.

'They will have by now, you can bet a day's pay on it.'

'I hope that left side gunner is okay. I didn't mean to get them like that.' Driscoll, the other commando, looked sorrowful.

'You did good boys; they could have bloody well sunk us. Don't be downhearted.' Gibbs patted each of them on the shoulder. 'Let's get this thing packed away; I doubt we will see any more of them today.'

Then Hook saw the securing strap hanging over the rail. The nut and bolt that held the strap to just behind the muzzle break were missing — he deduced that it was nothing more than the components working loose over time.

Gibbs was kicking the empty brass shells over the side of the boat, when someone yelled from behind them.

'What on earth happened?'

Traske was on the bridge, looking stunned.

'We got attacked.' Hook informed him. 'Catalina, with RAF markings.'

'Did you shoot at it?' Traske demanded.

'Yes, we hit her left engine and caused cosmetic damage.'

Traske made his way to Hook, being careful where he trod as he moved around the sergeant major and the two lads packing away the ammunition.

'I guess we are a lot closer to the coast than we thought,' suggested Hook. Traske shook his head.

'Catalinas don't need land, providing your shooting didn't puncture below its waterline. They can patrol constantly, as far out as they like.'

'Really?' Hook wasn't sure to be impressed or worried.

'Yes, they just need to arrange rendezvous with ships for fuel and supplies. They land nearby and then motor over to the vessel in question.'

A horrifying prospect dawned on Hook.

'Could they follow us into La Rochelle?'

'If I was their pilot, I would stay well away from any port facilities in German hands. Catalinas are good, but they are slow, and the Germans would shoot her to bits before she lined up to attack anything.'

'Okay.' Hook was content. Both he and Traske looked out into the distance. The faint oily streak on the horizon marked the aircraft's progress.

'You hit her, you say?' Traske asked.

'Yes, the boys are worried they hit the crew. Not that we will be able to find out.'

'Yes, well... you didn't shoot them down, that's the main thing.'

16

Hook made his way back onto the bridge, where Fearl was already taking sun shots with the sextant. One of the NCOs was with him, with a stopwatch, a notebook and pencil. Fearl dictated and the man copied his words down. The two commandos that operated the flak gun remained on the bridge as both Hook and Traske went below. Gibbs remained on the bridge to ensure the men were okay.

'Bet when you joined up, you never thought you'd have to shoot at your own side, eh?' The sergeant major felt that gallows humour was in order to bring the boys back onside. They were tough men, but also human.

It was Temple that replied.

'Never thought I'd be on a German U-boat either, they never mentioned that when we volunteered.'

Gibbs squeezed the man's shoulder. 'You have a point there, I never considered it either.'

*

Down in the control room, Hook was pulling off his rain gear when one of the men let him know that Mr Rayner had information for him. Traske took it upon himself to join him when Hook set off to see Rayner; after all, he *was* the commander of the boat.

Hook and Traske squatted down in the gangway, looking in at Rayner as he finished decoding a message. Morse code continued to transmit as Rayner grabbed a pencil, scribbling down what it all meant. Both Hook and Traske were trained in Morse, but anything in German, that was Rayner's job. The young officer noticed both of them waiting.

'Sorry gents, bear with me, the message is quite detailed.'

'Take your time,' Hook reassured him, mindful of the recent confrontation, and with all cards having been laid on the table, knowing how useful Rayner actually was.

Rayner set about decoding the further information, with a sense of urgency. He then set it neatly onto paper in block capitals, headlining it 'captain's eyes only'. He then handed it to the senior officers.

Hook read it first, then passed it to Traske. The commando captain cursed aloud.

'Fuck.'

Rayner nodded slightly. 'Yes, sir, it certainly changes the playing field.'

'How long do you think we have to respond?'

'Twenty-four hours, give or take, I haven't responded yet.'

'Good, do not acknowledge receipt yet. They will naturally assume that we are too deep to pick up messages.'

Hook felt a presence behind his right shoulder. He turned to find Gibbs, eating one of the many bananas onboard U-911. The sergeant major stopped chewing, looking at all three of the officers.

'What?'

Traske handed him the piece of paper. Gibbs read the bold pencilled font, slowly. Hook could see the man's eyebrows rising as his eyes followed the text. Gibbs then looked at his company commander.

'Why on earth do they want us to sail into the Med?'

Both the senior officers and Gibbs looked at Rayner, who sat upright, immediately defensive.

'Don't ask me, I have no idea why.'

'Before you joined us, was there anything the Germans were up to in the region, not including Tunisia?' Traske asked.

Rayner could tell he was on a hiding to nothing, trying to keep any information from them. He nodded.

'The Germans have been evacuating Tunisia for some time, whilst fighting a rear guard against us and the Americans.'

'Where are they going?'

'Sicily. The entire garrison has been carrying out considerable defensive preparations since the middle of last year.'

Hook leaned forward. 'So we are winning in North Africa?'

'I would appear so, sir.'

'What does this have to do with us redeploying into the Med?' Gibbs asked.

'Probably to attack our invasion shipping,' Traske said.

'Invasion?' Hook looked at the commander, who gave him a menacing smile.

'Our advance onto Sicily.'

'Gentlemen, please excuse my lack of enthusiasm.' The sergeant major stepped in. 'To get into the Med, we need to squeeze past Gibraltar. Half the bloody Royal Navy is there, and we just happen to be on a German submarine.'

Hook took the paper from Gibbs, screwing it up with both hands.

'We are not going into the Med. We carry on to La Rochelle. They don't know if we have received the message yet, nor will they turn us away as they are aware of our need for a dry dock inspection. But there is another factor that now presents itself.'

'What is that?'

'Families and friends of this boat's crew will probably be told that their loved ones are not due home anytime soon, and therefore will not be on the quayside when we arrive.'

'Good point,' Gibbs nodded.

Morse began to dot and dash rapidly, making all four of the men flinch. Rayner fumbled for a pencil, scribbling the meaning down as quickly as it came through the speaker. Hook hoped it was not a message demanding that U-911 acknowledge the message and divert to the Tunisian coast. The last thing they needed, with an overloaded German submarine, was to try and get past their own side in the narrow Gibraltar Strait.

Rayner began to decode the message. His fingers worked quickly, noting the meaning of the German message in English, and once completed he handed it to Commander Traske.

'Convoy co-ordinates, sir.'

Traske took the paper, studying it for a few seconds before getting up and heading for the control room.

Hook and Gibbs followed him as he clambered through the bulkhead hatch and made his way over to the chart table. Mr Fearl made room for the commander as he put the piece of paper on the table and fingered the co-ordinates written on it. Hook observed Traske at work, doing what he did best, commanding a submarine. With ruler and compass he measured current position and the contact details. After a minute or two, he nodded his contentment, putting the compass down.

'Convoy far to the north. We shouldn't run into it.'

'How many U-boats are tracking it?' Hook asked.

'So far, three. We would make it four.'

'Indulge me for a minute, sir...' Gibbs began. 'If we were a German crew, would the convoy be close enough for us to join the pack?'

Traske ran his finger over the chart once more before answering the sergeant major's question.

'If we had the right size crew, and we went hell for leather on the surface for as long as we could, we *could* be in position by the early hours of tomorrow.'

'So even if we wanted to, given our current load, we would have no chance of getting there in time?' Gibbs asked.

'Not a chance, Sergeant Major Gibbs.'

'Thank you, sir.'

'Mr Rayner will be receiving a tonnage score in the morning, let's not forget that,' said Traske.

That fact had not been lost on Hook.

U-911 ran on the surface all day, without any interference from allied aircraft. Hook took his turn on the bridge. The day was beautiful. The storm had cleared the air, and the fresh weather front made Paul Hook feel rather upbeat about his lot in life. Soon they would be on their final leg into La Rochelle. He knew his men would perform in a way true to the spirit of the British Commandos, but he was a little uneasy about how the submariners and Rayner would perform once off the boat. Hook found himself pulling and twisting his full beard. All the men, even the younger men, had grown a full set of whiskers, and looked very much the part. A U-boat crew returning from a war patrol. Pale skin, sunken eyes, matted beards and filthy bodies.

He took some time to think over what they would be doing and wearing during the raid. He would be up on the bridge with Traske and Rayner as they pulled up at the pens. Rayner would be able to inform them what people were saying on the quayside. Those in the conning tower, and 2 Troop on the forward decking, would be in battledress with their weapons slung behind their backs. They were to only have webbing belts and their water bottles fitted; magazines and grenades would be stuffed into their jackets and pockets. Hook didn't envy the Bren gunners, for their weapons were cumbersome, and their large magazines would have to be wedged inside their battledress. Rain gear would cover each of them. The intention was just to give the appearance of a bloated and overweight crew returning from life below the waves.

The remainder of the company would all be sporting standard British equipment. No rifles, just Bren guns and Thompsons. They were to ensure their bergen rucksacks were not overloaded, as that would delay men disembarking from the sub. With all those not on submarine duties upon the quayside, the last two men off the boat would ensure they had cast the ropes off, allowing Traske and his ad hoc submariners to attack the dry docks and U-boats within, damaging them enough to put them out of action, for the short term at least.

Hook was confident in his plan. He was confident in his approach, of allowing his troop commanders to plan the finer details of their own particular tasks. He knew that all of his men could navigate over land, and cause much trouble for the Germans along the way. The opposition was great in number, but not in terms of infantry quality. He would be foolish to think the British would have it all their own way, but he knew that if you fought hard enough and were aggressive in the execution of your mission, strong opponents tended to second-guess themselves, giving you the edge.

Tunisia had provided a different kind of opposition. The Afrika Korps were good at what they did. They were battle hardened, but weary. Hook knew that the Germans were planning to leave North Africa at some point, Rayner confirmed it. When his predecessor, Major Phillip Bird, had briefed them for the raid on the dock facilities in Tunis, Hook knew that would be a tough nut to crack. The captain was not himself part of the main attack on the shipping moored in Bizerte harbour. His job was to have 3 Troop in a fire support position, to give covering fire to Bird and the other two troops as they withdrew from laying their hull charges on the ships. The charges did their job and did it well — the ships sank at their moorings, rendering the port useless to the Germans. Unfortunately, Bird and the men were met by a well organised German force that fought and chased them all the way to their exfiltration point on the northern coast.

Because the fighting was at close quarters, Hook and 3 Troop had not dared fire, for fear of killing Bird and the rest of the company, so Hook opted to return to their landing craft instead, and rejoined the battered company out on the Royal Navy frigate that brought them to Tunisia. There, Hook was informed that Bird was dead, cut down on the beach as he provided covering fire for the men as they clambered aboard their landing craft. Hook, as second in command of the company, knew that he was now in command. Gibraltar was a very brief respite as he was tasked to board *The Rosa*, bound for the Azores.

Now, whilst the weather was good and the area clear of allied aircraft and shipping for the time being, Hook chose to remain up on the bridge as the men rotated through their watch routine. They spoke of home, the mission, life after the war, as if they were on a cruise ship, rather than a stolen German U-boat, full of British commandos bound for the La Rochelle U-boat pens.

17

Commander Ronald Traske had U-911 surface run through the night, keen to make good time into La Rochelle. He was concerned that the longer they stayed out in the Atlantic, the greater the chances of their being either attacked by their own side, or of the Germans becoming aware of their intentions. The stranded German crew back in Velas had been given plenty of time to get word to their masters, and his opposite number was not at all happy about his men having to hand over their service caps to the enemy. Traske was aware that Sergeant Major Gibbs had been somewhat diplomatic about it — well, as diplomatic as army warrant officers could be. The German captain was now one of those up on the ship's rail, watching as Hook and his men rehearsed getting off the boat as quickly as possible. The men were being trained in use of the deck and flak guns, which was just as well given the Catalina attack.

The day and night surface run had made up time on the run into La Rochelle. At first light, Traske had them dive to periscope depth as they drew near the French coast. Plotting the next leg, Lieutenant Anthony Fearl informed Hook and Traske that they were twenty-four hours away from the mouth of the estuary that would take them into La Rochelle docks. The time for contemplation was over. Hook and Traske had the men drilled and prepared in the final hours before their raid began.

The commandos carried out as much battle preparation as they could, given their location. They had no room to do much physical training, only press-ups and sits-ups in the gangway. Weapons were stripped down, inspected and cleaned before being rebuilt. Hook insisted that no weapons be loaded until they were on the verge of launching their attack. NCOs and their officers went through the particular tasks they were to undertake in the pens. The 1 Troop submarine crew made their final checks under the guidance of their submarine officers. Once these preparations were complete, the officers and many men of U-911 rested as best they could, wrapped in their own thoughts.

Hook had seen his fair share of action, but he was concerned about showing fear in front of the men. They were all scared in their own ways, and Hook believed strongly that any man about to go into battle who stated that they were not afraid, was either a fool or a downright liar.

Gibbs found the captain wedged behind the mess table, leaning against the wooden fittings and peeling a banana.

'You're going to turn into a bloody banana one day, Sergeant Major!' joked Hook.

'I'm just preparing for the bloody long walk out of town, never mind the fighting.' A mouth full of banana made speech difficult.

'Are the boys okay?'

His mouth now void of fruit, the sergeant major spoke more clearly.' Yes, sir. They are ready to go. Nothing we haven't done before.'

'Please gather the mission commanders; I would like to update them on developments.'

The troop commanders, along with the submarine officers, squeezed into the wardroom while the sergeants remained with the men. Once all were present, including Gibbs, the captain made his announcement.

'We attack at first light.'

The officers blinked, looked at each other, and then looked back at Hook. He continued.

'Darkness is confusing, for both them and us. If the RAF decide to hit the place while we are there, or are arriving, I fear the entire facility will be wide awake and out in force.'

'But daylight would almost guarantee a larger opposing force being already out of bed,' Rands challenged. Hook nodded.

'There is that to consider, but I have made up my mind. We sail into the pens at first light, when the chances of air raids are minimal. The night shift will be falling into bed, so we could exploit that fact.'

Hook's men knew better than to argue the matter for long. They knew the officer in command had made up his mind, and the men would just get on with it, despite their own reservations. They would never follow blindly, but a commando company was neither a dictatorship nor a democracy.

The final stretch into La Rochelle dragged. Traske was reluctant to surface until they were at the mouth of the estuary. He made it clear that he would like to remain submerged and push further in, but the Germans had been in France for a number of years and could well have anti-submarine netting and mines in place.

Just before first light, they finally arrived at the estuary's mouth. At periscope depth, Traske could see that it was twilight, the sun making itself known on the eastern horizon. He had the chief surface U-911 nice and gently. With the men restless and itching to get off the boat, the majority of them were already getting their fighting gear on, although not yet loading their weapons. 2 Troop was already in fighting gear, their battledress jackets stuffed with magazines and grenades. They drank greedily from their water bottles before refilling them from the sub's fresh water supply. Glazed in sweat, they made small talk as they ensured they had their German crew caps and rain jackets. Lieutenant Rands and Sergeant Grice took time to inspect them; not so they were smart enough to parade, but to make sure they had what was required for the attack.

Hook and Gibbs also sweated under their combat loads, and Captain Hook was dressed like any other member of the crew. Traske carried that look off a little better, for he had the swagger and demeanour of a submarine captain, and rightly so.

Lieutenant Rayner looked nervous; Hook patted him on the shoulder.

'Unsling your weapon; we can have ours by our feet on the bridge.'

Rayner was clumsy as he fought his way out of the Thompson sling. It got caught up on the pipe work he was leaning against and he became frustrated. Gibbs helped.

'Nice and easy, sir. You'll do just fine.' Gibbs' usually gruff demeanour gave way to fatherly reassurance.

'Thank you, Sergeant Major.' Rayner straightened himself up, resting the Thompson on the chart table. Lieutenant Fearl was in battledress, his submachine gun also on the chart table. His navigation skills were not required for the remainder of the voyage. With the sun coming up, Traske would enjoy, at least for a short while, a panoramic view of La Rochelle. He had studied the maps sufficiently to know where the lock gates for the pens were. He would give directions from the bridge.

Hook and Gibbs toured the hot, crammed submarine, shaking hands with all of their men. Both of them were impressed to see that Corporal Steer, head bandaged, stood with the others, geared up and ready to fight. Those who had been lightly wounded in the Velas attack were also ready to go. 3 Troop wore their regular battledress, their bergen rucksacks full of ammunition and rations. They had not made them too big, as getting out of the deck hatches in a hurry would be a real problem if they had too much to carry. The members of 1 Troop not acting as submariners were also wearing their usual British equipment. Hook had decided they would not bring their helmets, and had the men leave them in Gibraltar. He had always preferred to fight bareheaded. He had fought enough Germans in the past to know that they had a strict dress code, always fighting with their helmets on — with his own men *not* wearing theirs, they could identify the enemy without worrying about shooting at their own side.

Once they had both returned to the control room, Hook took the handset from the commanders' console, which opened the intercom to the entire submarine.

'Gentlemen, this is the Officer Commanding.'

Hook allowed a pause, scanning the sweating faces before him. Traske smiled and winked. His job, save the final run in, was now over. He had delivered them to the target. Until further notice, this was now Hook's mission. The commando captain put the handset back to his ear.

'We are about to make the final run into La Rochelle. Our passage here has been far from comfortable, and I thank you for enduring it. When the time comes, we must all give one hundred per cent to achieve our mission. You know what you have to do, make no hesitation in the execution of your orders. There will be civilians in there, and I trust you to do what is right, not what is easy.'

Hook paused long enough to notice Traske wince. His men knew what they needed to do; he trusted them to get the job done.

'Once we have done our job in the pens, you are to get out of La Rochelle by any means. You know which way you are going, just get yourselves there as soon as you can. I will not wish you "good luck", for I feel luck is nothing more than a wish by those that think success happens by accident. This is the type of mission we all volunteered for. So let's get this done.'

Hook rang off. There were no cheers and chest beating; his men didn't do that kind of thing.

Traske took the time to scan the area through the periscope once more, before ordering the hatches open. As he traversed, he spoke to no-one in particular.

'I think the RAF has paid La Rochelle a visit in the night.'

'What do you mean?' Hook asked, interested.

'I can see lots of smoke coming from the town.'

18

Traske led the way up the ladder, opening the hatches as he went. Once up on the bridge, he helped Hook through the hatch by taking his Thompson, and Hook in turn helped Rayner. Temple and Driscoll joined them, for their skills on the flak gun would be required once the shooting started.

The small group donned their soft German caps, Traske wearing the cap of a U-boat commander. Their rain coats looked a little bulky, hiding their battledress and equipment. They looked each other over, and exchanged compliments on how scruffy they looked, their beards putting the finishing touches to their disguise.

The flak gunners prepared the ammunition containers so that they were close to hand, but out of sight as they entered the pen facility. They had to make sure nothing gave them away to their reception party. Men from 1 Troop ensured the deck gun was ready for action. An eighty-eight shell loaded into the breach and extra shells were laid at the base of the conning tower, covered by a blanket. The gun crew, which consisted of three men, had to be certain there was ammunition ready to go.

Hook, Traske and the others took in the vast panorama of the estuary. The wind was up, a spray flicking over the deck, making the rain gear masquerade all the more credible. All appeared quiet and unremarkable, given the smoke billowing from the town, perhaps even the U-boat pens themselves. Traske gave the order to advance and in a matter of seconds, U-911 began to move forward at a leisurely rate, white water and spray breaking over the tip of the bow.

'Gents, do you think you might need this?' Gibbs called after them. Hook spun around to find the sergeant major head and shoulders out of the hatch, waving a large red, white and black German flag.

'Found it under the chart table,' he grinned through his scruffy, matted beard.

Temple and Driscoll took the flag and found the rope and pulley the previous crew had used to hoist it up the periscope mast. With the flag fluttering slightly in the brisk air, U-911 looked even more the part. As they sailed on, Rayner spoke.

'When they sent the new key settings for today, they repeated the message for us to divert into the Med.'

'Did you answer?' Traske asked as he scanned the distant La Rochelle through his binoculars.

'No, sir.'

'Good.'

'Either way,' Hook added, 'it's too late to worry about that now.'

As they made their way further into the mouth of the estuary, 2 Troop began to get themselves up on deck. Rain coats and caps were pulled into place. Hook tried his hardest not to be too critical of how bulky the men looked, with their weapons slung underneath their raincoats. The Bren gunners pushed their cumbersome weapons as far behind their backs as possible. Mr Rands and Sergeant Grice checked the men over, before finally checking each other. Satisfied that the men were as ready as they were going to be, Rands and Grice shook hands with their men, not to mention the three from Bamber Cross' troop who would operate the deck gun. Rands then moved to the base of the conning tower, looking up at Hook.

'Here we go then.'

'Ensure, Mr Rands, that you have two men ready to throw the mooring ropes please,' Traske asked politely as he leaned over the lip of the bridge. Grice was already taking care of it as Rands turned to address him.

As they drew in closer to La Rochelle, Hook, with binoculars to his eyes, could see some damage in the town, but the majority of the fire and smoke was further north, in the area of the general port facilities and perhaps the pens.

'You never know, the flyboys could have done most of the work for us,' Traske chirped optimistically.

Hook didn't answer. He continued to scan further to the north, and the source of the smoke columns. Only when he was sure the pen area was not in the smoke-filled area did he lower his binoculars and reply.

'If only we could be so lucky.'

As the initial breakwater came into view, two more men clambered up onto the bridge, each armed with a Bren gun.

'The sergeant major said to come up here and be ready to defend the bridge, sir.'

Hook and Traske looked at each other before nodding their approval. One of the two new men called down for rain gear. In a matter of minutes, they too looked like all the others.

As they sailed closer to the breakwater, Hook and Traske could see that the pens had, in fact, been hit in the raid. The barrage balloons, some damaged and limp, bobbed about, attached to their tenders. Until they cleared the breakwater, they would not be able to see what had been hit. The breakwater had U-911 moving further north in order to enter the port facility. As they cleared it, Hook was stunned to see the damaged inflicted by the RAF.

Buildings around the edge of the main port basin burned. Fire-fighting crews with horse-drawn fire tenders fought to get them under control, their machines fed by the sea water. Some of the larger ships moored up alongside the quayside were also alight. Other ships were casting off, to avoid being consumed by the quayside flames.

The lads standing on deck couldn't help but look about the place in wonder. Even those up on the bridge were in awe of it all. From the rails of the nearest ships, crewmen waved at the submariners, who instinctively waved back. Hook, too, nervously waved, mindful of the dangers of an eagle-eyed German sailor spotting something amiss on the submarine.

'U-boat coming up, starboard side,' Traske informed everyone in a remarkably calm tone. Hook's heart missed a beat at the sight of the U-boat heading towards them. It was certainly not a situation they had considered. He kept his own counsel as Rayner was gently ushered forward by Traske.

The oncoming U-boat crew, some beginning to clamber into their hatches, began to wave and whistle. Rands' men played along, waving back, as did Hook and those on the bridge. With a forced smile and casual wave, Hook hissed to Rayner through gritted teeth.

'Hope your German is as good as you say it is, Rayner.'

The waving continued, as the sea-bound U-boat passed on U-911's starboard side at fifty metres. Its crew, clean shaven and looking fresh, shouted a torrent of what could be best described as abuse to their U-boat comrades. It wasn't until some of the outgoing men dropped their trousers in mocking sexual references that the commandos got the idea of what was being shouted at them. Amid the spray and smoke that dominated the port basin, Hook's men returned hand gestures, for attempting to copy the real U-boat crew could well have given away their true identity, not to mention their real intentions with regard to the pens.

Rayner leaned over the bridge rail, in an attempt to hear, above the din of high-spirited crewmen, what those on the bridge of the other submarine were saying. During a lull in the banter, even

Hook could make out the crew on the opposite bridge shouting and waving at them. Rayner replied in kind.

'They said to go straight for the main lock, as the protected lock is still not ready.'

'Really?' Traske was surprised. His mind flashed back to the images of the facility they had examined when they planned the mission, he was content that the protected lock had been identified, and its use planned for.

The German bridge crew continued to shout at them. Rayner burst out laughing, hollering back with a friendly wave.

'What did they say?' Hook asked, his wave no longer as enthusiastic as it had been.

'They said we look like shit, and should have gone into the Med for some sun,' Rayner beamed.

'What did you reply?' Traske enquired, no longer waving.

'I'm not sure I should repeat it, for it may appear out of turn.' Rayner now looked a little sheepish, despite his features being partially hidden under a filthy beard.

'What did you say, man?' Hook demanded, irritated at the reluctance.

Rayner swallowed before speaking. 'I wished them happy hunting.'

Traske scowled at the young officer. Rayner shrugged his shoulders. 'It seemed fitting, given the situation we find ourselves in, sir.'

Hook shook his head as he puffed out his cheeks and pushed his cap back on his head. They were as good as in the lion's den now, and had to press on. They had appeared credible to a fresh and rested German crew, so they could appear equally convincing to whoever they encountered at the lock. Those fighting fires on the quayside were too busy to stop and wave, for they were trying to save what structures they could. The crews of the ships were too preoccupied with their chores. As far as they were concerned, U-911 was just another submarine returning from a war patrol, its crew ready for hot showers, good food and an excursion into town to drink and whore their pay away in time for their next mission.

19

Movement on the breakwater caught Hook's eye. A flak gun position pirouetted slowly, its crew looking up. Seeing them reminded the commando officer that they, too, had to be aware of the airborne threat. Should the RAF return, U-911 would be fair game.

He began to scan the overcast skies, quietly hoping the RAF was content with what they had done the previous night. He returned to scanning the route ahead; no-one had yet identified the lock. A headland of sorts jutted out from the right side of the port basin. Beyond that, columns of smoke were billowing, coloured from a dark black to a charcoal grey. The fire fighting crews were now getting the better of the flames.

As they cleared the headland, the more traditional lock came into view first. Open to the elements, its outer gate still open. Beyond it, Hook identified the swing bridge pulled out of the way for sea-going traffic. After a short period, the gross concrete encasements of the protected lock came into view; these were, no doubt, of similar construction to the open lock, but encased in concrete several feet thick, with an aperture either end for Hitler's precious U-boats.

Between the two locks, something flickered bright orange. Hood gave Traske a nudge.

'What's that?'

Traske looked at the area the captain was pointing to, before pulling his binoculars up. He focussed on what appeared to be one of the dockers waving a signal flag, ushering U-911 to keep over to the left. Traske lowered the binoculars, speaking as he did so.

'Someone is waving us into the open lock. Why we are not using the other one is anyone's guess.'

As they drew closer the docker, who stood at the end of a short concrete jetty and wrapped in wet weather gear to protect him from sea spray, began to shout. His free hand was cupped around his mouth in an attempt to amplify his words. Rayner cocked an ear to receive instruction before nodding, and giving the shouting man a thumbs up.

'He says not to moor up in the lock. They will get us through as quickly as they can.'

As they crept through the outer lock gate, some dockers who stood with the resting fire crews came over to the left side of the lock. The water line in the lock had the submarine sitting below the apparently jovial dockers, who, to the relief of Hook and his men, spoke in French. He knew that his men perhaps knew a little French, and he didn't care much for what Rayner understood. Using the language issue as an excuse not to speak to the dockers, he merely stared. The French men were quite animated in their crude German as they tried to spark up some kind of conversation with the men gathered on the deck beneath them.

One of the men holding the bow mooring rope, apparently unaware of what was to happen in the lock, went forward and prepared to throw the line to the dockers above. Hook's heart and stomach turned over as Rayner bellowed at the commando in mock German anger. The man was surprised at the reprimand, as were his comrades standing near him, for they all looked up at Rayner and then back to the scolded soldier. Rayner berated the commando in German some more, before Sergeant Grice moved carefully around the ranked men, waving the scolded soldier back. The dockers were laughing at the crewman's predicament as he rejoined the others.

Rayner looked quickly to Hook.

'Sorry about that, sir,' he said. 'I thought things were about to get really ugly.'

Traske stifled a nervous chuckle as Hook patted the young officer across the shoulders.

'Good thinking. Glad you spotted it.'

Hook looked to the stern of U-911, willing the outer lock gates to close more quickly. After a few long, agonising seconds, they finally shut. All they could do now was wait with bated breath as the water pouring into the lock from the U-boat pen basin began to lift the submarine. Some of the dockers grew bored of trying to talk to the filthy, exhausted submariners, and began strolling back to the men gathering up their fire hoses. As U-911 lifted, the heads of those standing on the deck came level with the lip of the lock quayside. Hook nervously looked at the dockers, who were now chatting with each other, and the demeanour of his men. They looked uncomfortable as the higher they rose, the more exposed they became.

Traske and Hook scanned the immediate area for armed German personnel. Besides those manning flak gun positions, there was no one nearby that posed a real threat — for the time being. Traske leaned in towards the commando captain, his voice low.

'What if they raise the alarm right now?'

Keeping his voice hushed and measured, Hook instantly replied.

'They will quickly die, and this mission starts right here, is that good enough?'

After what felt like an age, the inner lock gate began to open. A brief sense of relief washed through Hook as they began to move into the pen basin. Hook took in what was about them. Many of the buildings around the basin were still on fire, fire fighting crews trying their hardest to defeat the flames. The quayside to the left of the basin was totally open, save for two flak guns that concentrated on the cloud base above.

Hook pulled the binoculars up to his eyes. The flak guns in question were like oversized machine guns, capable of putting out a rapid rate of fire, and could probably engage ground targets should they need to. They were surrounded by sandbags that came up to the waists of some crew members. Hook quickly flicked between the two emplacements. Both were laid out in the same fashion. The crews manning them did not appear to have their personal weapons on them, but Hook and his men could not discount the fact that they may have them. If they abandoned the main flak gun, they may well fight from their position with their own weapons. Commandos would never assume the enemy was not prepared to fight man-to-man, regardless of service or kudos. He lowered the binoculars, signalling for the attention of both Temple and Driscoll, who stood ready to use the U-boat's own flak gun.

'Both flak guns on the left. Take care of the left one first.'

'Yes, sir,' Temple answered confidently. □ The gun is loaded, we just need to unlock it, cock it, and we can then engage.'

Satisfied, Hook then looked at the main pen facility, which appeared undamaged by the air raid. Seven pens across the eastern end of the basin, with a long concrete jetty on the right side. Each pen had a large white number painted above the opening. Of the seven before them, two, which were numbered three and four, had their outer dry dock gate in place. Hook nudged the elbow of Traske, who also had binoculars in front of his eyes. Traske described what he could see.

'One U-boat in number one. Two and three are empty. Four and five are in dry dock, I can see the top of one conning tower in each. Six has two inside. Seven is empty.'

'Shoot torpedoes into the empty ones, too. That gives them either damaged pens or unexploded torpedo issues.' Hook said. Traske lowered his binoculars.

'That's the plan, I would prefer the unexploded torpedo issues, and we shall soon see how reliable their torpedoes are.'

'What pen are you parking this thing in?' Hook asked, referring to U-911, as he too lowered his binoculars.

'I'm planning to ram it between the two in number five. Twist some metal for them. Number one is too isolated if you are slow getting through there.'

'Fair enough, nothing like changing the plan as it unfolds!' Hook sniggered a little.

Traske leaned over the bridge rail. 'You're going for the conning towers and the dry dock gates, boys. Start from seven and make your way across to one.'

The deck gun boys, waiting along with 2 Troop, gave the thumbs up.

Both Traske and Hook were suddenly aware, not only of the flak gun emplacements on the reinforced concrete roof above the pens numbered one and seven, but also of what appeared to be several armed personnel strolling about up there, as well. Hook counted a dozen, not including the flak crews. The two men who stood holding Bren guns, below the bridge rail, let the captain know that they were also looking at the rooftop threat.

'We've got it covered sir, don't you worry.'

U-911 was approaching the long concrete jetty that ran into the main building between pens seven and eight. Pens eight to ten looked incomplete; they had yet to have a roof built. Steel rods of various lengths pointed skywards, leaving what would in time become the interior of the pens open to the elements. Content they need not be considered in their plan, Hook turned his attention to the ship moored on the right side of the jetty. Her stern was very low in the water, her rail not more than perhaps a metre from the water's surface. She smouldered slightly, nothing more. What *did* have Hook a little concerned was the sheer number of German personnel and dockers working feverishly to

144

get her empty of whatever cargo she held, before she ended up on the bottom. Crates of various shapes and sizes were crammed on the jetty. Hook did not need his binoculars to see that the German troops helping had their personal weapons slung behind their backs. He counted another dozen or so, split between the jetty, where most of them stood, and the ship's rail.

Hook looked down at the men of 2 Troop, who were gingerly rearranging themselves to face the approaching jetty on the starboard side. Hook caught the eye of Rands, who gave him a worried look. The shooting would have to start almost as soon as the gangways were put in place. Rands then gave the captain a friendly smile, which strangely gave Hook comfort.

'Open outer tube doors,' hissed Traske down the conning tower hatch to those awaiting orders in the control room. The 1 Troop men, along with their submarine mentors, had no idea what was happening outside. They responded to Traske's commands, and no more. Those not tasked with operating the submarine stood poised in their fighting gear, their bergen rucksacks at their feet, ready to clamber out into the fight. The men sweated profusely, some cuffed the sweat from their eyes as the sergeant major walked amongst them, giving them reassuring words to keep them focussed.

'Straight up the ladder boys. Don't mess about. Get out of the way and start shooting if you have to.'

The lads responded to Gibbs' advice with pursed lips and forced smiles. Lieutenant Chris Joyce, commander of 3 Troop, could see nothing more through the hatch that would lead them up onto the deck behind the conning tower, than an overcast sky amid smoke. His men were lined up — as much as the tight quarters would allow. Some of them were hyped up, stamping their feet and slapping the shoulders of those in front. Most cussed under their breath, through gritted teeth.

It wasn't the action they dreaded, it was the waiting.

20

The bow of U-911 came level with the end of the jetty. Another docker, wrapped in rain gear, waved them in towards the left side. Hook took a deep breath, wiping his sweaty palms on his battledress trousers. Any second now, he knew that 2 Troop would let all hell break loose.

The docker and a man who appeared to be a German officer, were shouting in unison at the crew. The lads standing on the deck looked at each other and shrugged their shoulders back at their antagonists. Rayner focussed on what the officer was shouting. He nodded and gave the officer a thumbs up.

'The German gentleman...' Rayner paused, stifling a little nervous chuckle, 'wants us to make ourselves useful and help get the ship unloaded before she goes down.'

'Oh, *does* he now?' Hook was amused. Traske fought his own nervous laughter by whispering orders down the hatch, for the submarine to stop. U-911 continued to drift as the commandos holding the mooring ropes threw them to the dockers, who stood with their hands outstretched. Meanwhile, the German officer was growing all the more agitated, his body language and his tone suggesting to Hook and his men that they were not working fast enough to assist with the stricken ship. Hook was poised to clamber down the external conning tower ladder.

It was now just a matter of time.

Dockers heaved two gangways onto the deck of U-911, one forward and one aft of the conning tower, just as they had predicted. The German officer, along with two sailors who did not appear to be armed, came stomping down the forward gangway, and his animated arms and dialogue were clearly not expressing welcome.

Yet as the officer verbally assaulted Lieutenant James Rands of the British Commandos, his rant was suddenly cut off with the appearance of a Colt .45 automatic pistol, not two inches from his face. The German officer stopped abruptly, which caused the two inattentive sailors behind to stumble into him. Rands fired one shot, the bullet smashed through the nose of the German officer, blowing out the back of his skull, all over the faces of the two bunched up behind him. The jaw of the sailor directly behind shattered, as the ballistics of a .45 calibre round did what they had been designed to do.

The third German on the gangway was stunned as the bodies of the officer and his comrade fell backwards, knocking him from his feet. He had not even landed on his back by the time Rands fired the remainder of his Colt magazine into his chest and head. Hook was sliding down the conning tower ladder as Rands led his troop of men off the submarine. Rands dashed for the first cluster of shipping crates that took up most of the jetty at the other end of the short gangway, changing pistol magazines as he went. 2 Troop followed him, each holding their Colt in both hands. The dockers and troops on both the jetty and the ship's rail were stock still in those first vital seconds, as they tried to take in the scene before them. They had heard shots ring out, and were presented with men stampeding off the U-boat, a number of them lying on the gangway. Those on the ship looked up at the troops patrolling the roof of the pens, unsure of what had just happened. As they began to gather their senses, they remained slow to react to the U-boat crew members who were scrabbling behind the crates and fighting their way out of their rain gear. What was now taking the German onlookers aback was that some of the U-boat crew were firing at those workers moving crates about on the jetty.

Hook staggered over the dead men on the gangway as Rands' men began to fire at the enemy personnel on the jetty. As some of 2 Troop struggled out of their rain gear behind the crates, others, yet to uncloak themselves, engaged those nearest to them with their Colts. Troops and dockers alike fell, in a hail of .45 rounds.

As Hook shuffled out of his rain gear, he caught sight of 3 Troop scrambling out of the stern deck hatches, their bergen rucksacks hampering a rapid disembarkation. Bren gun and Thompson fire dominated the air about the captain, as Rands' men did not wait for officers to lead them. Those who were now out of their rain gear were already shooting at those on the ship's rail and were advancing on the dead and dying men who lay amongst the splintered wooden crates.

Sergeant Major Gibbs was chastising the men of 3 Troop, who were scrambling up the stern deck hatch ladders.

'Get a fucking move on, let's go, *let's go!*'

As one of the Bren gunners scrambled up the ladder, an almighty snap rendered the man inert.

'What's the fucking hold up?' Gibbs roared.

'Man down. Doyle is hit,' came back numerous shouts.

'For fuck's sake!' the sergeant major replied, as he shoved his way forward. Doyle's legs hung still for a few seconds, then began to thrash about, kicking the man behind him in the face.

'Get him down and out of the way!' Gibbs commanded.

As the two front men fought to free Doyle from whatever had hold of him, he simply thrashed and kicked all the more. The men trying to free him shook their heads.

'He's caught up on something, sir.'

'Right, wait there,' the furious sergeant major hollered. He fought his way past Doyle's thrashing legs and made for the conning tower.

As Gibbs emerged onto the bridge, he was welcomed by chaos. Traske crouched low as he peered over the rail. Two men were chugging away with short, controlled bursts from their Bren guns, the spent casings clattering onto the bridge floor plate. His ears were then buffeted by the deep bass drumbeat of a heavy calibre weapon — the flak gun. As Gibbs clambered out of the hatch, he caught sight of Lieutenant Rayner crouched behind the Bren gunners. He jabbed the officer in the buttock with a clenched fist.

'Mr Rayner sir, why are you not on shore with the captain?' he bellowed over the gunfire. The officer spun around.

'What?' Rayner cupped an ear. Gibbs shook his head. 'Never mind, follow me, sir'

As the sergeant major slung his Thompson across his back, he felt a rough hand on his left shoulder. He turned to see Traske, his face white as a ghost.

'Sergeant Major, we must get these men off quicker, we are a sitting duck...'

Gibbs cut him off.

'We *are*, don't you worry about that.'

Gibbs clambered down the conning tower ladder, his ears ringing as Driscoll and Temple fired short, booming salvos into the flak positions on the left side of the pen basin, large calibre brass shells clattering around their feet. As he got to the deck, Gibbs looked up and was pleased to see that he would not have to go back up and fetch Rayner; the officer was only a few rungs above him.

The sergeant major made his way around the base of the conning tower to where Doyle was caught in the aft deck hatch. He saw the soldier crumpled over the lip, grimacing in pain. Gibbs knew the lad had been hit. The deck around him was pockmarked and splintered from incoming fire. Doyle opened his eyes just in time to see his company sergeant major stomping over to him. As Gibbs grabbed him by his webbing yolk straps,

Doyle ground his teeth in pain as he was heaved out of the hatch. Doyle was one of the bigger men in the company, but that didn't stop Gibbs grunting and cursing him as he dragged him over to the base of the conning tower. Doyle was now out of the line of German fire from across the basin, and from the top of the pens.

'What are you playing at, Doyle?' Gibbs chastised the wounded man. 'You are holding up the show.'

'Sorry, sir. The fuckers up on the roof got me, I think.' Doyle grunted through bloodied teeth. Gibbs pulled Rayner closer to him.

'Help to patch up Doyle; I will get 3 Troop off this fucking tub.'

As Rayner went through Doyle's battledress for dressings, the sergeant major walked over to the crew hatch. With no regard for his own safety, he peered into the darkness below.

'Well don't just fucking look at me, give me your bloody bergen,' he roared at the man at the bottom of the ladder.

Rayner had Doyle's bandages in place as best he could. The big commando had been hit in the shoulder and the hip. His wounds were not life threatening, but his mission was certainly over. As he helped the pain-stricken Doyle back into his battledress jacket, he couldn't help but watch in awe as Gibbs stood at the hatch, in full view of the enemy, dragging bergens out so their owners could make a swifter exit. What was even more incredible, was that the commandos in question shuffled over to where Doyle sat against the conning tower, pulling their bergens on as they mocked him.

'What have you got Toby, fractured eyelash?' one NCO chuckled as he scrambled off the U-boat, and took cover with other 3 Troop members who were getting themselves organised among the crates, thanks to the sergeant major's selfless, if perhaps foolish act.

Lieutenant Chris Joyce was organising his men as they scrambled off U-911. James Rands' men were already fighting their way off the jetty, which gave his troop more room to get spread out. As another two men joined Joyce, he was aware of someone calling his name.

'Mr Joyce, sir,' hollered a gruff voice. It was Joyce's radio operator who pointed out the source of the shouts, that could be heard over the fire fight in which Rands' men were now embroiled, further along the jetty. The person shouting was the sergeant major, who was waving one hand as he yanked another bergen out of the hatch. Even Chris Joyce could tell that he wasn't happy.

'Don't just bloody sit there, get on with the mission! These boys will catch up.'

Joyce took that as his cue to get off the jetty as quickly as he could. Those who were ready followed him, as he dashed from crate to crate. They continued to attract fire from the German troops up on the roof. The Bren gun fire from the bridge of U-911 was effective at keeping the flak crews pinned down, but for individual men darting back and forth up there, it was a different matter. 3 Troop slowly gathered strength and momentum as they got off the submarine, and went straight into the fight. They stepped over the dead dockers and Germans carefully; mindful that they could be wounded and still have fight left in them. However Joyce knew, in the back of his mind, that Rands was a hard bastard among officers, and would not have let the enemy have that chance. The enemy bodies they did step over, were well and truly dead.

21

Joyce had not got far when he spotted other men, in British battledress, either lying still or writhing on the ground.. One still had his rain gear on. This told him that Rands' troop had taken casualties, but as he slowed to see to them, a harsh voice from behind stopped him.

'Keep moving, we deal with them once the mission is complete.' His troop sergeant, Daryl Pelton, reiterated the order. 'Keep moving, we can't stay on this bloody jetty.'

Knowing that Pelton was right, Joyce led 3 Troop towards the entry into the main pen building, which was littered with more dead and dying men from both sides.

The three men operating the deck gun fought like hell to get the weapon into the fight, despite the Germans shooting at them from the roof of the pens and the flak gun positions to their left. With nothing to engage in pen number seven; they diverted their fire to the U-boat moored on the left side of number six, and as they fired their first 88mm shell, their hearing exploded into a muffled whine.

A flurry of sparks from the base of the target conning tower confirmed a hit. They fired another shell into it for good measure, but could not engage the U-boat moored to its right, for they did not have the angle to hit the conning tower. With their own voices muffled, they hollered up at Traske on the bridge to move the submarine so they could continue the engagement. Traske waved in acknowledgment, for he too was growing very anxious about sitting still for too long.

Thankfully, heavy return fire onto U-911 had not materialised at that point. The lads on the Bren guns, not to mention Temple and Driscoll manning the flak gun, were doing a fantastic job of keeping the German flak gunners busy. It was the individual riflemen who were the main threat. Whenever Traske tried to read the battle unfolding before him, a sharp snap would crack at his ear, notifying him in short order that someone's aim was improving. He bobbed and weaved into a position where he could see Sergeant Major Gibbs, who was now at the base of the conning tower.

'We need the ropes off now!' he shouted. 'We are a sitting duck here, get off the damn boat, and get the ropes off!'

Gibbs nodded at the submarine commander and began to chastise Rayner into helping him get Doyle off the boat and into some cover on the jetty. Traske watched as they slowly lumbered over the gangway, each with a shoulder in the armpit of the towering Doyle, who was between them. Another loud snap flicked past his head, causing him to flinch — the shots were getting closer. Both Bren guns instantly fell silent, only the deck and flak guns were still in the fight.

'Davey? Davey?' one of the Bren gunners called, the bloodied head of his dead friend in his hands. 'Davey?'

Traske went to him. He had not witnessed close combat before being seconded to Hook and his commandos, but he knew a dead man when he saw one.

'He's dead, man; get back on the damn Bren.'

Traske did not want to seem insensitive to the commando's plight, but they had Germans shooting at them from above, and they needed to be taken care of. As the distraught soldier took up arms again and fought back with more vigour, Traske pulled his own rain gear off, draping it over the head and torso of the dead man. Traske pulled the fresh Bren magazines from the man's pouches and battledress jacket, putting them next to the living soldier's right boot.

He patted the man on the right knee. 'Extra magazines for you,' he shouted over the din of machine gun fire. The angry and distressed commando made no acknowledgement, for he was too embroiled in avenging his friend.

Doyle winced as he was put down behind the crates. All of his equipment, including his bergen, had been taken off the U-boat. Rayner helped the wounded man get as comfortable as possible as Gibbs peered over the crates. He could make out 3 Troop, along with those selected for the raid from 1 Troop, as they made their way into the pens. He could also see German troops bobbing around up on the roof, taking pot shots at the submarine. He saw the waving arm of Traske, who risked getting hit by the very same men.

'Gibbs, I need those ropes off *now*!'

The sergeant major left his own bergen where it was, and with his Thompson in both hands, sprinted for the bow mooring rope. He slid in beside it. Placing his weapon on the ground by his right knee, he fought with the thick rope in order to release it from its anchor point. The Germans on the roof spotted him, and before long, rounds snapped and whizzed into the ground around him. Dull, splintering thuds rippled around as the bullets penetrated the timber crates. With the first rope off, grabbing his weapon, Gibbs clambered to his feet and made for the stern rope with intense rifle fire cracking around his ears. Gibbs had never known a submarine to seem so long, as he dashed as hard as he could for the next anchor point. A burst of pink mist blinded him, an almighty hammer blow rendered him deaf in his right ear. The force of the impact spun him anti-clockwise like a top, landing heavily on his back, and his Thompson clattered as it cart-wheeled over the quayside and into the water.

'Gibbs? *Gibbs*?'

The shouting of his name was muffled, and he couldn't recognise the voice. He opened his eyes. As his vision swam into focus, he could see Rayner, who was rather animated, next to what appeared to be Doyle, sleeping.

'Gibbs? *Gibbs*?' The shouting continued. This time the voice sounded more acute, and annoying.

'Yes I can bloody hear you!' He responded in a traditional warrant officer bark.

'Stay still, Sergeant Major, don't have them fire at you again.' Rayner was getting on his haunches, ready for the sprint of his life. Gibbs pointed at him with his left hand.

'You bloody well stay there, Mr Rayner, do you hear me?' Gibbs' command was stern, despite his current predicament.

He rolled onto his left side, his right arm trailing behind him. The sudden movement sent a thunderbolt of pain through him. He cussed through gritted teeth.

'Fuck, that bloody hurts!'

Rayner watched the sergeant major clamber to his knees, his shattered right arm hanging lifeless. The young officer winced as he anticipated the next bullet, that would surely finish the man. It didn't come. He watched Gibbs shuffle on his knees to the anchor point not more than a metre away, and begin to remove the second — and thankfully — final rope.

'Rayner!' roared Traske from the bridge. 'I need that bloody rope off now!'

'What's it fucking look like I'm doing?' Gibbs roared as he fought with the rope one-handed. With a loud grunt from Gibbs, the rope slid off the anchor point and down the side of the U-boat, which was now free.

Traske had the submarine engines set into reverse, bellowing his instructions down the conning tower hatch to the chief petty officer, who stood behind the two drivers. They responded to the chief's orders, a little hesitantly at first, the battle raging outside being something of a distraction. Roger Toil, the chief, was not one for land combat but his ability to remain calm under stress allowed both of the commandos sitting in front of him to relax as he told them what he needed them to do. Traske, meanwhile, who was exposed to the ferocity of German return fire from two sides, bellowed his instructions to the torpedo room via the bridge's intercom.

'Standby to fire torpedo number one.'

Lieutenant Price responded to the commander's orders verbatim and with a professional calm. The torpedo had long been loaded as a matter of routine, since leaving Velas, for practice drills when the rookie crew had hand-cranked the projectile in and out of the tube. With the outer torpedo doors open, and the firing solution set, they awaited the word.

As the boat lumbered back, Traske was subject to several near misses from German troops who had arrived on the left side of the basin in two trucks. They poured out of the open-topped vehicles, most taking up firing positions among the sandbag fortifications of the flak guns, which were now crewless. The sole surviving Bren gunner ignored the threat they posed, keeping his focus on the rooftop defenders. As U-911 slowly gathered momentum, opening the arming distance for the torpedo pistol to arm, Traske got the attention of the flak crew, making sure they were engaging the new arrivals in the flak gun position.

Conscious that the deck gunners were exposed on their left-hand side, Traske shouted at them to watch themselves. They looked in the direction the commander indicated, but there was little they could do. They continued to fire shell after shell into the U-boat that was now exposed to them on the right side of pen six. With both the U-boats in pen six now smouldering from their conning towers, the deck gunners switched their attention to the dry dock gates of number five.

'Fire torpedo number one,' Traske ordered through the intercom, a snap of another close shot muffling his left ear in a high pitched whine. He did not hear the repeated order from Price, but felt a slight vibration as the torpedo left the tube. Traske risked his head to perch high enough to identify the tell-tale wake of the torpedo on its way into pen seven. The deck gunners stopped their shooting to watch the wash of the torpedo as it propelled away. Traske cursed himself, for he knew that U-911 was still too close for the torpedo to arm. He was not surprised when, after the predicted travel time of the torpedo had passed, there was no detonation. He fought with his inner coward to hold his nerve until the submarine was closer to the inner lock gates, otherwise Hook and his men already in the pens would have to fight their way in and out of all the U-boats that were moored in there.

22

Gibbs crawled in next to the unconscious Doyle and the panic-stricken Rayner.

'You are no good to the mission sat there, sir. Get yourself up the jetty and join Captain Hook.'

Rayner looked down at the filthy, exhausted warrant officer. He could see the man wasn't going to get out of the pens, with or without Doyle. Gibbs looked the young officer square in the face with an expression that showed a man resigned to his fate.

'Looks like I'm not getting away with this one,' he grunted as he acknowledged the dark humour to be found in the current situation, an action that caused him to wince. His shattered right arm and shoulder blade would require a hospital.

'The Germans have orders not to take commandos prisoner Gibbs, you know that, right?' Rayner could do no more than imagine what they would do to both of the men slumped beneath him. Gibbs closed his eyes and nodded slightly, then the firing of the deck gun out in the basin made him flinch.

'Well, they had better do the job properly then, hadn't they?'

The sergeant major offered his left hand, which Rayner took. Despite his condition, Gibbs' grip was like iron. The hand shake was firm. The wounded man ended it.

'Enough of this soppy shit, Mr Rayner. You and my boys have a U-boat pen to wreck.'

*

Captain Paul Hook found himself crammed behind all sorts of building materials that were lined up on either side of the jetty as it ran into the main structure. Pallets and crates of piping and sheet steel were stacked high, waiting for a labour force to finish pens eight to ten. Hook was thankful that it afforded his men cover from fire, but that 'luck' proved bitter-sweet. The German sailors and troops had now recovered from the initial shock of the attack and were also using the materials as cover, blocking their path. The din of rifle and machine gun fire inside the structure echoed around, buffeting everyone's ears. NCOs and men hollered to each other as they fought to overcome the Germans who were growing stronger with every passing minute. Those who had been hit in the earlier exchanges, British and German, lay exposed in the central aisle. Some lay still, most writhed in agony as they were hit again and again in the continuous fire fight.

The Germans raised the stakes when they began to lob stick grenades at the commandos. Hook could hear them clatter amongst men and materials. With nothing else for it, the British troops dived for cover across the aisle to escape them. They detonated with a chest-punching pulse, rendering everyone deaf for a few seconds as the over pressure punished the eardrums of both attackers and defenders.

Some of Hook's boys were not quick enough to get out of their way. Few were killed by the grenades, but many got hit one way or another by their fragmentation. Recognising that to remain where they were was as good as suicide, some of James Rands' men were bold enough to throw their own grenades, and as the Germans dashed about to avoid them, Rands and his men advanced aggressively. The grenades had knocked the wind out of most of the Germans holding the British at bay, forcing them to give ground and abandon the battle-littered corridor for more favourable positions in pen seven, and in the offices that dominated it on a mezzanine gantry.

Rands and his men gathered themselves at the entrance to pen seven. Hook moved up quickly behind them. His radio operator, Corporal Alfie Parch, was among the wounded who were dragged to the left side of the corridor. Hook shook his head mockingly.

'Parch, does this mean I now have to carry my own radio?'

The wounded man, already nursing a lit cigarette between his lips, grinned.

'You can if you want sir, but the thing is knackered. Some bugger put a hole in it when we first got off the boat.'

Hook grinned, then explosions within the pens snapped him back to the mission at hand. The explosions were loud and the blast that rippled implied that they were powerful. He knew Traske and the boys would be getting on with shooting up the U-boats at their moorings. He moved forward to speak to Rands, whose left hand was now sporting a crudely-applied bandage.

'Mr Rands, what have we got in pen seven?'

Rands beckoned him closer to the thick drab concrete threshold that separated them from the pen in question. Hugging the wall on their left, with Rands in front, they both leaned out enough to spy the wrought iron gantry that bordered the mezzanine offices above. They both flinched as the helmets of German troops occupying the offices bobbed and weaved beneath the long, exposed windows.

In between the shell detonations further into the pens they could hear hushed, excited whispers in the pen area, in both German and French. Hook knew that his men had planned to clear the pens in a certain fashion, and it was not his style to change something before they tried it— but the dominant position of the elevated offices changed things. He turned to one of Rands' NCOs who stood bloodied but poised, his Thompson gripped tightly in both hands.

'I need Mr Joyce up here; he needs to clear the offices.'

*

Traske called for the U-boat to stop at the far end of the basin. Submarines never stopped on a sixpence, so he had to ensure he called it early enough that she didn't drift into the basin quayside. He called orders for the chief to steer her slightly to port.

As she moved, Traske felt very exposed as he looked up at the over-arching cranes that lined the right side of the basin. So far, no German troops had moved around to that side, concentrating their forces on the roof of the pen, or on the left quayside among the flak positions. More trucks had arrived, their cargo of troops pouring out. Most dashed either into the main building, or up the external stairs onto the roof. There was not much that he could do about it, anyway. The Bren gunner was now running low on ammunition, so was husbanding what he had left. The deck gun crew were slowing their rate of fire into the pens as they reversed further away from them, too. Traske was impressed with the gunnery of the deck gun crew. They had damaged three U-boat conning towers, and had shot up the dry dock gates on pens four and five. He couldn't be certain they had fractured the gates, hence the requirement to hit them with torpedoes.

Traske was pleased with his decision to get more distance before firing torpedoes two and three, for they swam straight and true into pen six, exploding at the rear of the two U-boats moored in there. He knew there was little chance of hitting them in the bow; the torpedoes must have glanced down between the two U-boats before exploding in quick succession. The concussion of the torpedoes had warped the sterns of both boats, enough to convince Traske that they had been damaged in the process. It would be down to Hook and his men to take a closer look, and if required, to board them with their thermite grenades.

With firing solutions set for torpedo number four, he ordered Price to fire it. As it left the tube, Price's newly-trained crew worked like dogs, feeding the next round of ☐ fish' into their respective tubes. They cursed and sweated getting them in. They had found it too hot to work in that environment with all their battle gear on, and were stripped to the waist. Some drank greedily from their water bottles between loading and firing sequences, complaining that life as a torpedo man on a submarine was like working in the devil's kitchen. The irony of this was not lost on them, and they reminded each other that they had done enough missions on the North African coast to *think* they knew what heat was... until they came aboard U-911.

Traske monitored the progress of the torpedo through his binoculars as it swam towards the dry dock gates of pen five. He had forgotten to start his stop watch when it left the tube, and was now at a loss as to whether or not the deadly 'fish' would arm in time. He estimated the pending explosion was overdue.

Just as the deck crew fired the gun once more into the conning tower behind it, the lock gates burst skywards in a hail of timber and iron. The concussion of the explosion punched the water surface before it, then retracted back in upon itself as it poured into the dry pen behind.

Ecstatic that the pen was now flooding, Traske called on the intercom.

'Great shooting men, standby tube number one.'

He then hollered down the hatch.

'Chief, let's have her slowly to port.'

With 1 Troop making short work of both the U-boats and the pens, the raiders' progress within the building had come to a halt.

23

Hook was alerted by a commotion behind him, and turned to see Joyce, Sergeant Pelton, and Lieutenant Rayner. He frowned at the latter.

'Where is the sergeant major?'

'Wounded,' Rayner explained. 'On the jetty, with a lad from 3 Troop.'

Hook pursed his lips, nodding. He knew the risks. He beckoned Joyce and Pelton forward, then directed Joyce to the problem at hand.

'They are in the office and the machine shop beneath it. We saw movement into the shop before we could fire. There may even be more troops in the pen area.'

As they observed their target, Joyce and Pelton began to devise a plan to deal with the machine shop and offices simultaneously. Hook waved a hand.

'Rands will deal with the offices, just get into the machine shop and clear it out.'

Pelton spun on his heels and called forward one of his NCOs, plus men. Grice, Rands' troop sergeant, did the same. The plan was simple; Bren gunners of both formations would move quickly into the pen area and engage whomever they encountered, whilst Joyce and Rands, plus their respective teams of eight men each, would assault the offices and machine shop respectively.

Once the assaulting troops were ready, Hook gave them the thumbs up. As the assaulting groups dashed though the threshold and onto their targets, shouting and commotion erupted in the pen. The Bren gunners scrambled through, some taking up fighting positions behind various submarine components on pallets and large wooden crates, whilst others slid onto their bellies, firing their Bren guns which were supported by their bipod legs. Those German troops who were firing were quickly overwhelmed by the Bren gunners, some hit in the initial exchange; others dived behind cover and remained there, not contributing to the fight.

Rands leapt up the metal steps two at a time, and was almost level with the office windows when the shooting started. As he got near the office door, which was already open, a stick grenade clattered onto the landing. Rands instinctively grabbed it, and lobbed it back in through the door.

Frantic calls in German and French filled the office as the grenade went off, the overpressure blowing out the windows, winding the assaulters. Rands did not wait for the rest of his men to catch him up, and proceeded into the offices on his own. With his Thompson in both hands, the shoulder butt wedged under his right armpit, he staggered into the open-plan office. He kept both eyes open as he focussed his assault on the exposed profile of a German sailor, clambering to his feet in the wake of the grenade attack. The man didn't have any chance to focus himself before he exploded in a burst of Thompson fire, collapsing back onto the floor quicker than he had got up.

Rands then switched his attention to the next man at his left, who was now raising his hands, helmetless, shouting something in French which Rands did not understand. He too was felled, by another burst from the officer. As Rands identified another threat to his left, he turned to engage the German, who then erupted in bullet strikes as Rands' men fanned into the room, their bursts aimed and short. No wild firing like panicked conscripts. The enemy force defending the offices was few in number, and quickly overmatched by the commandos.

Satisfied they had secured the offices; Rands went to the shattered window frames and called down to the captain. Beneath them, all hell still reigned in the machine shop.

'Offices clear!'

Hook responded with a thumbs up, as he helped two men drag Rands' appointed NCO out of the pen. In the rush up the stairs, he had not even noticed the incoming fire, which found the man behind. The floor beneath his feet thudded as secondary explosions in the machine shop became more frequent. Rands was content that there was enough concrete between the fighting downstairs and themselves. Had the shop been built like the wooden offices they stood in the situation could have proved troublesome, with the potential for fragmentation to penetrate the floor beneath them and vice versa.

The fighting beneath them petered out, and one of Rands' men called out to him.

'Sir, one of the dead looks like a docker.'

The soldier looked sad. Rands, aware that he had killed the man in question, walked over. He looked down at the body; he was without any emotion, but acknowledged that his men were not all like him.

'Wrong place at the wrong time. It happens.'

The soldier didn't say anything more, and went back towards the door.

Chris Joyce emerged from the machine shop, deaf and shocked. His hearing was slowly coming back to him as he watched the company move as one into the pen. Movement above caught his attention, as Rands and his men descended. Hook approached the shell-shocked troop commander.

'You okay?'

Joyce led him back in to the machine shop. It reeked of oil, cordite and the fresh, coppery tang of blood. Hook was shocked to see the devastation that lay before him. Two of Joyce's men were clearly dead; some of the others were wounded to the extent that they could not continue. An NCO in the assault group was pulling a screwdriver from the dead hand of a docker, before throwing it across the room. German troops and French dockers, dead and wounded, littered the entire shop.

'The bastards came at us with hammers, screwdrivers, saws... you name it. That was just the bloody French.'

Joyce stumbled, and was caught by Hook. The captain lowered him to the floor, seeing fresh blood soaking through the crotch of Joyce's battledress. Hook pulled out his clasp knife to cut open the material. Joyce's underwear was bloodied and soiled, the smell catching Hook's breath. As the young officer slumped against one of the shop workstations, Hook fought his way through the underwear. He was shocked at the scale of the injury. Joyce's entire groin area had been peppered with shrapnel, probably from a grenade. The blood wasn't pumping from the wounds, which suggested to Hook that no arteries had been hit, but it looked messy, and could potentially have spoiled the 'prospects' of the young Joyce.

Hook looked the wounded officer square in the face. Joyce knew that to be carried out of the pens under fire was not an option. Hook stood up; looking over his shoulder to the first commando he laid eyes on.

'Get him bandaged up. Someone fetch me Sergeant Pelton.'

As two men dressed Joyce's wounds, Hook went back out into the pen area. Both the sergeants and the NCOs had got their men into fighting positions. Hook knew that he had now lost the element of surprise and momentum. He needed to get his men moving through the pens before more German reinforcements arrived.

Wailing loudly from the roof of the pens was a klaxon, alerting the entire garrison of La Rochelle that an attack was in progress. It gave the same sound as a typical air raid alarm, and Hook was optimistic that local German units would be reluctant to move in fear of an air raid — but he knew they would soon learn of the real method of attack, and close in on the pens.

Traske was still in the fight, the impact of torpedoes and deck gun shells continued to echo through the facility. He could also hear the short drum beat bursts of the flak gun. They would keep the German troops at bay, for the time being at least.

Rayner, along with Sergeant Pelton, strode over to him. Hook explained the predicament Mr Joyce was in, and the harsh reality that he would have to be left behind so others could get on with the mission. Pelton went into the machine shop to see his troop commander, Rayner remained with the captain.

'Anything I could help with, sir?'

Hook shook his head, smiling as he did so. 'I don't think so, Mr Rayner. Thank you. I have enough command elements in place, but we could do with extra muscle.'

It was the politest way Hook could find, to tell the man to shut up and follow everyone else. The young lieutenant was good at what he did, but Hook and his company were good at what they did, which was causing trouble.

Rands had men taking a peek into the next pen. Hook allowed Pelton and his men to catch their breath in the machine shop, as he ascertained what was waiting for them in pen six.

24

Movement had some of Rands' men calling out in excitement. 'Enemy front, enemy front... ' The last part of the message was drowned out by a fusillade of fire from those up front. A few German sailors, attempting to get away from the moored U-boats, were cut down by the commandos as they made a dash for the door to the rear of the pen. Their intentions in pen six now clear, Rands' men made for the nearest submarine. Hook followed a little behind, with Sergeant Grice placing his Bren gunners in position to cover the U-boat beyond and the wide threshold that led to the next pen. Hook picked his way through the gunners, and moved closer to Rands' assault group as they boarded the submarine.

The conning tower smouldered somewhat, thanks to the gunnery skills of the boys working the deck gun on U-911. Kneeling down behind a stack of engine components, Hook could make out U-911 loitering at the other end of the basin. The deck gun did not appear to be firing, but he could hear the flak gun as it strafed the quayside with tracer fire. German troops in amongst the sandbag emplacements bobbed and weaved, firing back at the submarine out in the basin. Tracer and sparks flicked off the conning tower with increasing regularity. Hook could only hope that Traske was okay, and that he was still able to keep the increasing troop numbers outside the pens pinned down.

The din of an almighty explosion rippled through the pens. Loud enough to have even Rands and his assaulting troops steady themselves as they dropped in grenades through the crew deck hatches. Rands was a hard man, but when they dropped the grenades in, they were instantly greeted with hysterical screaming and shouting from within the submarine. The commandos stepped away from the openings as the grenades went off, the concussions punching out of the hatches, and the screams instantly rendered silent.

As his men scrambled in, ready to meet whatever fight was left in the stricken crew, Rands turned to his company commander.

'Why on earth are they still on board? For the love of God!'

Hook shook his head; the whole concept was lost on him. His men had not got into the pens as quickly as they would have liked, so there was no reason for the German sailors to still be aboard. They could have evacuated the pens, or at least grabbed weapons to defend their submarine.

Rayner joined Hook behind the stack, just as battle began within the submarine. Shouting, screaming, machine gun fire. It continued for quite some time, shouts in English becoming all the more dominant as the fighting went on. The chatter of Thompsons petered out, followed by the shouting soon after.

Rands waited for the assault force to return, and it wasn't long before the first sweat-glazed face appeared. It was an NCO, who clambered out before turning to take the Thompson of the man behind as he too exited the U-boat. Six men had entered the submarine, and to everyone's relief, six climbed back out.

'You're not scuttling the boat?' Rayner called, instantly regretting his outburst as Rands gave him a hateful glare. Outsiders did not tell commandos what to do. The assault team shook their heads as one, but it was the NCO that spoke.

'No need, she is taking on water from the stern, and flooding quickly by the looks of it. Commander Traske's shooting appears to have done the job on this one.'

'Are they all dead in there?' Hook asked the NCO. The man didn't look at the captain. Head down, he nodded slowly. That was good enough. Rands patted him on the shoulder.

'Good lad, you don't have to like it, just get the job done.'

'Yes, sir.' The NCO replied quietly.

Without having to be told, they climbed back onto the walkway and jogged over to the other U-boat. As they picked their way through the bodies of its crewmen, who had tried to make a run for it, another explosion punched through the structure.

Ears ringing, Hook turned to Rayner.

'How many bloody torpedoes did we have on that thing?'

Rayner grinned. 'I'm sure we had twelve.'

As Rands' group climbed onto the next U-boat, they were alerted to hands appearing on both the bridge and the deck hatches. German voices kept calling out, the same thing over and over. Hook and his men had been in enough action to know when the enemy was begging you not to shoot. Rands cussed through gritted teeth.

'Get them out of there, quickly.'

His men began to berate those trying to surrender. Keeping one hand on their weapons, they grabbed the drab tunics of the sailors, heaving them out onto the deck. Hook knew this was going to make things difficult if he didn't get control of it quickly. He had Rayner follow him back towards the threshold, calling for Sergeant Pelton as he went. Pelton was already out of the machine shop, reorganising his men, when he heard the call.

'Pelton, get these prisoners into the machine shop, quickly,' the captain ordered.

'Prisoners?' Pelton was most puzzled.

Pelton joined Rayner and Hook at the submarine in question. Rands' men were on the verge of being overwhelmed by what appeared to be a collection of not only German sailors, but also French dockers, who had taken shelter with the Germans when the attack began.

Rands sought out Rayner, even though he was beginning to doubt the man's value.

'Tell these clowns to get off the fucking boat, Rayner. We are scuttling this thing.'

Rayner spoke quickly in both German and French to entice the scared men off the submarine deck. German and French men alike were panicked, fearing execution at any moment. Rayner raised his voice to get his instructions over to them, and before long they began to comply, assisted by plenty of pushing and shoving from Rands' men. After the last prisoner left the deck, an NCO prepared a grenade.

Rands held up a hand to hold him off.

'Are there anymore inside, Rayner?' There was still enough noise for Rands to have to bellow.

'What?'

'Make sure there are no more.'

Rayner understood what the irate officer was referring to, and fought his way through the melee of men shuffling, their hands above their heads as they made their way over to Pelton and his men. Rayner climbed aboard, calling into the hatches using both languages. The commandos strained to hear voices from within. Rayner called into the submarine one more time. No answer. Rayner had not even got his head away from the hatch, when the grenade the NCO was holding fell past his right ear, clattering as it hit hard surfaces on his way down. The lieutenant scrambled back a little, giving Rands a glare.

Rands stood away from the hatch. He gave his fellow officer a sarcastic grin and then flinched as the grenade detonated.

Pelton's men were about to receive the prisoners from the U-boat, when movement at the far end of the pen caught Pelton's eye. Before he could warn anyone of the danger, tracer bullets screamed through, flicking off metal and concrete with a shrill whizz. One of Rands' men, armed with a thermite grenade, erupted in a bright flurry of sparks as a bullet hit the incendiary grenade in his pouch. In those opening few seconds of the German ambush, men were hit; pink and green mist burst as they fell, one man screamed his life away as he was engulfed by the intense welding heat of the struck grenade.

Hook was on his belly, crawling for the nearest crates in a bid to protect himself from the incoming fire. His choice of cover was poor, as bullets punched through the crates, hitting men and concrete beyond. To his right, his men struggled for a position from which to fight back, and to his left, Rands and his small group stood stock still, mesmerised by horror. Hook found the strength to roar above the din of the fire fight.

'Scuttle that fucking boat, *now*!'

25

Rands suddenly snapped out of his trance, the orders of his company commander punching through the fog clouding his mind. He composed himself as his men clambered down into the belly of the U-boat. Their mission remained the same, no matter what was going on outside.

Hook could not kneel up due to the risk of getting hit, and had to wait for the incoming German fire to lessen. His men, recovering from the initial shock of the ambush, began to regain some control. Firing, communicating through shouts, they repeatedly changed position to avoid fire, whilst also making it hard for the enemy to determine the size of their force.

Pelton, his blood coming up in violent coughs, lay in the open with the dead and dying men, British, German and French alike. He felt no pain, but could only lie still as the battle raged mere inches above him. The bodies of the dead and dying flinched as they were hit by wayward shots. Daryl Pelton could not tell if he had been hit again, for he felt nothing at all. Lying face down, his head turned to the left, he could see Rayner looking straight back at him from behind crates of submarine components; crates that were continually hit by bullets, the timber splintering all over Pelton's' numbed, inert frame.

Rayner watched the commando fade away, the man's life pooling underneath him in a dark, clotting mass.

Hook crawled on his belly to the men behind a pallet of metal components that afforded better cover than the splintered and perforated crates he had originally chosen. Breathing hard, and sweating profusely due to the effort, the captain found himself in the company of a mixed group of six men from various parts of the company. Two of them had Bren guns, the remainder their standard Thompsons. Every man had a Colt .45 pistol.

One of the men was Sergeant Ross, who was in command of those 1 Troop members not tasked with submarine duties. Hook was pleased to see him. He climbed onto his haunches, cuffing his brow.

'Sergeant Ross, what can you see?'

Ross, leaning out of cover slightly, tried to see what he could of the Germans occupying the far end of the pens. The snap of a near miss had him flinch. He looked at the captain, shaking his head.

'If my wife hears of this, she's going to go mad.'

Despite the circumstances, the men in the group managed to chuckle as they fired bursts at the enemy. There was virtually no cover that would allow them to move, so they had to stay low. Ross risked another look. After a few seconds he leaned back to the captain.

'It's hard to tell, a dozen maybe. They are slowly moving towards us. I've seen movement in pen two; I don't think they know how strong we are, hence their reluctance to rush us.'

Hook nodded, He had to take Ross' information at face value. He deduced that the enemy troops' reluctance was due to their inexperience. They could be garrison troops, sent in but unfamiliar with the layout of the pens. That could be to Hook's advantage — he just needed to figure out how.

A flurry of boots, clattering on concrete, made Hook and the men flinch. Rayner slid in behind to join them, his face flushed with exertion. Hook bit his bottom lip as he acknowledged the young officer. He needed to get his men out of the pens. The longer they took, the greater the likelihood of increased German strength in the town as they withdrew.

Hook felt a nudge on his left bicep. Rayner was pointing over to Rands and his men, who were now climbing out of the submarine. Rands waved frantically, giving a thumbs up in between waves. Hook waved back, hoping the man could see him. That was another U-boat taken out of the Atlantic for the time being. Rands led his men off the U-boat and back towards the main corridor, an area that was alive with the hornets of bullets and tracer rounds. Hook watched as Rands just stopped short of exposing himself to the battle.

Rands was limbering up for a dash back into the fray, when one of his men called out from behind him.

'Mr Rands, sir, look at this.'

It was a large steel door. It was on runners, so that when it opened personnel could move between pens instead of walking the long way around, through the pen threshold, every time. The sliding door was not locked or secured in any way, which enticed a couple of his men to pull it open slightly and see what was in the next pen. Rands followed them in.

The dry dock gate of pen five was shattered, enough to allow basin water to come rushing in. The U-boat, which had been undergoing heavy structural maintenance, sat heavy in the water, the side panels having been removed allowed the seawater to consume her.

All manner of equipment floated alongside the drowning boat. Her conning tower smouldered; the puncture marks of 88mm deck gun rounds pock-marked her superstructure. Rands acknowledged the skill of the 1 Troop lads on board U-911, who continued to bombard any enemy troops on the quayside with their flak gun. Rands still had the problem of having to get his men past the U-boat in front of them without having to go into the main corridor.

He looked at the dry dock gate. It had been compromised by the torpedo attack, but the footplate on top, and the somewhat buckled hand rail, were still in place. If he was to take his men across the dock gate, there was a chance of getting fired at by those on the quayside, but it certainly beat the other option.

Rands had made up his mind. He went back into pen six and called for those of his men embroiled in the gun battle in the main corridor.

'2 Troop. 2 Troop . On me. On me!'

Traske had been joined by the company sharpshooters on the bridge. The Bren gun ammunition was all but gone, save for a few magazines the gunner would need once they disembarked. The men in the torpedo room continued to feed the insatiable appetite of the submarine. An advantage of their relentless efforts was that as the torpedoes were loaded, it allowed them more room to move about. The stifling, cramped conditions of the journey had tested them to the limits of their mental endurance. They were comrades one and all, but after a long period of being crammed together, their senses of humour were failing, and heated exchanges between men of all ranks were becoming increasingly frequent. Yet, the discomfort of the voyage could be forgotten as they loaded the torpedoes into the tubes.

Up on the bridge, Traske kept his head and shoulders as low as possible as the two sharpshooters picked off any Germans not in suitable cover. Pickings were slim, as the enemy men did not give themselves away easily. The flak gun now having run out of ammunition, one marksman engaged those on the quayside, the other focussed on the roof of the main building. The deck gun crew, now down to single rounds, chose their targets wisely. They had done what they felt was enough damage to the U-boats in the pens.

Traske was informed that the last torpedo had been loaded, as he scanned the innards of the pens with his binoculars. Targets were plentiful, but he had to verify the progress of Hook and his commandos within. As he scanned, the commandos down in the belly of U-911 began to get their land fighting gear ready. Their secondment to the silent service was almost at an end.

*

'What does he want?' Hook called to Rayner, nodding in the direction of Rands and his assault group. Rayner cocked his left ear, attempting to grab what the waving officer wanted.

'2 Troop, on me, quickly!' Rands hollered across the pen. His body language showed exasperation. Behind their cover, both Rayner and the captain crawled closer to Rands' group. The movement attracted fire from an unknown source as they kept low behind smashed crates and stacked pallets of fruit and vegetables intended for patrol-bound crews, but thankfully that fire never found its mark. Now a little closer, Hook could just about make out what the irate troop commander wanted. Hook immediately scrabbled back, calling for Sergeant Grice.

'Sergeant Grice, I want all of 2 Troop back here, right away.'

The sergeant was not one to question orders, but given their current predicament, he did give the captain a second look to confirm that he was serious. The hesitation irked Hook.

'2 Troop, Sergeant. If you please.'

Grice nodded his capitulation and scrambled away, calling for the men in question. Hook moved back over to where he had sight of Rands, giving him a thumbs up. Rands returned the gesture. The firing from the commandos lessened, as those of 2 Troop still capable of fighting crawled like possessed men on their bellies back to where Hook was waiting. The fire fight had all but petered out, both sides taking pot shots at the other in an attempt to gain the upper hand.

As the men slid in beside the captain, he congratulated them for doing so well.

'Good effort boys, catch your breath, I need you to join Mr Rands over there.'

He pointed over to Rands and his small group. Grice and the men nodded their understanding as they either changed magazines on their weapons, drank from their water bottles, or did both. Hook was confident the fire had lessened sufficiently for him to get onto his haunches, his Thompson in both hands.

'Listen up, lads!' he bellowed to the men. 'When I say so, 1 and 3 Troop are to give covering fire to 2 Troop, as they are going left, do you understand?'

Calls from various men confirmed that his orders had been heard and understood. As he allowed a pause, he could hear the Germans shouting to each other at the other end.

Rayner grabbed the pouch of the commando captain.

'They are translating what you just said... go now, *go now!*'

The lads of 2 Troop didn't wait for the covering fire, and began to scramble out from behind the cover, making best speed for Rands. The fire from 1 and 3 Troops spluttered into life, and was violently returned in kind by the Germans. Tracer screamed and snapped all over the position.

In the mad scramble to the left, one of Rands' Bren gunners was hit, the impact toppling him over the low chain-link rail into the water-filled pen. His comrades would also die if they stopped to help, and so they pushed on, with others also hit in the hail of bullets.

Hook cursed himself for having betrayed his intentions to the enemy; he should have known better. He peered over at the running group, two of whom had fallen and now writhed on the floor. He willed them to remain still, so to not attract more fire. As he panned right, the sheer violence of the German ambush became clear. Many of the dead and dying were members of 3 Troop. Dockers and German sailors, who had not been hit, braved the German bullets to drag wounded men of both sides out of the line of fire. Hook could not help but admire them, as they continued to help the un-wounded commandos apply dressings to the pain-wracked men. With 2 Troop now regrouped with their troop commander, Hook had to let Rands get on with what he had in mind.

Hook's plan was beginning to falter; he had to get his men out of the pens, and out of La Rochelle.

26

The footplate across the dry dock gate was only wide enough for the men to cross in single file. With his troop down to nineteen men, Rands decided to lead one group of ten, including himself, and Grice would take the remainder. 2 Troop's NCOs were the brunt of the casualties so far, those NCOs that Rands did have left were still up for the fight, but did not complain when an officer and a sergeant stepped in to lead from the front. Grice's men covered Rands' group as they clattered across the footplate.

The Germans on the quayside were too preoccupied with the U-boat shooting up their positions. The quayside flak gun nearest the pens burst in a flurry of sparks and secondary explosions, as the U-911 gunners found their target. The Germans on the flak gun nearest the basin lock began to abandon their position, fighting a withdrawal between the buildings still smouldering from the RAF raid. The sight lifted the spirits of 2 Troop.

'C'mon lads, we can do it, let's go!' Grice roared as he led his group over.

The U-boat was now consumed by the flooding sea water. There was no need for any of Rands' men to scuttle her. Stern heavy in the water, the rear deck hatches now swallowed the North Atlantic in a relentless torrent. Rands and the men were content. One less U-boat to prey on the convoys.

Hook and Ross noted that the German troops occupying the far end of the pens were beginning to withdraw. Hook could see them moving off in ones and twos, to the left and then out of sight. He could not be sure whether they were leaving the building itself or just regrouping in pen one. Rayner stuck close to the captain, not wanting to be left behind at any point. Sergeant Ross took the initiative, and had 1 Troop make a push forward, level with the threshold between pens 5 and 6. Only when he had eyes on Rands and his men on the far side of the pen, did he wave forward Hook leading Rayner and the remains of 3 Troop. With heavy hearts, those fit to fight had to leave the dead and wounded for the time being, until they could be certain that it was safe to tend to them properly. Hook also chose to leave his new-found prisoners. The sailors and dockers were unarmed, and did not seem to want to resist the efforts of the British in any way.

The breached dry dock gate of pen 4 had caused the same fate to afflict the U-boat within it as had been the case in pen 5. Cautiously, Rands and his men made their way through the large, heavy, sliding partition door. No-one was in the pen. 2 Troop flooded through and over the dry dock footplate. The Germans on the quayside had either gone, or were staying behind cover, knowing that any observed movement would attract the wrath of U-911. As Rands led his men to the next partition, which separated them from pen three, a loud speaker whined with feedback, before a German accent crackled into dialogue.

'British commandos... British commandos.... British commandos...'

The sinister voice repeated the same words over and over. Hook, Ross and the remainder of the company moved up carefully, the threat of another ambush ever-present.

'British commandos... your mission is over... you have nowhere to go...'

The voice over the loud hailer repeated its message '...your mission is over... you have nowhere to go...'

'Germans!' roared a few of the 3 Troop men, as movement around the threshold of pen one alerted them. Everyone took cover. Hook and Rayner slid behind a motorised trolley to their right which was pulling several trolleys in its wake, like a small train. Each trolley was carrying a torpedo. Rayner puffed his cheeks as he exhaled.

'Not the best choice of cover, if I may be so bold, Captain'

'Agreed.' Hook carefully eyed up the opposition troops who were dashing about, taking up fighting positions. He couldn't tell if the Germans he observed were sailors who had raised their game, or garrison troops called in to support them. He acknowledged that there was nothing rookie about them. Both sides kept their communications to a hush, each trying to anticipate the next move of the other. The last thing Hook needed was a standoff. It would favour the Germans as more troops arrived.

He needed to get out of there, it was just a question of *how*.

The Germans made the first move, lobbing numerous grenades ahead of them. The commandos flinched as they anticipated the explosions. The grenades popped and fizzed as off white smoke belched from their innards, rapidly filling the wide, high-ceilinged corridor.

'Hold your fire lads, hold your fire!' hollered Sergeant Ross. The Germans' boots could be heard, clattering on the rough concrete floor as they moved about behind the smoke, yet no firing commenced. Hook was feeling his pulse race, yet still his men held their fire, and their nerve. Rayner fought to keep his hands from trembling. He gripped the Thompson hard enough for his knuckles to grow white with the effort.

'C'mon you bastards,' Hook hissed under his breath. 'Let's see what you've got.'

As the man-made smoke began to lift, drifting out into the pens, the white haze grew thinner and Hook strained to see where the

Germans were. It was now possible to pick out the features of the far end of the pens... then muzzle flashes erupted from cover much closer to the commandos than before. Bullets snapped past the British in a violent and erratic stream, ricochets flicked and screamed randomly off hard surfaces before embedding themselves in soft materials such as wooden crates, fresh produce and dead and dying men. The commandos responded in kind, their aim a little better due to being static and somewhat more rested than the assaulting Germans.

Stick grenades tumbled into the British positions; some deflected into the water of their own accord. Others exploded behind the commandos, close enough to punch the wind out of those nearest, whilst a few of the British took the very bold move of stepping out and kicking them back at the throwers. None of their kicks were of rugby quality, for they spun top heavy in various directions, but they were enough to put the Germans off their aim, and have them take cover.

As the grenades detonated amid the German cover, Hook's men began to push forward, firing short, rattling bursts from their Thompsons as they went. Those handling the larger and more cumbersome Bren guns held their positions until the lead men got into fighting positions, which allowed them to follow on. Hook took the opportunity to move up behind his men, happy to get away from the rather exposed torpedoes.

As the follow-on commandos moved up, some slid and stumbled on the many empty bullet casings laying over the ground. The German offensive was stopped as soon as it began. They had not expected the British to move in so close to them, for each side had men hit as the commandos made their bold bound forward under fire. The dead and wounded had to stay where they were until the grim business of close combat was concluded. Hook, as well as his men, noted that the Germans were not falling back, as more dashed in from the quayside to reinforce the destruction of their British attackers.

Grenades, both British and German, were thrown as both sides fought to dislodge each other from their fighting positions. And when one stick grenade exploded amongst some of the 3 Troop lads, Hook began to dread the spectre of defeat. All the Germans had to do was keep his men engaged in combat — they would soon run out of ammunition. They had nowhere to go, and to try boarding U-911 to escape would only ensure their destruction.

'MG-42!' roared one of the men. Hook peered through the fire fight to see the Germans raising the stakes. Two machine gun crews shuffled in from outside, splaying the legs of their fearsome machine guns as they went. Belts of ammunition already hung from them, as their operators looked for fighting positions amongst their comrades.

'Shoot the gunners; get their fucking gunners!' Ross screamed at his men.

The concussion of an immense explosion in pen one pulsed through the facility, forcing the air from everyone's lungs as it went. Rayner and Hook were on their hands and knees, their lower guts burning as they fought to draw in breath. The men of both sides staggered to their feet, stunned by the sheer force of the blast that had washed over them.

Rands and his men, having not been hit by the blast, dashed towards the main corridor, the lead runners firing as they went. The stunned and shocked German troops were too slow to react to this renewed attack from a different direction. Some fell in the hail of bullets, but most left their weapons where they dropped and fell back towards pen one and the facility access to the quayside.

The main group of commandos gathered themselves, pushing forward to exploit the German retreat. They did not fire, but were wary of fire coming from the far side of pen three. Before long, they identified the profile of Rands and 2 Troop, who were shooting into the retreating Germans as they fell back through the concrete dust that hung in the air, thickly. Hook, the burning sensation subsiding from his gut, jogged on behind his men.

As he caught up with Rayner and the men, he could see Rands' men lined up in single file at the threshold into pen two, but could hear machine gun fire rippling around pen one. Bullet strikes on concrete, and pink mist bursting on running Germans, looked most peculiar considering none of his own men were firing. They were preoccupied with taking up the ground lost by the Germans.

Only when he stopped to catch his breath, did Hook hear a dreadful din of scraping and bending metal. Rands took a group of six men with him to investigate. Crouching as they moved through pen two, stepping over dead and dying Germans, they peered into pen one.

27

U-911 was not looking her best. Commander Traske had rammed her at full speed between the furthest walkway and the lone U-boat moored up. The impact of the crash had crumpled the bow, it was enough to render her useless to the Germans without considerable dry dock restoration.

The other U-boat had suffered a career-ending gouge along her starboard side, and numerous deck gun puncture wounds in her conning tower. Traske shook the hands of the men that had taken up positions on the bridge on the run in.

'Well done men, now it's time for what you guys really do well.'

'What do you mean, sir?' one of the commandos grinned. 'Are we not good enough to be submariners?'

'No young man, you are not, now get off my boat.' Traske winked and chuckled as he spoke.

With the bridge men providing security, Traske helped Lieutenant Bamber Cross to get his men and his officers off the crippled U-boat. Given the position in which she had finally come to rest, the ad hoc submariners, now back in their commando roles, had no trouble stepping off her deck and back onto terra firma.

'We've got friendlies in front of us,' called one of the bridge men. Traske moved from behind the conning tower to see Hook and some of his men. They looked like hell, but most were smiling. With men guarding the entrance to the facility, the reunited boys of 1 Troop stole a moment to shake hands and compliment each other on a job well done. With all but the dead and wounded of the company reunited, Hook took the opportunity to let them all catch their breath and regroup.

The captain was aware that it was not ideal to stay too long at the target, but to begin the push out of La Rochelle without taking stock of what they had achieved could spell disaster for the whole mission.

With 1 Troop providing security, Hook had the other two troops gather up the dead and wounded of both sides, and bring them into the machine shop. Even the dockers and German sailors who had been caught up in the fighting but survived unscathed, assisted with muted enthusiasm, fearing perhaps that the British would shoot them otherwise. The only dead and wounded not collected were those out on the exposed jetty and those in the first U-boat that Rands had boarded and scuttled. The pen facility had its own sick bay of sorts, for wounded crewmen needed support as they were moved to hospitals, and there were plenty of dressings and pain relief held in its pharmacy lockers. The stretchers that were stacked up in the stock room to the rear of the dispensary were used for the wounded. Hook did not intend to carry out the wounded, but should the Germans overwhelm his men, they would perhaps look favourably on the chivalry of the commandos they may capture.

With a crude battlefield clear-up concluded, Captain Paul Hook held a meeting with the officers and sergeants that remained. Hook looked at each in turn; they all appeared exhausted, but still very much in the fight. He acknowledged the loss of the sergeant major, Mr Joyce and Sergeant Pelton. Each troop had accounted for its dead and wounded, yet despite the fighting they had just undertaken, their fighting strength was still workable.

Standing beside one of the few intact crates of fresh produce to survive the fire fights, Hook patted the top of it to get everyone's attention.

'Gents, our time is short, but we need to get our ducks in a row before we make our next move.'

As the men around him fell silent, an eerie atmosphere filled the pens. The odd man from the company coughed here and there, and they could all hear the clatter of vehicles moving about on the quayside, but apart from that, all was quiet. Given how long and deep the pens were by design, the Germans on either side of the basin could not see in and it was too dark for those trying to spot them from the lock area. Hook went on with his address.

'We've done what we can for the wounded, and we have redistributed their ammunition amongst those of us that can still fight. Let's now talk about what we have achieved here, up to this point.'

He paused, surveying the destruction about him before going on.

'How many U-boats have we put out of action?'

'Including U-911,' Traske said, 'six.'

'Excellent. What condition would you say this facility is in now?'

'I would like to say written off.' Traske's tone was optimistic. 'We have given the Germans a big salvage operation to deal with if they want the U-boats dragged out of here, and the empty pens are damaged, or have unexploded torpedoes sat at the bottom.'

'That's what I was thinking,' nodded the captain. 'Let's not forget the ship sinking at the jetty, which now delays the finishing off of the other three pens from eight to ten.'

'I'm sure the RAF will already have chalked that one up,' grinned Rands. The others let out a little chuckle.

'Enemy forces, how many do you think we've killed or wounded?' asked Hook.

The officers and sergeants looked at each other, shoulders shrugged among those that had fought in the pens. The submarine officers kept themselves out of that part of the discussion.

'A troop, I'd say,' Sergeant Grice suggested, looking for support from the others. 'Thirty plus, give or take.'

Hook nodded. 'I ask this so that, should we get separated on our way to Marans, we can have the SAS boys report back to England on our battle damage assessment of the pens and its garrison forces. Remember, that figure could well go up, we've got to get out of here yet.'

They all nodded in agreement. Hook continued.

'We now need to get out of here. We have a few hours before it starts to get dark, and I really don't want to wait that long. The longer we wait, the more Germans are bound to turn up.'

Hook then turned to Sergeant Ross. 'Tell these guys what you and your men found for us.'

Ross cleared his throat. 'Another way out. It's a long shot, but better than going out of the front door with guns blazing.'

The officers looked at the sergeant, waiting for him to enlighten them. He turned to point at something close to pen four.

'That torpedo trolley we came across, they must have abandoned it as they drove out of their ammo bunker. They have a room full of torpedoes, deck gun shells — the works. They have a vehicle services hatch leading out to what looks like rail sidings. There is a bloody great crater just on the other side. The heavy shutters are punctured and pushed in, from blast by the looks of it. Just enough for us to get men out. There is a train wreck the other side. Must have been hit in the raid last night, it's still steaming like a bastard.'

The men standing before him blinked hard, looking perplexed. Hook gave Ross a nod.

'Show them.'

Ross showed the officers what he and the boys had discovered. The service bay shutters were buckled just enough to get two, maybe three of the men out at once. Outside the pen building was the jack-knifed wreck of a steam locomotive, along with its rolling stock. Its precious cargo of torpedoes had spilled all over the ground, and some lay at the bottom of a huge crater. The hit was clearly recent, as the erupted innards of the steam engine continued to bubble, boil and steam.

'The Germans can't be patrolling the wreckage,' suggested Rands, 'or else they would have discovered this way in.'

'Remember, they are most likely sailors, turfed out of bed to contain us until the army troops arrive,' whispered Hook. Rands turned to regard his superior.

'I suppose having the British commandos raiding the pens is good enough reason to let the army in to help.'

The officers grinned at each other. They knew that German protocol would have gone awry, the same had happened in Tunisia. Any German that could fire a weapon was deployed to try and cut off their escape route then, and there was no reason why it wouldn't happen here.

'When do you want to go?' asked Ross, inspecting the rolling stock for early sign of patrols.

'As soon as we can,' Hook answered. He held his binoculars up to his eyes.

'The rail line runs directly away from us, there is one on the right that runs parallel,' Ross informed him. 'Going by the photographs we looked at in Velas, to the north of the railhead behind the wreck there is a small industrial area, looks like factories. We could get in amongst the wreckage, wait until dark, then get the hell out of town through the factories.'

Hook pursed his lips. 'That's a long time out there. We haven't a clue what the bastards up on the roof can see. We can't have them looking down at us.'

Silence fell upon the officers. Those who had already surveyed the area crawled back, to allow others to get in position. Hook slid back far enough for Rayner to see the wreckage. The captain was in awe of the ordnance around them. He did not like the idea of fighting in that room; it would be better to get out amongst the wreckage whilst the Germans were preoccupied with the northern end of the pens, than have to shoot their way out later.

'When we go, we need to have the Germans think we are still in here,' stated Rands. 'Any volunteers to stay behind?'

'Me.' A firm voice commanded from behind them. Ross and all the officers snapped their heads round.

Gibbs, a Colt automatic in his left hand, his shattered right arm hanging useless down at his side, looked down at the crouched group. Wracked with pain, he managed to grimace his way through his words.

'Well sirs, you've certainly wrecked this place haven't you? I'm very proud of you all.'

Hook and the others clambered to their feet, mindful that the sergeant major was in no position to accept a handshake.

'Good to see you, Sergeant Major, thought the Germans had finally got you.'

Gibbs winced as he waved his good hand dismissively.

'They're going to have to try a little harder than that.'

'Did you get off the jetty okay? I mean, did you get Doyle into the pens?' Rayner was concerned for their colleague. Gibbs shook his head.

'I couldn't move him. He's alive, but the great lump can't walk, and I can't drag the man.'

'What Germans could you see?' Hook asked. Gibbs smarted as he adjusted himself, pushing the Colt into the top of his trouser waist band.

'Headless chickens mostly. None of them appear to know where they are going. They all want to hide amongst the flak gun positions. They must think the entire British Army is in here.'

'They could well be waiting for the entire German Army to help them out. This isn't good for us.' Rands pointed out. The sergeant major agreed.

'Well then.' Gibbs straightened himself up, wincing as he did so. 'You need a distraction.'

'What do you have in mind?' Hook asked.

28

'I will stay here with the wounded, anyone that can fire a weapon. The bastards are going to try and get back in, so we need them to think we are still here. In the meantime, all those that can walk out of here, get out through that knackered shutter, and make for the SAS rendezvous.'

Silence fell amongst the officers. Ross, feeling somewhat out on a limb, made his way out of the magazine to rejoin the company. Hook eyed Gibbs, whose facial expression said that he knew his time was up. The sergeant major had never been more serious.

Hook stepped forward. 'You do realise that, should they take you and the boys alive...'

Gibbs cut him short.

'With all due respect, sir, we are *all* aware of the consequences of being captured alive. It's a little late to start getting squeamish about it, don't you think?'

Hook could only agree with him. He gingerly put a hand on what he thought was an uninjured shoulder.

'You are one of a kind, Neil Gibbs, one of a kind.'

Mockingly, the sergeant major swiped his arm away.

'Captain, please... you are making me blush. I can't have the boys see me blush, so pack it in.'

The small group chuckled a little. Traske then stepped forward, offering his hand to Gibbs. The man took it suspiciously as he accepted it.

'You need able-bodied people to make our last stand look genuine. I will stay with you.'

Hook snapped his gaze to the submarine commander in surprise. The other officers, commandos and submariners alike, were just as shocked.

Gibbs shook his head in protest; Traske raised his other hand to cut him short.

'Sergeant Major, I wasn't asking for your permission. I will run about, shooting at whatever you tell me to, okay?'

'What are you playing at, Traske?' Hook eyed him with a frown. The submariner looked back at him.

'I'm a sub captain, Paul. Not a bloody commando. I don't fancy getting chased all over France, besides, you guys are better at that kind of thing. I've done my part of the mission. I got you here, and I did some damage.'

'Thank heavens for that,' chuckled the chief petty officer. 'I thought it was only me with that thought in mind. I'm staying, too.'

In quick succession, all of the submarine officers volunteered to stay. Hook and his own officers, including Rayner, exchanged bewildered looks. Traske turned to Hook, a defiant smile on his face.

'You now have a somewhat more credible distraction, so don't hang about too long.'

The submarine officers helped Gibbs collect Doyle from the jetty. The lad had lost a lot of blood, but was still able to use his weapons. Those leaving with Hook ensured they had collected what ammunition they could for their own weapons. The decoy group now possessed, for the main part, German weapons. Both

MG 42s were recovered from the smashed ruins of pen one and set up to decimate anyone foolish enough to try and rush through the quayside entrance. The remainder of those wounded who could still fight were helped into position, ensuring they could cover their respective fields of fire. The prisoners, along with those who were too badly wounded to contribute, sat in the machine shop.

As the commandos still fit to fight went over their final equipment checks, the loud hailer outside crackled and screeched into life once more.

'British commandos. You have nowhere to go. Surrender now and we will treat you fairly. We will give you medical attention, food and water. Your mission has failed. Do not make us come in there and destroy you all. British commandos, surrender now.'

The men looked at each other. One shook his head.

'They didn't say anything about cigarettes, so I'm not interested. Knowing my luck, none of the fuckers out there smoke.'

Some of the commandos sniggered aloud. Hook fought hard to suppress a grin. His men were as good as surrounded by a force that was under strict orders from their Führer to kill any commandos taken alive, and they were cracking jokes.

An NCO from Rands' troop voiced his opinion.

'I can't stand their coffee, and I doubt they have tea bags, so I'm out. They are going to have to catch me first, though.'

A tittering rippled through the men. Hook rolled his eyes at his officers, who were trying their best to appear detached from the comedy show. It wasn't working.

'Are you horrible lot still here?' growled Gibbs. 'You are making my pens look untidy. Piss off before I make you sweep it end to end.'

Sergeant Ross scanned the train wreck with binoculars. He had to be sure it was clear before he sent his men out to their potential deaths. The wreckage appeared clear, and he could not hear any German voices nearby.

Hook stood behind him, waiting for the sergeant to let him move. To the captain's right side, Gibbs stood, his shattered arm tied to his torso with a number of field dressings. His Colt automatic still tucked in his waistband.

'When you get home sir, tell Jean I volunteered to stay with the boys.'

Hook scoffed, raising an eyebrow to the man.

'Bollocks to that, she'll go flipping mad, you can tell her your bloody self.'

They grinned, shaking hands.

'All the best — give them hell,' said Gibbs.

'I will, don't you worry. But first, I need you to keep them busy for a while.'

'No problem, sir. Me and the boys will do just that.'

'Whenever you are ready, sir.' Ross whispered from below where he was eyeing the train wreck on his belly. Hook stepped around the sergeant, catching the eye of Traske, who stood to the left of the shutters. They exchanged nods.

'God speed Captain Hook. Give them hell.'

Hook grinned at the sub commander as he and the first group of commandos got down on their bellies and began to crawl out into the open exposed void between the building and the train wreck.

*

Rayner crawled as fast as he could through the shutters. The wide expanse outside made him feel very vulnerable as he crawled over cracked concrete that bordered the facility. Only when he heard the men crawling behind him scramble to their feet did he follow suit and dash for the huge crater that Hook and the remainder of the company had gathered in.

As he leaped in, gunfire erupted from the end of the pens. The last few men from the company were not put off by the shooting as they dashed over to join them. Rayner slid in next to the captain as they tuned in to their new environment.

The gun fight was, initially, a little confusing to Hook. He found it odd that both sides fired the soundtrack of German weapons, whereas usually he could distinguish between the opposing sides. In fact, that most of the deep echoing fire was coming from within the pens, with the fire outside more stunted and unremarkable.

Rands spotted movement through the broken and twisted rolling stock. He soon recognised more German army trucks, arriving with reinforcements. The new arrivals were energetic, clean, and moved with purpose, unlike the sailors who were clumsy in their actions.

Rands spoke quietly over his shoulder.

'Army troops have arrived.'

'How can you tell?' asked Hook.

'These fuckers look like they know what they are doing.'

Rayner looked at the captain following Rands' comments. The captain merely shrugged. He clambered across the large crater, which was difficult since some of the rail track lay warped and buckled across it. He then focused on the piled-up rolling stock that separated them from the industrial area. Fires still raged from the raid. Hook could see movement. He doubted it was more muscle arriving to deal with them; more likely fire crews, trying to save what they could. But he needed to be sure. He turned to his men, who were all poised to fight from their new position if required.

'Mr Rands, have your boys check out the factory area before we move out.'

An NCO and three men from Rands' troop crawled up next to the captain, just as horror erupted in the pens.

29

Gibbs knew that changing magazines on his Colt automatic would present a challenge. The idea of firing one-handed was nothing more than Hollywood nonsense. The silver screen would have the public think that shooting from the hip with a revolver in each hand was all the rage, with deputies and bandits hitting each other at hundreds of yards. Trying to fire a beast like the Colt .45 automatic with one hand, was like trying to fire a cannon from the shoulder. It kicked like a mule; flicking high right with every recoil. Shooting with both hands was not for the faint-hearted, either. Pistol shooting did not come naturally to most soldiers, and for Gibbs, who was not left-handed, his chances of hitting anyone with his weapon were now more remote than ever.

The Germans tried to get into the pens as soon as Captain Hook and the rest of the lads had got out.

The man moved with a sense of purpose amongst the ad hoc force. He had to be seen; the lads performed better when they knew the sergeant major was backing them up. The pain relief he had received had not touched his shoulder, every step sending a charge of agony through him like an electric shock. A sudden cough would bounce the shattered limb, causing Gibbs to absorb the pain through gritted teeth. He would not show weakness in front of the boys, for some of them were in a far worse state and yet remained cheerful — on the outside. He did his rounds, with every intention of talking to them all.

Doyle was awake, but weak from blood loss. His head swam as if he was drunk, but he refused to be sent to the machine shop.

'I'm not sitting in that abattoir, I'd rather fight,' he asserted to the sergeant major, who stood over him. Gibbs nodded at the man's determination.

'Good lad. We need to give them a show, so the captain and the rest of the boys can get away.'

'Yes, sir.' Doyle looked forlorn as he accepted his lot, at least for the time being. Gibbs winced as he squatted clumsily down to speak to the man at eye level.

'Now you listen to me, Doyle. Wounded or not, we still have a job to do. It's what we all signed up for. No-one said we would always have it going our way.'

The commando nodded. 'Yes, sir. You are right.' He nodded at the Colt in the sergeant major's left hand. 'Will you need help refilling that thing?'

Gibbs looked down at the pistol, hanging unnaturally in his weak hand. He stifled a chuckle.

'Probably do better to throw it at them.'

Both men grinned at each other. Gibbs awkwardly stood back up, his face contorting as he adjusted himself. He nodded at the German submachine gun in Doyle's hands.

'You going to be okay with that?'

Doyle held it uncomfortably in both hands, in the hand of a wounded man it looked to weigh a ton.

'I will be fine, sir. I've used it before, nice little weapon this, providing they get close of course.'

'Well let's not give the fuckers the oppor...'

'Smoke!' yelled some of the men in the forward positions. Those seated fought through the pain of their wounds to get into a fighting position. Traske and his submarine officers darted about, unhappy with their positions, desperately searching for better. As the white phosphorous smoke instantaneously billowed out of the grenade bodies, Gibbs scampered forwards to bolster the men in the front area, and to adjust the sub-officers, who were not ideally placed.

Behind the white fog, everyone could hear more grenade canisters clattering in through the main access from the quayside.

'Hold your fire boys, watch your ammo,' called Gibbs over his left shoulder, his Colt pointing directly at the smoke.

'Watch for movement!' yelled another voice.

The smoke began to lift and drift out into the pens once more. It was at this point that the commandos could hear boots clattering from concrete underfoot then changing to a hollow clanking tone as they contacted metal. The sound travelled up, over the top of the smoke. Those in the forward positions, including Gibbs, couldn't help but follow the noise.

Dread washed over the sergeant major.

'They are above us on the gantry, get ready!' someone called through the haze as it drifted through the pen. The smoke hid all but the noise of the Germans as they poured into pen one. The smoke was now thinning, and it was then that movement was detected by the commandos manning one of the MG42s.

'Contact!' roared the men as the captured machine gun let out its first long, rippling burst. Instantly, those Germans who were in its firing line crumpled and numerous bursts of pink mist struck home. In those opening seconds of the fire fight, more German troops ran into the unseen stream of bullets, their lives expiring instantly as the hail of bullets pulverised their bodies, gravity taking them to the ground. Those dead German boys had served no purpose other than to block the route for more of their comrades to rush into the facility, for they piled up quickly. The Germans wounded in the opening burst did all they could to scramble out of the firing line of the other commandos holding the line. Some made it to relative safety, without their weapons. Those who kept hold of their guns were less agile and died violently as a result.

Gibbs had only just managed to get into a position suitable to engage the running Germans with his Colt when the crate between himself and the MG42 crew to his left splintered and shattered from incoming fire. The left side of his face and neck smarted; his left ear throbbed as he slumped onto his shattered right arm. The action caused the tough warrant officer to growl in pain. His discomfort evaporated as soon as he saw the lifeless eyes of the two men that had been using the MG42. The Germans up on the gantry had done well to knock out the biggest threat to them, as they charged into the pen in small groups of four and five.

Gibbs scrambled to his feet, to the snap and scream of bullets just missing him and flicking off the concrete floor. He let fly with all ten rounds in his Colt magazine, the top slide shunting to the rear and staying there as the last hot brass case flicked out right in a spinning arc. The futile gesture against the German troops firing down from the gantry was enough for some of them to flinch and seek better cover, but it achieved no more. The sergeant major crouched back down as more German troops poured in. He was not left-handed, but had the dexterity to release the spent magazine from within the pistol grip. It clattered to the ground as he put the empty pistol into his right hand. Merely holding the heavy handgun sent a bolt of pain shooting through him, as he fought through his webbing pouches for another magazine.

Gibbs had no idea that he was one of two surviving commandos in the forward positions, as bullets snapped back and forth over his head. He gritted his teeth as he fed the full magazine with his left hand into the weapon, holding it clumsily with the right. He felt the magazine click into place. He used the thumb of his right hand to push down on the top slide release catch; the tensioned spring within the Colt slammed the top slide forward, feeding the first round into the chamber, the hammer remaining to the rear, ready to fire. At any other time, Gibbs would have changed a pistol magazine without so much as a second thought, but with only one good arm, and not his leading arm at that, the effort was phenomenal.

Just as he went to stand, the chatter of German submachine guns behind him caused him to flinch.

'Right with you sir. Let's get the bastards,' called an NCO as he limped up to him at a crouch. His left hand was bandaged into a tight ball, the sling of the MP40 was around his shoulder, allowing him to push the weapon away with his good hand well enough to render it sufficiently stable to fire short bursts. Gibbs felt for the man, who would have his own issues when he, too, needed to change magazines. The pair of them fired with everything they had at those up on the gantry, oblivious to the Germans swarming across the ground floor towards them.

Then, as the top slide of the Colt locked to the rear once more, Gibbs noticed how exposed he was to the enemy troops no more than tens of yards in front of him. They fired, ducked and dived as they too were coming under accurate fire from the commandos and submarine officers holding their positions amongst the torpedo trolleys, fresh produce crates and submarine parts. Gibbs dropped to one knee as he began once again the painful, yet vital, process of changing magazines. The NCO beside him, patted him on the shoulder.

'Fall back sir, we are too exposed.' The man began to walk backwards at the couch, keeping his burst lengths short. Gibbs caught sight of frantic waving beyond the NCO, amongst the crates. The waving man was Commander Traske.

'Move back, you are too exposed, move back!' Traske roared, his profile made more prominent by muzzle flashes of weapons firing either side of him. The bullets snapped past close by, but he knew his men, wounded or not, knew how to shoot.

'Let's go sir, keep moving!' hollered the NCO, walking backwards while hunched over, providing covering fire as he went. His weapon soon ran out of ammunition, and despite his wounds, he slung the MP40 behind his back in one swift stroke, his good hand returning to view with a Colt automatic in it. The

NCO carried on firing at the Germans who were making a dash for the crates the pair of them had just vacated, in an effort to close the distance between themselves and the British. Gibbs put his faith in the men firing just past him as he slid in beside Traske, who was himself armed with a German carbine bolt-action rifle.

'Man down!' roared Traske, just as Gibbs was trying to talk to him. The message instantly caught Gibbs' attention, he turned his head in the direction Traske was pointing. The NCO with the MP40, who had covered his withdrawal, now crawled, slumped on his left side, blood trailing behind him. Incoming rounds splashed and snapped all about as his efforts exhausted him. He paused only to continue to fire his Colt at the German helmets bobbing behind the abandoned forward crates. As his top slide punched to the rear locked position, the NCO's head burst like a tomato, his war over.

In response to the death of a hardy commando NCO, the wounded men gave the advancing Germans everything they had. The enemy slumped where they fell, few were agile enough to dive back into cover.

Traske snapped off a shot from his carbine, at a German soldier dragging the MG42 from the dead commando. His first shot went high right, and by the time he fed a fresh round into the breach, the German was gone; so too was the fearsome machine gun.

'They've got the MG42!' Traske roared over his shoulder to whoever could hear him. As he looked back at the enemy troops bobbing about, snapping off shots, stick grenades tumbled in towards them. Most fell short, their throwers not daring to expose themselves longer than they had to, but others found their mark, clattering in amongst the commandos as they scrambled for better cover.

The concussion of the grenades pulsed through the wounded men. The crates and pallets in which they hid behind flexed and shattered by the sheer force of the detonations. Gibbs' head swam as he scrambled to get to his feet. As he went to stand, his face took one hell of a thump, ringing his ears, loosening teeth and making him see stars once again. The man crashed onto his back, his head bouncing on the concrete.

The dark profile of a soldier loomed over him. As his hearing became more acute, and his vision began to focus, he recognised the profile of a German standing over him, rifle muzzle pointing at his face, screaming at him in savage dialect he had never bothered to learn. He felt his left hand stamped on, in an effort to release the Colt from his grip and before he could look down, he felt the pistol ripped away. The sergeant major was now not only wounded

but unarmed and overwhelmed by enemy troops. His confused thoughts were punched out of him with a well-placed rifle butt to the face.

The lights went out.

30

There was not much Hook could do for the men left in the pens. The fighting sounded horrendous, but he was quietly confident that Gibbs, Traske and the others would keep the Germans focussed on that area, giving the rest of them some room and much-needed time to get out of the town.

Rands and his small group had been gone for a few minutes when the hissed call for the captain to come forward reached his ears. Cradling the Thompson across his forearms, Hook crawled out of the crater and into the twisted rolling stock piled up in front of them. Carefully, he picked his way between the buckled rails and wheels, seeing the soles of hobnail boots at eye level. The grubby, sweat glazed face of one of his NCOs caught his attention. The man put a finger to his lips before giving the captain the thumbs down hand signal. Enemy present.

Hook now tried even harder to not make any noise as he covered the last few yards to the prone commando waiting for him. The captain sweated profusely from the effort, and was denied any rest as the NCO began to slowly crawl away again. Hook knew to follow him. The route took them through shallower bomb craters, just as wide, but half as deep as the one the rest of the company rested in.

On the far lip of a third crater Hook, eyes stinging from sweat, identified the filthy, bare-headed profile of Lieutenant James Rands. The men remaining of his small group were spread out to the left and right of him, as far as the shell crater allowed. They were stock still. As Hook followed the NCO into the crater, Rands began to crawl backwards, extremely slowly. He and the NCO crawled past each other, the NCO taking Rands' place on the lip of the crater, moving in slow motion. Hook relaxed once in the deepest part of the crater, only then did Rands also relax a little, as he turned to talk with his superior.

'We've got a patrol out in front of us.' Rands' voice was hushed. Hook bit his bottom lip. Rands wasn't finished.

'Just shy of two hundred yards. Behind the rolling stock.'

'Strength?' Hook enquired.

'Just shy of a troop, maybe. Two trucks' worth. MG42 mounted on top of each cab.'

'Fuck!' Hook hissed, out of character. Rands could only nod in agreement.

'These fuckers are certainly army. They have one truck's worth on the road with both the trucks, like a roadblock, the other group is moving through the rolling stock wreckage.'

'Okay. How fast are they moving?'

'Steady. As you arrived, they stopped to talk with whoever is trying to put that factory fire out.'

Hook looked upwards, the only thing dominating his current position was the high, lingering smoke from the factory area, which they had to navigate their way through to get out into open country.

Hook leaned in to ask about dog patrols when the NCO, without so much as a glance at them, whipped his right arm down, clicking his fingers. The din of the fighting within the pens still dominated the area, and the thud of grenades announced a new phase in the German assault. Both officers crawled up to either side of the NCO, who pointed at what was unfolding before him.

The German patrol was moving again, men's lower legs visible as they too were careful where they trod. One of the machine gunners up on top of the trucks called out to the patrol, pointing in the general direction of the British in the shallow crater. Hook was somewhat alarmed initially, but took his time to read the German. The man was gesturing at something behind them. Hook fought the temptation to look behind him, for such movement could attract the attention of the very same German soldier. None of the small group of commandos moved a muscle. Instead they concentrated on the patrol coming through the smashed rolling stock, towards them.

The lead scout of the German patrol came into view. At such a short distance, just under two hundred yards, Hook could tell how clean and fresh the man was. It wasn't lost on Rands either that the enemy troops in front of them were new into the battle, and conducting themselves in a more serious manner than their Kreigsmarine counterparts. Garrison troops drafted in to intercept the British attackers. The lead soldier was armed with an MP40, others now coming out of the rolling stock had a mixture of that weapon and bolt action carbines. With just Thompsons and Colts amongst them, Rand's group could take care of the squad with little problem. It was the two MG42 they had in support that would be the issue. The commandos on the far right of the crater could suppress them, but to knock them out of the fight altogether would take some doing. As for pistols, the British would leave those to Hollywood film makers. A Bren gun on the right would be much better, but there was no way they could fetch one forward, not now.

The German patrol came closer.

*

Gibbs' face was swollen like a watermelon, according to Alfie Parch, Hook's wounded radio operator. To the sergeant major, it felt like it too. Traske, now wounded and dressed by one of the German medics that reluctantly tended them, explained that the German soldier who battered Gibbs senseless continued to hit him after he had passed out. A German NCO had pulled the angry soldier off him, striking his own colleague across the face. Traske went on to be rather complimentary about the German troops' conduct once that situation had been defused. The Germans called a halt to their violent assault as soon as they could see they had the better of Traske and the rest of the men.

'I am surprised...' Traske kept his voice low as German officers and men patrolled around them, 'that they didn't just finish us off.'

'Don't you worry about that sir,' Parch replied. 'They want to know how and why we are here first. These fuckers won't do it, they will hand us over to the SS or something like that, you'll see.'

Exasperated, Traske closed his eyes as he spoke to the pessimistic soldier. 'You know what Parch, in future just lie to me, I sleep much better when I don't know what's going to happen.'

Gibbs' throbbing jaw allowed him to chuckle, drool dripping off his chin. Parch wiped the sergeant major's chin gingerly with a dressing.

'You are okay sir, they didn't break your jaw, but they sure had a go, mind.'

The remark caused the man to chuckle a little more, squeezing Parch's shoulder with his good hand. For the time being, all Gibbs could do was accept his own defeat and try to recover from his beating enough to oversee his men. If they were allowed to live after the sheer nerve of their attack, life as prisoners of war would be something they all, as fighting men, would find hard to cope with.

As the German troops began to carry the dead and wounded out of the machine shop on stretchers, fresh-looking German officers, adorned with ribbons and medals and entourage in tow, were being shown around the wrecked pens by a man Traske assumed to be the assault commander. The young man looked filthy and exhausted as he pointed out key features, such as the ruined U-boats at their moorings. One of the brightly-coloured officers turned to a colleague, not half as decorated, and spoke in measured tones. The receiving officer waved to their combat-weary colleague to follow him, as he began to walk over to the battered and bruised British. The combat officer looked a little concerned, as if unsure of any reason to engage the enemy in conversation, but the freshly-laundered officer began to speak in excellent English.

'The generals would like to speak with the British officers please. Thank you.'

Traske looked at Gibbs, who was trying to get to his feet. The submarine captain put a gentle hand on the sergeant major's knee.

'You must rest, you've done enough.'

Gibbs lowered himself, nodding his acknowledgement to Traske, who was now on his feet, straightening himself and his bandaged head. Traske caught Parch grinning up at him, flicking an eyebrow to emphasise the bandage.

'What?'

'Don't forget to salute with head dress on, sir.'

'Fuck off.'

As Traske turned, Gibbs managed a hefty left jab into the bicep of the giggling Parch. The other submarine officers, all sporting their own bandages on various body parts, limped forwards to join their commander. The two German generals, one considerably older than the other, looked at the dishevelled enemy officers as if they had disturbed the generals' prior engagements. Members of their entourage were far more courteous. Professional nods were exchanged, but no handshakes.

The older general spoke aggressively at Traske, who acknowledged that his use of interpreters was admirable. Many made the mistake of talking directly to the interpreter instead of having them behind their shoulder, translating as they spoke. Traske kept his eyes on those of the general in question, as his aide spoke.

'The general demands to know how you come to La Rochelle.' The young Wehrmacht captain spoke excellent English. Traske gave the man the once-over. His apparent youth was questionable, given the medals he wore. Traske concluded quickly that the captain was either a soldier worthy of distinction from earlier campaigns, or just another arse-kissing fool. He answered the general, at a deliberate pace so his aide could translate.

'We arrived on board that U-boat, U-911.' He pointed at the bow-broken submarine capsizing in pen one. The aide glared at Traske as he spoke into the general's ear, clearly shocked at the answer.

The general looked furiously at his aide before storming off to look at the U-boat in question. The German captain skipped after him with the remainder of their group following on. Traske knew better than to wait to be pushed and shoved after them, so took a casual stroll in their wake. The furious general stood, hands on hips as he looked at the two wrecked submarines beneath him. He then blurted out more German, spittle flying from his lips as he glared at the British officers. The aide blushed with embarrassment as he delivered a far more measured question to Traske.

'How did you get into the basin?'

Traske had to be careful what he said next, so he kept it short, so that the lie would be easier to remember.

'My deputy and I were on the bridge, and we shouted at the dockers to keep the lock open as we approached. Another U-boat was putting to sea, so we exploited the situation.'

The general's face contorted even more as the captain translated the reply. Traske was not going to mention the fact that his men had been lined up on the deck dressed as rain-soaked German sailors. That revelation would ensure a swift handover to the Gestapo, the SS and then the firing squad.

'You are soldiers, how would you know how to command and manoeuvre a submarine, never mind one of our U-boats?' the aide demanded. Traske shrugged his shoulders, mindful he was dressed the same way as Hook's men.

'We made it our business to learn both German, and how to use the submarine.'

The general spoke more quietly, his face glazed in a shine of sweat as he fought to control his rage. The captain looked uncomfortable as he listened. The young officer lifted his chin, swallowing hard prior to speaking.

'What has become of the U-911 crew?'

Traske gave a slight smile. 'They are in the Azores. We sneaked aboard a supply ship delivering torpedoes from Italy. The ship was interned and inspected in Gibraltar, where we boarded.'

The young German officer spoke as Traske answered. The general kept his hateful gaze on the apparent commando stood before him. He barked a mouthful of German before Traske's answer was fully translated. His aide hesitated, due to the outburst; the general eyed him with disdain as he repeated his question. The young man turned to Traske.

'How did you know the ship was bound for the Azores?'

Traske had to think quickly, he had to ensure the compromised Enigma codes were not revealed, for that would undo all that Rayner had spoken of, and more. He kept it simple yet credible.

'We didn't. My men and I were in Gibraltar getting ready to ship to Malta when the opportunity fell into our laps, so to speak.'

'Why Malta?' the aide asked.

'Why not? Not like it's going to be yours any time soon.' Traske couldn't resist, and even the other submarine officers fought to stifle their amusement.

'The ship's crew collaborated with you?' The aide added a question of his own to the proceedings; flustered somewhat by the nerve of the commando. The general winced at the question. It was that question alone that made up Traske's mind about the man. Arse-kissing fool. Traske shook his head.

'We put the crew under considerable duress, they were not party to our plan.'

'Hmm' the German captain scoffed as he gave the old general a sideways glance. Red mist descended over Traske, who forgot his place.

'If it's all the same to you, herr captain, I'm not having merchant seamen punished for something that was completely out of their control. We shoved guns in their faces, and they did as they were told.'

The German group, as well as his own men, stood opened-mouthed at the British officer's outburst. The old general waved a hand to calm the conversation, himself having cooled somewhat. The young German captain, scolded by Traske, straightened his field cap, pushing his shoulders back a little. Pretending the whole thing had never happened; Traske looked into the eyes of the general once more, his demeanour a little crestfallen.

'It is with regret, that a few of the German U-boat crew fell in our assault to seize U-911 for our own ends.' Traske could tell by the young aide's demeanour and tone, that he relayed this to the general without emotion. The old man nodded, speaking quietly.

'Such things happen,' relayed the captain. 'Did you bury those men as you would your own?'

Traske shook his head. 'The locals took care of the dead. They conducted a small ceremony, the captured crew in attendance.'

The general nodded as he received what Traske had said. He muttered to the captain.

'How have you taken the crew into captivity? Whom have you left in the Azores guarding them?'

Traske felt he was not giving anything away with his next answer.

'They are unguarded. Both they and the Italian crew are still on board the cargo ship we hijacked. They have enough food and provisions to make their stay reasonably comfortable. The locals will no doubt assist them in any way they can. All we did was destroy their means of communication, to buy us time to get here.'

Traske gave himself a mental reprimand, for he was already treading a fine line. He derailed his run-away verbal train, before he slipped and spoke of their using German uniforms.

The old man straightened himself up, adopting a much sterner expression as he spoke to the covert submarine commander, his message relayed as he went.

'The general cannot guarantee that you and your men will not be taken into custody by the Gestapo. The nature of your attack makes explaining this to High Command, in such a way as to prevent that outcome, much more difficult.'

Traske nodded, his own officers had their heads bowed a little. The German captain offered more.

'Return to your men. We have many wounded to tend to, before we can have you moved to prisoner of war facilities.'

As the German group turned to leave, the much younger-looking general caught Traske's eye. A sly smile appeared upon his face. This one did not need an interpreter.

'All this destruction...' the sinister-looking man surveyed the entire facility before turning back to Traske. 'With so few men...'

Traske held himself mute; he wondered if the general knew something that he knew, too.

'Impressive, very impressive.' The German chuckled. Traske was unsure what to say next. The German had not finished.

'The fat, cognac-swilling experts in Berlin will not feel like breakfast when they hear of this superb mission. My compliments go out to you and your men, for even trying such a move. If only our own planners would even dream up such a coup. They will have to change their asset protection protocol now, you can be sure of that. Using a U-boat as a Trojan horse... remarkable.'

Traske said nothing as the chuckling general turned and walked away. Traske slowly turned to his own officers, who looked back at their superior. Chief Toil spoke first.

'Well, I wasn't expecting him to say that.'

The officers returned to the wounded commandos, who sat together sharing cigarettes that had, surprisingly, been given to them by some of their German guards. They had moved off a little, already bored by the duties. Gibbs pulled himself up into a more comfortable sitting position.

'How was your chat?'

Traske eased himself in amongst the crates, accepting one of the cigarettes offered by Parch. He waited for it to be lit; answering only when he had taken a long, greedy drag, smoke drifting from his nostrils.

'They wanted to know how we got here, so I told him. Hardly a bloody secret now, let's be fair.'

The smokers in the group took further pulls on their French cigarettes. It was Parch who spoke next.

'So, when do the SS arrive to shoot us all then? Old Adolf won't be happy with us for doing this to his precious bath toys.'

The group sniggered, knowing he had a point. Traske allowed the cigarette to hang from his lips as he spoke, ash dropping into his lap.

'The general, the older one of the two, does not appear keen to hand us over. The younger one, I don't know what to make of him. Looks like he would take much pleasure in shooting us himself.'

'I bet the old man is from the old school,' Gibbs said. 'One of the Kaiser's officers back in the day. He looks old enough to have fought in the Great War. I can't see them all being loyal Nazi followers.'

'What makes you say that?' Traske asked, pulling a flake of tobacco from his bottom lip. The sergeant major managed a shrug of sorts.

'Just a feeling I've got. He's too long in the tooth for command on the Russian front, hence he has a nice backwater number here. Well, he did until we arrived anyway. He doesn't look the sort to be scared of the Nazi boys, he was just as hostile to his aide as he was to you.'

Traske was about to add his own take on it when gun fire erupted outside, beyond the buckled shutters of the magazine. Traske turned to the German officers leaving the pens, the young general sneering at Traske with a sinister grin on his face, before barking orders at the soldiers who stood near the pen entrance. Traske turned to Gibbs and the officers.

'Don't expect them to be so nice after hearing that racket.'

31

Hook and his small forward group cut down the first three members of the German patrol. Rands and others were already moving their fire positions to fool those of the Germans that had survived the opening ambush into thinking that the British were many in number. The German troops loitering around their trucks moved forward at a crouch, spreading out as they went. The MG42 gunners up on the trucks were hesitant at first as they shouted for target indications, mindful of hitting their own. The British commandos hit a few more of the patrol as they made a dash rearward for better cover amongst the train wreckage. Some fell and remained still, others yelped as they were hit, crawling frantically to get to better cover, only to be hit again by the violent cross fire about them.

Hook was alerted to movement behind him. He was pleased to see the remainder of the company dashing forward to join his forward exposed group. One of his men was hit by the opening burst of the MG42 forward right of their line. In retaliation, some of the men strafed the two trucks with both Bren and Thompson fire. One of the German machine gunners was hit, the other ducked down out of sight, his movements thereafter unknown.

Hook crawled back out of the fighting line; he had more than enough men to fight on his behalf. At the top of his voice, he called for his commanders to move in to him. Despite gunfire and commotion reigning, Hook's commandos shouted their commander's orders to each other. As the likes of Ross and Rands crawled back towards him, the familiar snap of incoming rounds alerted Hook to events unfolding to his left. He was surprised to see more German soldiers moving about the shattered locomotive, and the first sets of jack-knifed rolling stock.

'Enemy left, enemy left!' the captain roared. The commandos nearest him flicked their heads left, identifying the threat that could impede their escape efforts. Hook stood fully exposed in the crater, firing short bursts from his Thompson as he shouted.

'2 Troop, peel left, peel left!'

As the command was passed among the men concerned, both Rands and Ross joined the captain in a standing position, firing their Thompsons. It allowed those 2 Troop members in unsuitable positions to re-orientat themselves against the new enemy threat, whilst the men of 3 and 1 Troops took care of the ambushed patrol and the truck reinforcements. In next to no time, the company was strung out in an L-shaped formation, the base of which faced those Germans coming from the pens to finish them off.

It was the familiar clunk of an empty magazine that prompted Hook to kneel back down in the crater. Both Rands and Ross followed suit. The captain spoke forcefully as he changed magazines.

'Ross, I want you to take 1 and 3 Troops, and clear the trucks and the train wreckage in front of your men. We need to get into that industrial area; we will have better cover in there.'

Ross didn't answer. He was off back towards his men at a crouch, changing magazines as he went. Hook turned to Rands.

'Engage the bastards around the train. Be prepared to peel right, following Ross into the buildings.'

'Roger that, sir.' Rands rolled onto his side before getting up into a kneeling position. As his men fought the increasing German forces gathering around the locomotive, the troop commander moved up and down behind them briefing them up on what the captain wanted to happen. Hook moved about to avoid being targeted by a keen eyed sharpshooter, noting that the Germans they were now fighting were more refined that those they had fought in the pens. Rands was probably right in his assumption that army troops had been called in to counter their attack. They did not give themselves away cheaply, but nor did his own men.

Hook turned his head frequently, monitoring both the progress of Ross' men as they moved slowly forward, dashing from what cover there was between them and the tail end of the rolling stock and the bullet riddled trucks, and the men strung out in front of him. The Thompson carriers moved here and there, changing firing positions, the Bren gunners doing the same, but not with the same agility.

The leading men of 1 and 3 Troops had made it as far as the rolling stock when they came upon other German troops on the forward edge of the industrial area, not three hundred yards further on. The buildings behind them burned wildly, the fire tenders, now abandoned due to the fighting, sprayed unaided into fires that overmatched their feeble attempts to soak the structures. Movement behind the smashed trucks caught the attention of two of the Bren gunners, and their bullets cut through the chassis, hitting those who tried to use them as protection. Ross was content the trucks no longer posed a threat to the commando force and called for men not to risk making an exposed dash to clarify. The incoming fire from the industrial area was heavy, but lacked accuracy. Ross' Bren gunners enjoyed easy pickings against a less experienced force, their pedigree unknown.

Then, as the Bren gunners scrambled for fresh fighting positions, Ross' entire force was punched flat by the blast of a colossal explosion that obliterated the largest burning building of the bunch.

The concussion of the explosion rendered the battlefield silent, save for the echo, of Biblical proportions, that rippled outwards. Hook's ears rang with an intensity he had never experienced before. As his men struggled to gather their senses, they were forced to find cover, not from incoming German fire, but from what remained of the factory building and now rained down about them. With all tactical considerations forgotten, the commandos, less those knocked senseless by the blast, huddled as small as they could to reduce the chances of getting killed by building materials falling to earth.

Hook hunkered down, his hearing slowly returning. The dull thud of heavy objects indicated a near miss, which in turn prompted profanity from those it almost killed or severely wounded. The captain found the idea of being killed by a stray roof tile a little absurd, considering what *could* kill any soldier in the midst of a war. As his hearing improved, he began to identify familiar voices calling upon their men, ensuring they were still fit to fight. Hook could only assume that the Germans they were fighting were in no better shape. He lifted himself up into a sitting position and was amazed to find those who were still able in 2 Troop to fight were still alive, their position littered with all manner of smashed and warped building material. One matter in particular was now causing consternation: what looked like torpedoes, minus their nose cones, were strewn about the place.

'Fuck getting clouted on the bonce by one of *them*,' one of the lads chuckled.

Comedy... It has always been all about the timing.

*

'What the bloody hell was *that*?' Gibbs bellowed, as the echo of the explosion magnified as it pulsed through the pens. The Germans guarding them were unsteady and dazed on their feet, unsure whether to join their comrades in the battle that was unfolding outside, or to remain with the prisoners. They hesitated for but a few seconds, time enough for Gibbs to get the measure of them. They were just young boys, probably too young to ship off to Russia just yet. The barking of other soldiers in pen one made the decision for them. They jogged away to join their unit as it gathered in pen one.

Gibbs clambered to his feet, painfully. Apart from about a dozen German troops gathered just inside the quayside entrance, there was no one guarding them. He turned to Traske.

'Are we making a break for it, or what?'

Traske got to his feet. 'Wait here; let me check the coast is clear before we make a mad dash into more bloody Germans.'

The submarine commander kept himself low as he made for the magazine. He kept to the right of the damaged shutters, getting onto his belly to look out, towards the train wreckage. He could just make out what may have been Hook and his men moving amongst the wreckage — he could not be sure.

He had not even accustomed his eyes to the late afternoon sun when German voices blurted out hysterically to his left.

Gibbs, along with some of the men, flinched as bullets splashed and screamed about the magazine. If the kids they called soldiers had known what was stacked up inside, they may have not have been so quick to open fire. The sergeant major clambered towards the magazine access door, his heart sinking as he found Traske, face down, his blood already pooling beneath him as German troops outside dragged his limp body outside, flipping him over as if he was a rag doll.

Two more Germans crawled in through the shutters, their submachine guns pointed directly at Gibbs, who slowly raised his hands as far as his pain threshold would allow. The German soldiers had looks on their faces that begged the commando to give them even more of an excuse to kill him. Gibbs nodded to them as he backed away from the threshold.

With a heavy heart, the commando sergeant major sat back with his wounded men, their escape route denied them. What caught in Gibbs' throat was that a man who had no formal allegiance to him, whom he had only met in the most bizarre circumstances in Gibraltar, had sacrificed himself whilst acting on a warrant officer's flippant, yet simultaneously serious, suggestion.

32

Sergeant Ross struggled to gather his senses. The world was swimming about him, his hearing muffled, his eyes yet to focus. The noise of battle seemed far away. To keep the nausea under control, he had to sit upright; not ideal in the middle of a gun fight, but his drunken stupor denied him all consideration of the risk. He felt rough hands pull him up straight.

'C'mon Sergeant, we are leaving. Get on your feet.'

The voice was full of authority; the man telling him to get up was none other than the captain himself. Ross' head swam as the officer hauled him to his feet. He wasn't ready for the sudden activity, vomiting as he rocked to his right.

'Come on Sergeant, we need to get out of here.' Hook was irritated at the conduct of a man he held in high regard as a good, dependable operator. Hook then put himself in check, quickly realising that Ross had been knocked flat by blast, along with the rest of 1 and 3 Troops. The sergeant's legs did not want to work, and it was a big ask for the captain to haul him along under fire. He carefully lowered the man back down, looking for Ross' Thompson as he did so. It was nowhere to be seen. Hook checked for a pistol, the Colt was still in its holster, not that Ross was in any state to use it.

Hook enticed the shell shocked sergeant to lie down. The cover was better for the pair of them, as rolling stock blocked the Germans' line of sight from around the locomotive wreck. Hook peered to his right, identifying Rands' men tending to their blasted comrades. Those not helping out were in fighting positions, but not firing. Movement caught the captain's eye further to the right. What he thought to be enemy troops were crawling and rolling about. None looked in any fit state to engage the commandos. After a few seconds, Hook recognised that most of the troops on the ground were not moving at all. The blast of the explosion had taken anyone in its path.

'Am I dead, sir?' a voice croaked. Hook flinched, looking for its source. It didn't occur to him that it would be Ross, as he raised a trembling hand up the captain's left shoulder.

'No Sergeant, you are very much alive, but you took one hell of a knockout blow when that bloody factory went up.'

'Are my boys okay?'

Hook tried his hardest to be upbeat, for he had already seen some of those dealing with the blast casualties shaking their heads in resignation. He nodded at the prone, bloodied man.

'They are fine, beaten up, but fine.'

A hacking cough had the man curling up into the foetal position, blood and bile hanging from his lips in strands. Hook knew Ross needed medical attention, but he wasn't going to get it there. Ross forced himself up onto his knees, cursing the gods as he did so.

'I think I have a hangover that could kill a small town. Where the hell is my weapon?'

Hook was impressed at his toughness, and helped to steady him.

'I couldn't see it anywhere, you have your pistol.'

Ross focussed on the men treating his boys. He knew some of them would be too far gone. He then regarded his company commander, with a resigned expression.

'I'm sure I can use one of theirs.'

Hook was tight lipped at such pragmatism. Both then flinched as fighting broke out once more. The Germans in the train wreckage were now recovering from the explosion. Those that could fight back, now fewer in number, went about their work with the same vigour as before. Those who had been hit by the blast but could now bear arms again crawled about, no longer match fit for the gun fight.

Unsteady as he got to his feet, Ross composed himself, Colt in hand ready to fight. He then staggered along the right side of the wreckage. As he came upon the first of his dead men, Ross came face-to-face with two German riflemen who had rushed a gap in the rolling stock.

Ross, with many hours of pistol range shooting under his belt, blasted both of them in quick succession. The Germans screamed as they crumpled, squirming in agony, having taken the heavy-hitting bullets to the chest. Ross, as roughed up as he was, did not waste more ammunition on them. They were down, and staying down. They whimpered as he knelt clumsily next to the dead commando. Without ceremony, he stripped the man of his Thompson and spare magazines.

He inspected the weapon to see what state it was in, and was saddened to see that the man had not even got a shot off from the magazine fitted. He then rummaged in the man's ammunition pouches for his Colt magazines, stuffing them into his own battledress jacket. The two wounded Germans coughed and gargled blood from between their teeth, blooded hands outstretched towards him in surrender. Only then did the commando sergeant come to realise that the blood-speckled faces of the men he had shot were very young. He wanted no more to do with them, and clambered to his feet. He turned to his right only to be faced with another German soldier who was shocked to see an enemy so close. He let off a burst with his

MP40 that snapped past Ross' left side, only to be smashed by several return bullets across his own chest and face. Ross' left ear throbbed from the closeness of the bullets. He flicked his head around to the left, and saw Hook's Thompson smoking.

'Thanks sir. I'm getting old,' Ross acknowledged. Hook nodded back at him.

'Let's hope so.'

The commandos were strung out all along the train wreck that led them towards the destroyed storage unit. German stick grenades cartwheeled between the rolling stock. Hook's men nearest where they fell either tossed them back or dived out of the way as they detonated. With the Germans now pushing hard, Hook knew he had to get his men into the industrial area, for the sake of having some cover to fight from. With the exception of a few bomb craters provided by the RAF raid, cover for the British was scarce. The Germans were now exploiting the wreckage for their own ends.

'Peel right, peel right!' roared Hook. 'Get into the buildings, move!'

As much as the commando captain wanted to haul all of his wounded along with him, he knew that would only serve to create more casualties. The combined fire from Bren, Thompson and Colt rippled into the German positions. One at a time, with Hook leading the move, the men got up from their fighting positions and sprinted as best they could behind those still firing. It was a well-practised and efficient manoeuvre that had served them well up to that point. He had trained his men long and hard enough to go against their human instincts to save a friend who had fallen. It wasn't just dead men they left, but also blast-concussed men who were just not coherent enough to respond to the situation, which was getting out of control around them.

More Germans attempted to assault through the wreckage as the commandos moved into the shattered buildings. Hook took up a fighting position at the first piece of decent cover, firing his Thompson at movement amid the rolling stock, his men dashing past his left side. The familiar clunk of an empty magazine had the captain kneel down behind his cover, screaming 'magazine!' for all he was worth. With no covering fire coming from him, the commando nearest him as he approached spun around, taking up Hook's role as fire support. Only when the captain, fresh magazine fitted, was back in the fight, did the soldier continue his dash into the buildings.

Sergeant Ross, not his usual agile self, was the last man in the line coming towards him.

'Last man!' he hollered as he jogged past, exhausted. The blast had greatly affected him. Hook followed him in amongst the ruins of various buildings — ruined not only by the RAF, but by the most recent explosion. Dead fire crews, stripped bare by the blast, lay motionless alongside their fire tenders. The explosion had killed Germans and French alike. His men, breathing and sweating heavily, were taking up fighting positions in and around the flame-licked ruins. Hook called out to them as he jogged through.

'Drink what water you have boys, take five minutes.'

Rayner, fighting to catch his breath from his sprint, found the energy to clamber to his feet and scamper after the captain.

'Have we *got* five minutes?' he gasped, only to have the captain turn on him, the glare already written across his face. Rayner immediately realised he was forgetting himself.

'That explosion knocked the hell out of them too. I don't think they will be in so much of a rush to follow us in here, for fear of more buildings blowing sky high.'

'But what if they do go up?' The young lieutenant pushed on. Hook, taking greedy mouthfuls from his water bottle, shrugged, not rushing to finish rehydrating himself. Only when he had his fill did he answer.

'Then none of us will ever remember it.' He winced as he rotated his torso to put his bottle back in its pouch. Rayner noticed fresh blood spreading across the left side of his battledress jacket.

'You're hit, sir.' Rayner gasped. The blood was already beginning to darken. Hook looked down at the wound.

'One of the bastards got me with his MP40. It hurts like hell, I just need dressings.'

Rands took command of the company as men treated the captain. Hook had taken a round straight through. It looked bad, but no vital organs or bone had been hit. Rands ensured the men were as rehydrated as possible, and he also checked on Ross, who was slowly getting back in to the swing of things. The other blast-wounded members of the company, who had managed to get to their feet and move, fared no better. Rands assumed they preferred to walk further into France as free men, not as prisoners.

Rands felt movement behind him, and turned to see Hook and Rayner walking up. Hook winced with each step, fully dressed once more. Despite the blood stain and the pain that made him grimace, Hook refused to let misfortune keep him from leading his men. Rayner, much to Rands' irritation, looked somewhat fresh, and would flinch and startle every time something within the ruins combusted. Rands asked why the captain was making his way back to the rolling stock.

'I want to see what they are doing with our men.' Hook spoke without looking back. Rayner looked sheepishly at Rands, who rolled his eyes before following on.

Carefully, all three of them got into position to look back at the rolling stock, along with the ground they had just evacuated. All three flinched as a grenade detonated in a deep crater. More stick grenades cartwheeled into other shell holes. That cruel act prompted commandos caught out in the open to make a dash for the buildings, only to be cut down by the rippling fire of at least one MG42.

'Bastards!' Rands hissed under his breath. The other men could only agree. They knew the Germans had passed the point of being chivalrous. They had commandos in custody, and yet there were still more running about the facility, causing trouble.

Hook snapped the other two out of their hate-filled thoughts.

'It'll be dark soon. We will make a break for it then. They won't be in a rush to find us in here. For all they know, there are bloody loads of us, all over the place.'

'We can't hang about too long.' Rands piped up. 'The RAF has wrecked the town, and we've come in here causing trouble. I can't see many French people being on our side anytime soon.'

Hook had to agree with his troop commander. It would not just be German troops they would have to avoid as they got out of La Rochelle; there were a lot of angry civilians to contend with, too.

33

Gibbs was trying his hardest not to give his best left hook to the German sailor shoving him. With every press of his rifle butt, the angry U-boat crewman would make sure the commando's damaged arm got a prod, as he helped his comrades herd their prisoners out of the pens towards a line of trucks. Their hands on their heads, the captured men were spat on, punched and kicked by their guards. Dockers, wounded in the raid but still able to vent their anger on the troublesome British, put the boot in as well.

It was the submarine weapons officer, Clayton Price, who caught a glimpse of what he could only assume were Gestapo, standing around two dark-coloured Mercedes saloons. Dressed in tailored suits and wide-brimmed hats, they were deep in conversation with both of the generals who had spoken to them earlier. The younger general was very animated, laughing with the suited men, whereas the old one appeared somewhat irritated by the whole conversation.

It was the arrogant young officer who had acted as interpreter that made Price look twice. He made his excuse to leave the conversation with the suited men and was making his way over to him. Both Price and Gibbs stopped, their guards trying to push them on.

'Leave them be.'

The German captain called to them in his native tongue. The guards acknowledged his orders, but carried on pushing and shoving the others. The young German officer did not look as smug as he had previously, as he stopped short of the two men.

'The Gestapo have intervened rather early in this whole affair. You will be taken to the town police station, in readiness to be handed over to the SS for administration.'

'*Administration?*' scoffed Price. 'Is that the long and clever word for it?'

The German looked a little forlorn. 'The general felt it only proper for you men to be held in Kreigsmarine custody, but commandos fall into an entirely different category.'

'Who said we were commandos?' Price pushed. 'We are in British uniforms, openly carrying our weapons.'

'The dockers at the lock claim you were in crewman rain gear, which makes your approach underhand. This dictates you are commandos, hence the Gestapo's interest in this attack.'

Price and Gibbs looked at each other; there was nothing they could say to that. The German waved them on, towards the trucks that were now being climbed upon by the men, their guards jostling and mocking them as they boarded.

'I'm not sitting in a French cell waiting for the SS to come and pick us up,' Gibbs murmured.

'Me neither.' Price responded.

As they drew near the rear truck, the Germans felt the need to push and shove the wounded warrant officer down the column. Split from the officer so early in their yet-to-be-hatched escape plan, Gibbs had to withstand the knocks to his injured side and come up with a way to avoid ending up in the police station. Once they were in those cells, they were as good as dead, for the

SS would certainly cater for a large group of prisoners. Gibbs found himself careering into the chief petty officer, Roger Toil, who was helping the more seriously wounded men up into the rear of the front truck. Straightening himself up, Gibbs gave the senior NCO a knowing nod. Toil smiled weakly as both he and other helping hands above him helped the one-armed Gibbs up into the truck.

The two German sailors that were to ride on the tail gate with them shouted and cursed, full of the power that the situation had gifted them. They had, up until that point in their short navy careers, been beneath the dark cold depths, fearing British destroyers in the terrifying game of cat and mouse played out in the North Atlantic. Now, they had commandos as prisoners, and these same young boys had been given a chance to wave the big stick.

Gibbs fought back the agony of his shoulder through gritted teeth as they manhandled him up onto the tail gate. Once inside, there was no room for him to sit. The rear of the truck had not been unloaded prior to its re-assignation as prisoner transport. Toil absorbed a few well-aimed rifle butt strikes to his own shoulder blades as he hauled his broad frame up into the truck. Gibbs shuffled a little to make room for the burly submariner.

'I bet when you are on shore, you spend most of your time on the rugby pitch,' Gibbs commented. Toil gave a much friendlier smile.

'With a frame like mine,' Toil beamed, 'front row all day long.'

'Good.' Gibbs replied. 'We are going to scrum on my say so.'

Toil frowned a little, puzzled as by the reference. Suddenly the penny dropped, his eyebrows raised.

'Oh right....scrum, indeed!'

The over-enthusiastic guards clambered up, shoving against both Toil and Gibbs, who could not help but fall against the battered and wounded men behind them. The guards' comrades raised the tailgate so they could lock it in position. The pair of them lit fresh cigarettes, still buoyed by their power.

*

It wasn't just Gibbs and Toil biting their lips at the arrogance of the two German sailors straddling the tail board.

'They've put all our men from the pens into trucks. They must be taking them to a secure location pretty soon.' Rands' chest heaved as did those of the other three men who had accompanied him on his rudimentary scouting mission. It was now dusk and Hook was glad to see the back of the sun. He rubbed his hands over his matted beard.

'It serves no purpose to try and rescue them; some of them can't walk, let alone fight.'

His words hung in the air, no one even contemplating his opinion.

'Besides,' Hook attempted to be a little more upbeat. 'If an opportunity presents itself, I'm sure they will take full advantage.'

A few stifled grunts came from the group. The company, or at least those who could still do some damage, were still rallied in all-round defence in the ruins of the industrial area. The majority of the fires had burned themselves out. The Germans had made no attempt to follow them into the area, probably from fear of further explosions.

With the light as good as gone, they now had to pick their way out of La Rochelle and head further inland.

'Get ready to move. I want 2 Troop leading, with Sergeant Ross and myself following up with the remainder of the company.'

As Rands went to leave, Rayner raised his hand a little. 'Where do you want me, sir?'

The captain looked at him, his left flank throbbing under the tightly-wound dressings. 'You stick with me. When we get to Marans, we will need to get our mission status relayed back to England. The SAS will have means to speak with home, so we can have them do it for us.'

As the company got ready for the next dangerous phase of the operation, a commotion caught the captain's attention.

'Trucks are moving, trucks are moving!' hissed the lads still on sentry duty. The men within earshot relayed the message, and so it reached the captain in a matter of seconds. Hook paused to hear the trucks gunning their engines, the pitch of their transmission rising as they changed gear. Between the shattered buildings, Hook could see the headlight beams bobbing to and fro. He had to think fast. Should they allow the convoy to pass, his men aboard going into German captivity, or stop the convoy, thereby giving his men a chance to turn their fortunes around?

Hook turned quickly to look at Rands.

'Lieutenant, stop the convoy; don't shoot until you have to.'

Rands instantly turned to the nearest commando. 'Talbot, fake a limp, Colt only. Let's get up on the road.'

34

The truck's suspension had not been designed for a leisurely cruise. It jolted with every pothole and ironworks the wheels hit, each sending a shock rippling through Gibbs' smashed shoulder. He hated truck convoys as much as he hated landing craft — it occurred to him to wonder why he had ever volunteered for The British Commandos.

The two young German sailors smoked their cigarettes with enthusiasm; they had yet to go a couple of minutes without one, since loading the truck. For reasons unknown to all in the military, it was quite normal to hurry troops into transports and then have them sit around for ages before the vehicles even began to move. Gibbs assumed that the German armed forces were applying the same protocol to the movement of personnel.

As the truck led the other three vehicles out of the pen area, Gibbs turned over in his mind the various means by which they could stop the convoy for long enough to let his men grab their chance at freedom. Not all could make that choice, which was unfortunate, but if those who could walk were able to get far enough away to cause a pain in the arse for the Germans, they would be doing what they had come to France for in the first place— causing chaos and disruption.

He felt the vehicle lurch forward violently as the cold brakes stuck on the cold drums; the gear change down made the lurching all the more violent. They must be approaching a checkpoint of some sort. Gibbs leaned forward, tapping the chief petty officer on the shoulder. Toil looked at him, face full of dread. Both men knew their bold plan would get them and others killed if it didn't work, but given that the SS would soon be making their acquaintance anyway... why wait for the inevitable?

As the vehicle rolled to a halt, Gibbs could hear German voices hollering aggressively at someone, or something.

The angry shouting ceased abruptly as the windscreen of the cab burst inward in a hail of bullets.

Gibbs roared as he ploughed himself into the chest of the German sailor facing him.

'*Scrum*!'

The two German troops riding in the cab didn't have a chance, as Rands and Talbot emptied their Colts into them. Both commandos moved up against the front grille of the truck, reloading their magazines. Other commandos joined them, returning their Thompsons to them. Hook and some of the others led the charge down the left side of the column, pumping the cab of each truck in turn full of bullets, their occupants decimated in the brief, violent action. The troops jumping down from their perches on the tail gates were cut down with equal ruthlessness.

Rands employed an age-old trick, and pretended to hold up a wounded man in the middle of the road. With his Colt-bearing hand out of sight, the Germans driving the lead vehicle felt empowered as they were apparently presented with two more wounded British to add to their tally — that naivety cost them dear. The Germans who had refused to pursue them into the burning buildings, clearly had not informed the convoy operators that the enemy was near the road.

The two Mercedes saloons at the rear of the column slewed broadside as they were punctured by a hail of Thompson and Bren gun bullets. Those passengers who survived the attack, which had blown the heads off their drivers, fought frantically to get out of the bullet-attracting vehicles, even for just a few seconds. Those that managed at this stage to get the heavy, warped, doors open were greeted by commandos stepping up towards the cars, firing short bursts into those that had so far refused to die quietly.

The Gestapo officers were dead before they could fire a shot.

Gibbs was helped to his feet by two of the raiding party, one of whom handed him a fully-loaded Colt.

'Here you go, sir. Loaded and made ready.' Gibbs, out of habit, inspected the pistol. The hammer was to the rear, indicating that it was indeed ready to be used. He carefully allowed the hammer to be released forwards with his left hand, conscious that the left hand wasn't his best.

'Cheers boys. Good to see you both.'

Toil was helped to his feet, a little concussed thanks to his own dramatic rugby tackle of the young German sailor who was now his prisoner. How the tables could turn when one did not pay attention. The young man was less arrogant now. His friend, with whom he had been sharing cigarettes, had managed to get up from his dive with the one-armed Gibbs, only to be cut down by the British raiding party moving down the column. The boy now tried his hardest not to cry — and failed. Hook made his way around the second truck, grabbing the sobbing German and hauling him up.

'English. Do you speak it?' The captain was not feeling generous and it showed in his conduct. The terrified sailor looked about the enemy soldiers before him, all of whom remained stony-faced, except one.

'What do you want to say to him, captain?' Rayner said.

The captain took a deep breath, blinking slowly, his wounds reminding him of his own mortality. He stared at the trembling, snot-nosed sailor.

'You are to get out of here. The SS are coming, and if they find out that you allowed us to escape, they will shoot you along with any of us they capture. Do you understand?'

Rayner translated. The sailor's eyes widened at the threat. He began to speak faster and faster in German, too fast for Rayner to keep up with him. The officer waved him to slow down.

'He is a Danish volunteer, he just wants to go home.'

'*Danish* you say?' Gibbs winced as he adjusted his strapped arm. Rayner shrugged.

'His German is basic, as if he has learned it. He doesn't have a regional accent or anything.'

Hook pulled the sailor in closer to get his attention.

'You had better get a move on, Danish volunteer. Go now!' Hook released the boy, who staggered backwards, too afraid to turn his back on the British men. Hook rolled his eyes, waving him away like an unwanted guest at a party. The Dane turned on his heels and sprinted for the open farmland. He was quickly absorbed by the darkness.

'It's a long walk back to Denmark from here,' laughed Gibbs. Hook shook his head.

'He will turn himself in to the nearest unit, no doubt, telling them everything that has happened here.'

'Why didn't we kill him?' asked Rands, who had just joined the group. Hook shrugged his shoulders.

'I think we will need the ammunition for later.'

With those that could walk taken from the trucks, it broke Hook's heart to know that those who were far too wounded to be moved would have to await the arrival of other German units. With dead Gestapo men slumped in the cars, not to mention the convoy personnel littering the area, the scene that greeted them could only encourage the SS to do what their Führer commanded of them when it came to commando prisoners. With heavy hearts,

Hook's raiding force patrolled and limped their way into the open countryside that separated them from their RV with the SAS.

The group spilt into smaller parties, to maximise the German hunter force effort that would be required to apprehend them. Rands and Ross led 2 and 3 Troops, respectively. Hook, along with Rayner, Gibbs and those submarine officers that could make the journey, led out what was left of 1 Troop. With sound navigation skills, and the tactical acumen to keep the German hunter forces at arm's length, Hook looked forward to seeing his men again in Marans.

They had completed their primary mission, now they were about to link up with the SAS and cause even more trouble.

As long as the Germans didn't get them first.

35

With his company broken up, making for the RV in their own ways, Hook fought through pain that refused to subside. He was confident blood loss would be minimal, but the pain pulsing through him with every step told him that the walk to Marans was going to be a long one. Going through the farmland and sunken lanes that made up the landscape was not much of a challenge for fit, motivated men, but the commandos under his charge were beaten up, tired, hungry and low on ammunition.

With the U-boat pens of La Rochelle now hidden in the darkness behind them, everyone was confident they could put good distance between themselves and local German forces now gathering at the site of the truck ambush. Their confidence was short-lived, however, evaporating when the bark of dogs carried on the night air. Hook knew the sound came from German army dogs, for they all began to bark as one, as if they had just arrived at the scene. Hook spun around to try and get a direction of whereabouts they could be.

He didn't have to try too hard. Way back in the darkness, numerous torch beams bobbed to and fro.

The Germans were pursuing them. The dogs would do their work.

'What do you want to do, sir?' a gruff voice, hushed, sounded in his right ear. The surprise of the question had Hook flinch in pain as he turned to its source. Gibbs was looking back at him.

'Those dogs will have them close the gap in no time at all, and most of us are not in any state to try and out-run them.'

Hook knew the sergeant major was right. If they were to get to their RV, they needed to level the playing field. He called for the group to halt, having them rally around him, facing outwards, weapons at the ready. He spoke quietly, despite the soundtrack of barking growing louder every minute.

'We need to ambush this hunter force coming up behind us. They have dogs, and we can't out-run them.'

The lads shook out, lined abreast facing the bouncing torch beams. Their training took over as Bren gunners moved to the flanks, the Thompson handlers making up the main group in the middle. The submarine officers crouched in a group just behind the commandos, as they were well and truly out of their comfort zone. Hook saw to them once he was content with the fighting positions of his men.

'Here, take these grenades.'

Hook handed Price four high explosive grenades. The submariner looked at them with fear, as if they were about to go off in his hands.

'When we open fire, throw them into the centre of the enemy troops, let the fragmentation do the work, got it?'

Price handed them out so the officers had one each. Hook turned back, to see the hunter force closing in on them. The meadow grass was just above thigh height. The moon appeared from behind a bank of low cloud, illuminating the entire area. With the light levels higher, Hook and his men could identify the dark profiles of those behind, pulled along by the scent-drunk dogs, their weapons at the ready to deal with any stray British soldiers.

Hook slowly dropped to a crouch, behind the centre of the main group. The sergeant major approached him from the right and came in very close to the captain's ear, his lips almost brushing the lobe.

'Bren guns have extra magazines. They are ready to go.'

Hook replied with a nod. He then hissed at the men crouched a few yards in front of him.

'On my shot. On my shot.'

The bright moon allowed him to see their heads nodding as they turned back to the approaching enemy. The barking grew louder, their handlers calling them to heel. The German troops were also shouting to each other, and the scene before the British resembled a fox hunt more than a pursuit of the enemy. The torches scythed across the top of the meadow grass, causing a number of the men, Hook included, to flinch. The Germans were just two hundred yards away, the dogs pulling out in front of them as the scent got stronger. Hook spun around to Price, taking the grenade from him.

The dogs were closing in; the main group behind them was just over one hundred yards away. Hook ensured the grenade's fly off lever was in the web of his hand as he pulled the pin. He got up on his haunches and identified the dog group, then threw the grenade like a cricket ball in amongst the dark mass of man and canine.

Hook crouched lower in the grass, just as the grenade detonated.

The dull thud of the explosion had the dog group punched flat. The dogs yelped and howled, peppered with thousands of shards of shrapnel. Their handlers lay prone, or writhed in deafened agony, as they fought to contain their pain.

Hook was up on his feet, ears ringing ever so slightly as he pulled his Thompson into his right shoulder, firing short, controlled bursts at the German troops behind the dogs. He caught them unawares, for they froze to the spot long enough for Hook to hit at least one. His own muzzle flash blinded him as he kept his standing position firm. The bright red blobs drifting across his vision denied him the sight of the Germans dashing right and left away from not the fire; not just Hook's, but that of the company.

The Germans were quick to go to ground, save a few that fell prey to the Bren guns on the flanks. Hook was back down on his haunches, changing his magazine, as his men mowed the meadow grass with disciplined bursts. Despite the din of the ambush, the dogs refused to die as they squirmed and yelped, their masters being either dead or in no position to let them off the leash. Hook turned to the submarine officers, who were hesitating over where to throw their grenades.

'Throw them into the fucking middle!' The captain roared himself hoarse as he competed with the din of his men's firepower.

The officers, clearly trained for sea rather than land, fought frantically with their respective fuse pins, before lobbing the grenades into the dark conglomeration of German soldiers. They bobbed up and down, snapping off shots as they fought to overcome the ambush they had found themselves in. The three grenades detonated in quick succession, each one sending their concussion wave pulsing through the Germans with enough force to render them inert for a short period of time.

The firing from both sides began to peter out. Any German soldier foolish enough to stand up in the full glare of the moon was cut down by both Bren and Thompson fire. Hook knew that, moon or not, they had to get the hell out of there.

'Sergeant Major?' Hook roared above the wailing of the dogs.

'Yes, sir?'

'Let's go, single file, and follow me. Brens at the rear.'

'Okay boys, you heard the man — let's go.'

Hook did not look back as he led his battered group out of the meadow. He was confident they had taken no further casualties, for Gibbs would have alerted him to the fact. The group continued on to Marans, and hopefully, their RV with the SAS.

*

The adrenaline of the ambush let Hook forget his wounds, but the same could not be said for others. Now the ambush was being diluted from their hard-marching bodies, their aches and pains began to return. Hook had not set too punishing a pace, but, unsurprisingly given the circumstances, the group had seen better days.

He considered what should be done with the men, once they linked up with their Special Forces counterparts. Firstly, wounds would need tending, ammunition must be replenished and weapons cleaned. The key ingredient of any fighting forces was the men, the equipment and their weapons.

More torch beams bounced and flicked in the distance behind them, and another German hunter force was catching up with another British group to the right. With the moon now tucked behind a long thick bank of cloud, the torches could be seen all the more easily. The barking of dogs echoed across Hook's group and they found it difficult to determine which of the two new hunter forces was directing them. The sound of gunfire rippled and popped through the night air, too distant to be focused upon them, but close enough to make them assume that one of the other groups was being engaged. The familiar thud of grenades began, the commandos again at a loss to know which side was using them.

Rayner was a few metres behind the captain as they staggered on, towards what looked like a cluster of farm buildings in the middle distance. No light came from the area, but that didn't reassure the young lieutenant, for the owners could either be asleep or away from home, or the place could be primed for an ambush. Rayner shook the last thought from his mind, putting his pessimism down to the distress of being chased by German troops with dogs, and exhaustion from all they had been through. Terrifying scenarios had run riot in his sleep- and food-deprived brain. Yet he had faith in the NCOs now leading the column, and both he and the captain had paused to try and determine the exact locations of the Germans following them, or the other groups.

The NCOs leading were trying their hardest to manoeuvre around the left-hand side of the unlit farm complex, but wide, deep and full irrigation ditches made progress painfully slow. The group came closer and closer to the buildings as they sought an energy-saving route across them. The commandos who had been wounded when fighting in the pens were really feeling the pace now. They were also without weapons due to their previous capture.

Thankfully, there were sufficient men in the group still bearing arms, the young Rayner included. He had fired his Thompson a few times in the pens, unable to confirm that he had hit what he was aiming at. The same went for the fighting amid the train wreckage upon leaving the facility. He felt in his heart that he had given a good account of himself during the raid, and that he had been open and frank with the officers when he was challenged on the journey to the target.

The group paused briefly to rest. NCOs and officers gathered in a huddle to consult sketched maps, whilst the remainder kept watch for the German patrols, drinking greedily from their water bottles. Those who had been stripped of all their fighting gear received water from their comrades. Hook was confident that their direction of travel was correct, the mapping provided in the target pack featured the very farm complex they stood next to. Hook had the men get ready to move out.

*

As the lead elements of the group came around the left side of the main farm buildings and courtyard, they were suddenly bathed in brilliant light. Instinctively, they shielded their eyes from the light, overwhelmed by whistle blasts and the aggressive commands from unseen German voices. As if on cue, dogs erupted their contribution to the shock action.

The commandos caught in the full glare of the lights slowly lowered their weapons towards the ground. Hook crept past those of the men who had not yet been discovered, who were along the side of the building. The men exposed on the road looked right at the movement of their captain, who was edging closer. They gave no indication that they were not alone, but snatched up their weapons in an attempt to use them.

They were hit multiple times by withering fire from unseen German soldiers. Hook watched those of his men who had been caught on the road crumple, pink mist registering the hits that took their lives before they even hit the ground.

Frozen briefly by the sheer violence of the action, Hook composed himself quickly enough to fish a grenade from an ammunition pouch. Pulling the pin, he lobbed it underarm with his left hand at a number of moving figures, silhouetted by vehicle headlights. As it chinked about on the ground, the dark figures froze for a split second before darting in either direction. The grenade concussion burst the headlights and forced the wind from the lungs of those too close for comfort. Hook stepped out from behind the building, firing bursts from his Thompson at any Germans he could see dashing between the chest-high wooden fencing that bordered the road-facing side of the farm complex, and the profile of what looked like an armoured halftrack troop carrier.

'Peel left, peel left, go go go!' Hook roared as he kept up the fire. Rayner, who had been tucked in behind him up to that point, swallowed hard as he dashed past the captain, taking up a kneeling position a few metres to the man's left amid the dead commandos. He then fired short bursts either side of the dark vehicle, for that was where he noticed movement.

The other commandos in the group who were capable of fighting filed out from behind the building, peeling in to the left of Rayner. Hook dropped to one knee whilst changing magazines, before continuing the fight from there. Rayner too had to contend with an empty magazine, his actions not as smooth and rapid as those of the commando captain, but the Germans were unable to find their mark in time. In what felt like a lifetime to the novice young officer, he was back in the fight, firing at the German troops trying to take up fighting positions to the left of the vehicle, in amongst the irrigation ditches and chest-high meadow grass.

The commandos who were unarmed did not wait to be told to cross the road and make for the fields. To stay on the road would mean getting killed, or at the very least being wounded or captured once more. With the walking wounded clear of the road, Hook lifted his Thompson barrel so it pointed straight up, whilst getting to his feet and dashing behind Rayner, screaming at him as he went.

'Peel left, peel left!'

Amidst the din of the fire fight, the snapping of barking dogs, whistles and men shouting at each other in English and German, Rayner followed Hook's example as he tagged on behind him, the commando to his immediate left wielding a Bren. The man had the weapon tucked under his right armpit as he fired short, chugging bursts. Then, an almighty snap rendered the Bren silent.

Rayner paused to look back at the Bren gunner. He was now writhing on the road, both hands to his throat, his blood pooling in a dark mass underneath his twitching head. Oblivious to the danger, Rayner was transfixed by the dying man.

A rough hand grabbed his shoulder, almost yanking him off his feet as he was bundled across the drainage ditch and into the long grass. Rayner fought to gather himself; his antagonist did not let up either their grip or their pace as they stampeded further into the field. Only when he was thrown to the ground behind other commandos, still fighting, did Rayner manage to look up and see the looming dark profile of the sergeant major.

'You stop to watch the show like that again,' Gibbs leaned down towards him to make himself heard over the gunfire, 'and me and you are going to have words, do you hear me?'

Hook, now in a better position to control the mini battle his group had been embroiled in, scampered up and down the fighting line as his men sought to suppress the Germans on the road. The dogs continued to give it their all, as another vehicle arrived to join the fray. Its high profile gave away the fact that it was a truck, but it disappeared from view before Hook could direct fire onto it. The gunfire was petering out, as ammunition became a concern, and the commandos reverted to shooting only at what they knew they could hit.

The unmistakable sound of the truck tail gate squealing and slamming in the down position gave away the arrival of German troop reinforcements.

Hook knew that it was now or never for the group to make off and get themselves to the SAS RV.

'Break clean, break clean, break clean!' he hollered, over and over. The signal was for the men to make off on their own to the RV, thereby rendering chasing them more of a problem for the Germans.

Hook was on his feet long enough to see his men respond to his executive order. A bright flash and a concussion that punched him flat was the next thing to consume his world.

His ears screamed a high pitched whine. Drunk from the explosion, his head swam as he fought to gather his wits. A series of heavy thuds rippled through the ground. As his hearing returned, he could make out what he thought were voices, but soon sounded more like barking. His vision, saturated by drifting red blobs, made the search for his Thompson impossible as the barking got louder. Hook abandoned the Thompson for his Colt, and no sooner had he grabbed the pistol with his right hand, than a dark mass leapt at him.

He instinctively raised his left arm to defend himself, but his senses returned with a vengeance as teeth penetrated his

battledress sleeve, the momentum and mass of the German
shepherd taking him down.

36

Major Dan Simmons watched with interest as the day unfolded. His squadron of sixty SAS men, who would normally be training local men to attack the German garrison near La Rochelle, found themselves diving for cover as the entire area erupted like a kicked-over hornets' nest.

The SAS men were not entirely sure of the reason for the sudden upsurge in activity. Even their recently seconded French volunteers found the information coming out of the port town disjointed and confusing.

Initially, Simmons had dismissed the early activity as mere reinforcements, brought in to assist with the aftermath of the bombing raid the night before. But as the day grew older, the Germans stationed around the hamlet of Marans became increasingly agitated.

It had gone noon by the time Simmons had a reasonably clear picture of what was developing in La Rochelle, but he found it a little hard to swallow. The signals coming out of the burning town spoke of a 'commando' raid on the U-boat pens at La Pallice, on the northern outskirts. The SAS men, who ranked from trooper, up to the solitary major that was Simmons, found the idea absurd — suicidal, even. More signals, sent at great risk to the originators who would normally have packed their RAF-delivered radio sets away at first light, repeated the same message, continually. A commando raid was indeed in progress in the U-boat pens.

'Well that's going to fuck things up around here for a while now, eh sir?'

Trooper Brackpool, Simmons' signaller, shook his head in dismay, for what the so-called U-boat raiders were currently doing threatened to shatter a fragile armistice between the local French resistance forces and those of the German Garrison Command.

'You are not wrong,' Simmons agreed. 'What the hell are they playing at?'

The German colonel, more than content that his command was in France and not the Russian Front, had been brought to the table by local partisans who, in exchange for the ending of mass arrests and the handing over of downed allied aircrews, vowed to not attack the Germans' French lovers, or troops leaving on or returning from leave. This agreement had been brokered by Simmons and his squadron, who had parachuted in six weeks earlier. They found themselves amidst a turf war between the French volunteers and the German army. Tit-for-tat killings were increasing in brutality with each passing day. One factor the French exploited was the honour and integrity of the German colonel.

He had seen his fair share of mass shootings in the Ukraine, and was not about to endorse the same methods in western France. He was a family man, and found it difficult, even when his soldiers were being ambushed almost on a daily basis, to use civilians as leverage. He insisted that his junior commanders raise their game, and they took the conventional fight to the partisans.

In theory, such doctrine was straightforward, but in reality it was difficult to enforce without dragging the local population into the fight, which would simply aid the terrorists' recruitment drive. One of the female volunteers happened to be sleeping with the colonel's adjutant, who after much cognac revealed, whilst lying in bed with her, that the colonel had been threatened with a Russian command if he didn't get his occupation zone in order.

Even if he was tough on the locals, the colonel's own men were battle-weary from the Eastern Front, and had no problem with their role in the relative backwater outside La Rochelle, save for terrorist incidents against the unwary, which were simply the price of occupying foreign lands. As far as the average German soldier was concerned, it sure beat being in Russia.

It was the threat from German commanders in Paris that gave Simmons no alternative but to intervene.

The German High Command had Waffen SS divisions that needed respite from their relentless operations on the Eastern Front. If one of those divisions were to be shipped into the area for rest and refitting, the entire plan for Simmons' mission would have to change.

The Resistance fighters he was training were enthusiastic, but no match for a battle-hardened division known for its brutality with regards to prisoners of war, let alone partisans. They were content to pick fights with a weary Wehrmacht unit, which had weak commanders, but to employ the same approach to the SS would lead to their certain annihilation.

Simmons masterminded the meeting between the local resistance leaders and the German garrison command, which neither he nor his men attended, and both parties agreed that to have the SS deployed into the area would seriously compromise what quality of life they did have, given the circumstances. The colonel and his men would be shipped back into Russia, and the SS would be the new masters.

A truce of sorts was agreed, in principle. The Germans insisted that no paperwork was in place, since should it be discovered that a deal had been struck with the enemy, it would be a one-way ticket to Stalingrad or the firing squad, for the colonel.

Secretly, when not in the company of the French, Simmons and his men had already discussed what they would do should the SS send units to La Rochelle, even if that was just to rest and refit. Poring over their maps, they agreed the roads that would be blocked, prior to their arrival. They would then ambush the Germans, causing as much damage to their convoys as possible before withdrawing deep into the French countryside, merely to pick the moment at which to strike again, at a later date.

As for the railway lines, the squadron would blow key bridges and chokepoints just as the train was about to cross. They would then finish off whatever the crash didn't, killing as many of the SS men as they could before they were overmatched by sheer weight of numbers. It was a fact not lost on any of the SAS men, that the SS could take out their need for revenge on the local population, blaming partisans for the action. It would be a dreadful outcome, but in acute circumstances it would be necessary. As for the Resistance fighters — they could do as they pleased.

In the six weeks since their arrival, Simmons and his men had knocked the French volunteers into some sort of a fighting force. Their tactics prior to the Britons' arrival had been far too ambitious for the mob-like organisation, members of which spent most of their time between their so-called missions brawling with each other. None of the partisans trusted their comrades, fearing the presence of a German agent in their ranks. They had next to no tangible contact with their own so-called leaders, who were directing the insurgency from Paris, many of whom were too terrified to travel as far as La Rochelle for fear of being arrested by the Gestapo. It was a plea from Paris, via a number of agents, to the Cabinet Office that had Simmons and his squadron mobilised for the mission.

The SAS squadron, along with bundles of allied weapons and ammunition and a slab of French francs worth nearly half a million pounds, had been dropped into the French interior via Dakota aircraft, in the dead of night. The drop was chaotic, since the partisan landing party didn't know how to use their marking lamps properly, resulting in the RAF dropping two thirds of the SAS men into wetlands. Simmons' second in command, Captain Scott Woods, along with four very capable troopers, all drowned before they could get out of their parachute harnesses.

The slab of money had almost pulled Simmons below the surface of the flood water. It was only his ability to hold his breath for a long time, and slick handling of his combat knife, that spared him the same fate.

The opening meeting between the SAS squadron and their prospective allies had not started well. The French were most sorrowful for the deaths of the five men, and went to great lengths to help bury them, and make the other soaked SAS men feel welcome. With his men as dry as they were going to be, Simmons began the task at hand. He was in France to build the La Rochelle Resistance into some sort of fighting unit, so its members could then direct their attention to attacking the German garrison that dominated the area.

Initially, all the French wanted to do was snipe at the Germans; they did not have the appetite to get embroiled in close combat with them, where the vast differences in fighting quality would reveal themselves. The SAS men took their 'on the job' students deep into the forests, so they could conduct live firing training without half of the German army coming to see who was there. In a very short period, it became clear that the enthusiastic novice snipers could only just about shoot straight, never mind hit key targets at long distance with precise fire. The Resistance fighters were therefore taken back to the basics, learning to hit a target at one hundred yards. Only after considerable amounts of ammunition had been consumed, did the students progress to more elaborate shooting.

Despite the reasons for Simmons' trip to France, he had yet even to get a look at the enemy he was tasked to disrupt. Acting as early warning against German patrols, he had some of his squadron members on sentry duty well away from the training area, linked by radio sets, fewer in number than he would have liked, due to the almost disastrous parachute insertion.

Once Simmons was satisfied the French volunteers could shoot straight, he had his NCOs instruct them on the use of knives and explosives. Deer, caught in traps built by the SAS men, gave the students a live subject with which to try out their knife killing skills. The squadron sergeant major, a huge Scotsman who had been a gamekeeper before the war, made short work of one deer with his blade, as a demonstration. Given the lack of deer, and the large number of students, Simmons picked those whom he felt had too much to say for themselves during shooting training. The mouthy French men soon became mute, when they were put to the test. They made a real mess of killing the deer, two of which had to be dispatched by the sergeant major after he had endured sufficient calamity as the knife-wielding partisan lacked the physical strength to wrestle the animal to the floor and kill it outright. The French man, now less boisterous, re-,joined his comrades. None mocked him, for they feared being chosen to kill the final deer.

Since the use of explosives would certainly encourage German intrigue, the students were disappointed to learn that the lessons in that area would consist of theory only — for the time being. They would be supervised by SAS men on their first live demolition mission.

Content that the Resistance fighters of La Rochelle were now as good as they were going to get, the SAS finally began their primary task. Disrupting the enemy.

*

Simmons squatted next to his signaller as more messages were decoded, from operators in the town. It was the middle of the afternoon and the thud of a colossal explosion rippled through the air from the direction of the coast.

Signals coming out of the town told Simmons that commandos had blown up the German torpedo assembly depot. Simmons shook his head in exasperation, then gave his signaller a nudge. His voice came through gritted teeth.

'Any signals from England that may have warned us of this fucking commando raid?'

Brackpool shook his head. Simmons knew the man would have told him if there had been such warning. He cursed the top brass in London for their meddling and began to gather his thoughts regarding the breakdown of the local truce, and opportunities for hitting the Germans hard before they could react to the events unfolding in the area.

Darkness had fallen by the time the action in the town reached its climax. Operators sent signals to Simmons that spoke of British troops now running from German hunter parties with dogs. The last thing the SAS needed was for stray commandos to be wandering the area, leading the Germans into the SAS' area of operations.

'Sir?' The voice came from outside Simmons' crude command post. Fallen logs had been stacked up and staked to make a fort of sorts, draped in a green parachute canopy. Simmons emerged, to see one of his NCOs standing before him.

'What's up, Campbell?'

'My boys have grabbed what appears to be a British soldier. He claims to have come from La Rochelle.'

As Campbell spoke, the squadron's sergeant major wandered over and stood between the two men.

'Is he armed?' Simmons asked.

'Yes, sir. Thompson, and a Colt automatic.'

It was one of the commandos, Simmons deduced. He looked at his sergeant major.

'What do you reckon?'

The sergeant major turned to Campbell.

'Blindfold him, then bring him in here. There may be more of the fucking idiots wandering about with German patrols sniffing after them. Have Sergeant Cole put his troop on watch for any more wandering in here.'

The SAS corporal turned and walked away. The sergeant major turned to speak with his squadron commander.

'Please don't tell me we have to babysit these clowns as well?'

Simmons shrugged. 'Maybe they know something we don't. Won't be the first time we have been the last to know.'

A few minutes later, both Simmons and the sergeant major spotted Campbell, plus one of his troopers, leading a blindfolded soldier through the surface-running tree roots that spanned the forest floor like a giant web. As they pulled up in front of the major, he eyed the prize. The blindfolded man was indeed dressed as he expected other British troops to be. He doubted he was being used as bait by eagle-eyed German patrols out in the open farmland.

With a flick of his head, Simmons had Campbell pull off the blindfold. The soldier blinked profusely as he sought to focus within the dim interior of the thick French forest.

'Anything you want to share with us, young man?' Simmons' question was curt, devoid of any hospitality.

'Plenty, sir,' grinned Rayner. 'Plenty.'